WITHDRAWN

The One I've Waited For

Also by Mary B. Morrison

The Crystal Series
Baby, You're the Best ** Just Can't Let Go ** The One I've
Waited For

If I Can't Have You Series
If I Can't Have You ** I'd Rather Be with You ** If You Don't
Know Me

Soulmates Dissipate Series
Soulmates Dissipate ** Never Again Once More
He's Just a Friend ** Somebody's Gotta Be on Top
Nothing Has Ever Felt Like This ** When Somebody Loves
You Back ** Darius Jones

The Honey Diaries Series
Sweeter Than Honey ** Who's Loving You ** Unconditionally
Single ** Darius Jones

She Ain't the One (coauthored with Carl Weber)
Maneater (anthology with Noire)
The Eternal Engagement
Justice Just Us Just Me
Who's Making Love

Mary B. Morrison writing as HoneyB
Sexcapades ** Single Husbands ** Married on Mondays
The Rich Girls' Club

Presented by Mary B. Morrison
Diverse Stories: From the Imaginations of Sixth Graders
(an anthology of fiction written by thirty-three sixth graders)

The One I've Waited For

MARY B. MORRISON

KENSINGTON PUBLISHING CORP.
www.kensingtonbooks.com

To the extent that the image or images on the cover of this book depict a person or persons, such person or persons are merely models, and are not intended to portray any character or characters featured in the book.

DAFINA BOOKS are published by

Kensington Publishing Corp.
119 West 40th Street
New York, NY 10018

Copyright © 2017 by Mary B. Morrison

All rights reserved. No part of this book may be reproduced in any form or by any means without the prior written consent of the Publisher, excepting brief quotes used in reviews.

All Kensington titles, imprints and distributed lines are available at special quantity discounts for bulk purchases for sales promotion, premiums, fund-raising, educational or institutional use. Special book excerpts or customized printings can also be created to fit specific needs. For details, write or phone the office of the Kensington Special Sales Manager. Attn.: Special Sales Department. Kensington Publishing Corp., 119 West 40th Street, New York, NY 10018. Phone: 1-800-221-2647.

Library of Congress Card Catalogue Number: 2017940680

Dafina and the Dafina logo Reg. U.S. Pat. & TM Off.

ISBN-13: 978-1-61773-080-1
ISBN-10: 1-61773-080-7
First Kensington Hardcover Edition: August 2017

eISBN-13: 978-1-61773-081-8
eISBN-10: 1-61773-081-5
Kensington Electronic Edition: August 2017

10 9 8 7 6 5 4 3 2 1

Printed in the United States of America

To a friend named David James

Acknowledgments

My world revolves around family, friends, and fans. I cannot thank you enough for supporting my literary career. The words I pen, stories I create, are a gift from God.

A special thanks to my editor, Selena James; Steve Zacharius, Adam Zacharius, Lulu Martinez, Vida Engstrand, and everyone at Kensington Publishing Corporation for doing an amazing job!

There is no way I can repay Julie Brown for taking our adorable Yorkie, King Max B Byrd, into their home when I relocated to Atlanta. Letting me continue to visit Max every time I'm in Oakland is priceless. I could not have shared Max with a more loving family. Dude is so spoiled. Thanks a million times infinity.

I've adopted over a thousand aspiring and published writers into my circle. April 2015, I started a Facebook group to inspire my fans, family, and friends to write. The name of my group is Mary B. Morrison's Write a Book in 90 Days Challenge.

Many of you have a story to tell. Some don't know where to start. Others have a difficult time committing to the process. Encouraging you to do something you're passionate about is one of my ways to give back. By the time this book is in print, some of you will also be published authors. I'm looking forward to becoming your fan!

Always cheering the loudest for my son, Jesse Byrd, Jr.; his first novel, *Oiseau: The King Catcher*, was published in 2015, retitled in 2017, *King Penguin*. His content is for ages twelve and over. I've said it before and I'll say it again, "God gave me the right child." I continue to pray all great things for Jesse and his beautiful wife, Emaan Abbass.

I have amazing siblings. Wayne Morrison, Andrea Morrison, Derrick Morrison, Regina Morrison, Margie Rickerson, and Debra Noel, I love you guys. My in-laws Angela Lewis-Morrison, Dannette Morrison, Roland Johnson, and Desi Rickerson are the best. I appreciate all that each of you has added to our family over the years.

John Ferguson, rest in peace, brother-in-law, you are truly missed.

My unmarried husband and true friend, Richard C. Montgomery: with an upstanding man like you in my life, I may never say, "I do."

My gurl squad: Vanessa Ibanitoru, Carmen Polk, Brenda Jackson,

To the amazing women in my life: Barbara H. Cooper, Felicia Polk, Kimbercy Marie, Aje Huru, Yevonna Missy Johnson, Gricela Christian Chambers, Christal Jordan, and Numbiya Aziz.

There are so many people I need to express my gratitude to, so let me say, "If your hands prepared a meal for me, and/or you sent prayers for a healthy recovery, I'm am eternally grateful."

Kendall Minter, no entertainment lawyer reps like you and I'm blessed to be your client. You've supported me on levels that I can never repay you for. Congratulations on the release of your book, *Understanding and Negotiating 360 Ancillary Rights Deals.*

What's life without social media, baby (pumping both palms toward the sky)! I can never have enough supporters, but I can say, "I love you!" McDonogh 35 Senior High Class of 1982, the mighty Roneagles celebrated our 35th reunion.

Wishing each of my readers peace and prosperity in abundance. Visit me online at www.MaryMorrison.com. Sign up and invite your folks to do the same for my HoneyBuzz newsletter. Join my fan page on Facebook at TheRealMaryB, follow me on Twitter at marybmorrison and Instagram at maryhoneybmorrison.

This is novel #3 in The Crystal series

Shhh . . . Men are more insecure than women.

PROLOGUE

Mercedes

My pussy. My prerogative.

Our marriage certificate did not dictate where my husband dipped his dick.

Divorce? Legally separate? Coexist for our kids' sake? Fake it? God knew I tried forgetting her face. That was the one thing I could not do.

Her dark skin, brown eyes, lash extensions, full mocha lips, thick brows, high cheekbones—the circus was missing an animal. I was sure of it. Only a savage beast would knowingly lie with another woman's man. Short, slick, jet-black mane, parted on the right side, waved from her hairline to the nape of the neck.

All that effort and his mistress wasn't feminine enough to win a local beauty pageant let alone a Miss America or Miss Universe contest. There was a wrestling, weight-lifting, or bodybuilding championship belt waiting to decorate her petite, muscular six-pack. I was sure of that, too.

A piece of paper was not his license to share his dick and control my vagina. The tension in my neck created the onset of a migraine. Hate was demonic, yet an appropriate description of what I felt for his bitch. Not him.

"Excuse me, Mrs. Crystal." Rising from her seat, the voluptuous receptionist leaned against the counter as I approached her. "We can't proceed without your authorization. We need you to fill out the questionnaire, then sign at the bottom, please."

Her slender fingers held a clipboard with one letter-sized sheet of paper attached, then she pointed a pen toward me. Nobody forced me to do anything, including my husband. Intentionally, I made her wait.

Signing would release their corporation of liability. There were a few implied exceptions. Negligence. Misrepresentation. Satisfaction guaranteed was a dying consideration soon to become extinct. I was sure of that as well.

In retrospect, I wished reassurances would've come with executing my license.

Repeat after me. The words the pastor spoke on our wedding day marinated in thought intensifying my headache. 'Til death do us part? *Ha!* I'd stood at the altar and taken that idiotic vow, as did all the other couples who were divorced, separated, cohabitating, or foolishly breaking and making up all the damn time but underneath their façade they didn't trust each other.

My dear God! What was the point of it all when my husband didn't take his commitment seriously? Honor and obey. Forsake all others. Meaningless! Every single goddamn word he regurgitated to our minister as he held my hand and slid this—I stared at the diamond solitaire and infinity band on my finger—didn't mean shit!

Stop it, Minnie! Get out of your head before it explodes, girlfriend, my alter ego commanded.

I couldn't or I didn't want to. Either way it didn't matter that "Lovin' You" by Minnie Riperton was our wedding song. If anyone had told me my husband would cheat on me, I would've called them a liar! Sadly, this was my reality.

I was here and he was probably grinning in her ugly pug mug.

I blew a shot of hot carbon dioxide into the receptionist's face, and she fanned the space between us. *Really, Mz. Thang?* That was my way of releasing my stress. Scrolling my eyes down toward the text, thinking I better get air instead of snatching her ass from behind the counter and choking the shit out of her.

Narrowing my eyelids, I said, "You swiped my Luxury Black Card upon my arrival fifteen minutes ago. Show some damn respect."

Silence lingered.

Refusing to look up at her, I did not have to defend my impeccable oral hygiene against her rudeness. No apology was warranted. If she valued her job, she'd swallow her thoughts and get over it.

"Is it blue?" I inquired, looking at the blank signature line until the letters blurred into a blotch. Striving daily to be a perfect wife, whatever that meant, I struggled to find a reason for me to have a paradigm shift and forgive him.

I couldn't find a plausible justification. Perfection was unattainable for people who weren't upstanding like me.

"I'm sorry?" She frowned with one last wave—captured in my peripheral—that was closer to her face. Turning her back, she took a deep breath, exhaled, then stared at me.

Young. White. Semi-attractive. Big boobs. What was she sorry for? The unbuttoned white coat revealed she had an ass bigger than mine. A female in her employable position possibly earning barely above minimum wage could come up overnight by fucking my husband. She probably had several socially degrading profiles sporting practically naked photos of herself in a G-string swimsuit. I was almost sure of that.

Whores were the reason I was here. They enjoyed sucking dicks and surfing online! Plenty of Fish. Match. eHarmony. Black People Meet. Desperate, horny, sleazy, unscrupulous jezebels hunting for men on dating sites disgusted me!

Sternly, I replied, "Blue. Is the ink?"

As one of few to maintain a 4.0 GPA up to and through college, I believed unnecessarily starting anything over was a waste of precious time. Filling out a form, reverting to being single, I did my damnedest to get everything right the first time. Filing for divorce was an embarrassment I didn't want to become my future.

Birthing kids out of wedlock was worse. Thank God I'd gotten procreation out of the way. Having another baby didn't mean my man would stay. My mother was living proof of that not one, two, or three, but four times. Maybe I should have had a tubal ligation.

Sighing heavily, I elaborated, "I only sign my name in blue ink."

There went that hand of hers swatting as though flies flew out of my mouth. She pinched her nose, held it for three seconds.

Bitch, do it again and watch me snatch your fingers and bend them backward. Her brows drew closer as though she'd heard my thoughts.

"My apology, Mrs. Crystal."

If she was my assistant, I'd fire her right then. One "I'm sorry" was *one* too many. I scanned her head to chest, my breasts rising as I inhaled. Felt my nostrils flaring a little. I shook my head. The strawberry matte lipstick smeared across her full lips was inappropriate for an establishment that primarily serviced women.

Picking up a blank piece of paper, she scribbled, eyed me, then retorted, "It is blue," handing the pen to me. The moment I held the ballpoint she let go. I took a deep breath. She stepped back.

Fuck you too! I screamed in my mind.

Was my decision to come here out of spite and for revenge? You damn right! After learning of my husband's indiscretions I didn't need his input. What I was moments away from doing would slice his heart in half and I'd happily watch him slowly bleed as he'd become emotionally distraught. The way I cried myself to sleep without him by my side last night, the night before, and the night before that was my deciding factor. He did not deserve to enjoy any parts of my vagina.

There were only five *yes or no* queries. I circled *no* for each one. Angrily, I scratched up, down, up, down. Quick strokes, right left right tore a hole in the paper. I heaved. Slapped the pen onto the clipboard.

"There," I said as though she were to blame for my being here.

The receptionist nodded. "You won't have any regrets, Mrs. Crystal."

Mrs. Crystal. Hmm. Not for much longer. The title was all I had to change. I'd never taken his last name, Bannister.

I rolled my eyes at her. Hissed, "How do you know what I'll have?" This time her brows lifted toward her reddish hair. For the first time I noticed her freckles, small nose, brown lashes, the band on her ring finger, wondering if white women had it easier in their marriage. I was tired of looking at her plastic ass—she didn't have to tell me.

I told her, "I'll have a seat and wait for the doctor."

Checking my messages, I saw that none were from my husband. A text registered from the private detective, Dakota Justice, whom I'd hired to spy on Benjamin. She was the reason I knew his every move.

I read, **He's at The Cheetah strip club**

At one p.m.? I replied, **Is he with her?**

That skank mistress of his had no class.

He's alone. At the bar. Drinking.

Probably waiting on Arizona to get there. Dakota sent me a selfie. That cheered me up, a little, seeing her disguised in a man's suit.

I messaged Dakota, **Buy him 10 lap dances.**

I wanted to see how far my husband would go with a complete stranger and how his mistress would feel if she walked in and saw another woman grinding on his dick.

CHAPTER 1

Benjamin

Why did I have a wife if I needed a mistress?

A text registered, **Pick up the twins. I'm with a client.**

That woman's level of inconsideration made my blood boil!

Early in our courtship her bossiness was cute. I voluntarily followed her lead. She immediately declared an exclusive on me, and my dick. I fell into her trap. Let her pick out her engagement ring and our wedding bands. On our honeymoon she'd planned what she'd referred to as *our* pregnancy. Before the first anniversary, I was twenty-five with two kids. Today I know for sure, I'd married the wrong woman but I wanted to do the right thing.

Wished I'd waited.

"Hi, handsome." A soft hand caressed my shoulder. "I have several complimentary dances for you."

Pivoting my barstool sideways, a gorgeous, topless tender with perky gumdrop nipples smiled at me. Automatically, my shaft slithered down my thigh.

Exhaling my frustrations into my lunch—a glass of cognac— what was I fighting for? I'd done my time. Five years. One-fourth of a life sentence of disrespect substantiated my desire for a divorce based on good behavior. What the hell, tomorrow wasn't promised.

"Sure. Let's take it to a private room," I told her, covering my glass of water with a paper napkin to reserve my seat at the end of the bar.

I picked up my liquid gold, led the way to private room number four with the two-way mirror. That way I could see when the person I was waiting for arrived. Reclining on the leather sofa, I spread my thighs, interlocked my fingers behind my head, watched her shake those beautiful breasts in my face. Her nipple grazed my lip. I didn't move but my dick did.

She turned around, touched her toes, slowly slid her thong over an amazing ass. Red polished nails spread her chocolate cheeks. Her pussy was plump like she'd suctioned it with one of those vagina pumps. I squeezed my head to keep from leaking precum in my black boxer briefs. Coming off of a drought with the Mrs., it didn't take much to get me off these days.

My wife, she didn't get it. She hated when I told her what to do, yet our entire relationship she was a dictator without boundaries. Her consulting business compensated her for thinking on the behalf of others. I wasn't one of her damn clients!

Soon as the song ended, I said, "Thanks. That was nice."

"You want another?" she asked.

I'd learn the costly way that females got paid by the song. And since my wife hired a detective, everything that happened to me without my initiating it, Dakota was either directly or indirectly involved. "Whoever picked up this tab paid more than I would've dropped today. Keep the change."

She purred, "You sure?"

I stood, shook all three of my legs. "I'm good, sweetheart." Exiting the room, I reclaimed my spot at the bar.

Swallowing a mouthful of Courvoisier, I attempted to drown my disgust. "Ahhh." The burn in my throat felt good. I slid my empty glass in the bartender's direction. "Man, let me have another."

"What you gon' do, bruh? Keep coming in here numbing your problems or deal with her ass?" he asked, putting drink number three in front of me.

Before I signed a divorce decree, I had to be sure I was doing the best thing for my family. At some point I had to tell my wife, *I'm not your damn child.* If I told our kids to go to bed, she'd let them stay up another fifteen minutes. One. Five. That shit was fucking pointless!

"My dad never left my mom. I love my kids, man. Being a father is my number one obligation. A divorce would mess me and them up."

The bartender shook his head. "That let's-stay-together slave mentality is nineteen twenties, thirties, and forties. I tell you the same shit every time you in here. Leave that controlling bitch! Let her be the muthafuckin' boss of her goddamn self! Let her see what life is like without you, dude. If she gets some act right after a separation, take her back on your terms. If not, bounce the fuck on with peace of mind. You a good dude. Get your own spot."

Whoa.

I was tired of being humiliated in front of her mother, sisters, my parents, our friends, and her challenging me never registering as a problem to her. When I ignored her, the second we were alone (if she waited that long), I was definitely hearing "Benjamin Alexander Bannister," instead of "babe" or "honey."

Visualizing having my own spot again, "Umm, umm, umm." That short-lived wyld-with-a-*y* life after college, best to leave those bones buried.

Benjamin. The kids. Get them now! my wife texted.

I was over her immature antics. Mercedes wasn't the only person who could employ a private eye. "She's here," the bartender confirmed about the woman I was waiting for.

No need to look over my shoulder, I knew the second I inhaled her fragrance. Tori Burch perfume was added to my list of preferred scents on a lady the day we'd met. The woman I'd put on payroll glanced at my cell.

"That wife of yours is cute as a toy poodle," she commented, as I pulled out her stool.

Toya sat beside me at the bar, overlapped her long, sexy legs. "We don't have to meet at my place of business every afternoon. Let's get out of here and conduct this meeting away from your wife's master hiding over there in the corner dressed like a dude hawking us. We can go to my house. If you'd like," she said, touching my thigh.

The boldness in her tone mimicked lots of Atlanta women. Her

cotton candy–pink lipstick matched the color of the dress that
crept up to her ass when she wiggled on the seat. She tugged at the
hem, but there was no way she could hide the definition of the
track star muscles etched in her thighs. I loved the feel of a firm
body.

Her attire was more suitable for midnight hours or for performing on the stage that was to our right. Meeting Toya—that was her
government name—while standing in line at the Starbucks on
Piedmont off Peachtree one day, changed my shallow impression
of strippers.

First a square, white paper napkin, then a copper mug with her
usual Moscow mule was placed before her. "Hey, Toya. You look
and smell edible as always," the bartender said, taking a whiff of
the sweetness floating through the air.

No man stopped to get a whiff of my wife. Not even me. Said
something about she stopped wearing perfume not wanting to of-
fend any potential clients who may have allergies. What was her excuse for ditching the lingerie, thongs, seductive outfits, and high
heels she'd worn before I'd proposed?

Oh, that's right, now that she was a mom doing all the freak
nasty things she used to do to please her husband was inappropriate. I did not marry for my wife to put others before me! That included our children.

Two o'clock in the afternoon and I was at the one place I didn't
have to worry about my wife showing up. That woman was too
prideful to police my laptop, or cell, too prudish to go with me to
a strip club worried about what others would think . . . of her . . .
so she hired a spy. She'd forgotten about my feelings.

An occasional display of jealousy from her would instantly
stroke my ego. Let me know she still found me desirable. Had that
luxury with my mistress. No longer with the Mrs. Out of all the
places in the ATL, I was at a titty joint deciding whether my marriage was worth salvaging or should I get from under Mercedes's
snitch across the room and go to Toya's house and chill.

The bartender replaced my empty snifter with another cognac.
"This one is on the house."

Prior to my wife's employing a detective to snoop into my whereabouts, the only times I didn't get my kids from school was when I was out of town on business. Needed to start my own computer tech firm. The upside was I worked out of the office, seldom had to travel out of state to corporate in Miami.

I replied to her text, **I'd love to sweetheart but I'm extremely busy.**

If a legal separation was what she wanted, I was not going to fight her on it. She'd have to adjust too by getting her children or making other arrangements.

"You are so damn fine," Toya complimented. "I have got to let you taste my sweet pussy."

Gently stroking my tie, she turned it sideways, read the label, "Zegna," then nodded. "I can't understand these women in Hotlanta, man. So what if you dipped your dick into another female. You're still a keeper in my opinion. Your wife gon' find out when she start sifting through the pile of worthless dickatunities out here. Look at this."

She held her phone in front of me, played a video. I watched a long-framed athletic, dark-skinned man fucking doggie-style. "Damn, he's wearing her ass out!"

Toya said, "His ass out."

Instantly, my stomach churned. She ended the video, then said, "And the guy on top fucking dude in the ass is married with two daughters."

The bartender added, "Tried to tell him. His stock is Wall Street worthy."

"Your wife ain't stupid. Based on your looks, income, and personality, Benjamin, you're in the top two percent in the A."

Toya's words made me feel special. Odd as the compliment may have sounded, I needed to hear a woman acknowledge something about me was appealing.

Smiling on the inside, I asked, "You think so?" swirling my drink.

Scanning the room, she replied, "Dudes park in the lot waiting for us to open our doors and legs. It's packed every day with horny men who enjoy getting lap dances for lunch, seeing pretty pussies, booties clap, titties smack, and chicks twirl hard nipples in their face and these men aren't close to being fine as your sexy ass."

Tilting her head to the right, Toya continued, "That table over there. Those overweight execs are regulars, they're happily married and they have a different group of women with them almost every time they come in. That's so they have somebody to touch or fuck if they want to bust. But truth is, most of the times men just want to enjoy the company of beautiful women." She touched my thigh. "Benjamin, you're entitled to have a side if your wife isn't performing her duties. My offer still stands." Casually, she tagged on, "It's the ATL, Daddy."

True that. Nodding, I knew what she meant.

"You're either the one he's cheating with or the one he's cheating on. Black. White. All the men in Atlanta have situations that women have to deal with," she said.

Thought about my mistress. She was the coolest. In lots of ways Arizona made my marriage better. It would be easy to get rid of her but my wife didn't give me an incentive. My motivation to do the right by Arizona was fading.

The hottest female in the club was next to me. She twirled the edges of her wavy, black hair extensions that draped down opposite sides of her exposed diamond navel ring. Wondered how she gripped the pole with those wicked pointed pink nails.

Long lashes fanned in my direction as she blinked several times. As I watched her curl the tip of her tongue to the edge of the mug that was covered with condensation, saliva coated my inner jaws.

I swallowed the guilt of being where I shouldn't. Pondered leaving my wife for my mistress. Toya's sexy mannerisms kept my heavy nuts glued to my seat. Under no circumstance was I going to put my lips on the clit of this stripper but I couldn't lie. I wanted to. Her outer labia were just as juicy as the lips on her face.

Sipping my cognac, I told her, "No, thanks. Irrespective of my dilemma, I do have this on my finger." I twisted my wedding band several times.

Easing those nails under her dress, she said, "If that makes you feel better about not hitting this," then she smeared her pussy cream under my nose.

The bartender laughed.

Toya mumbled, "Men," then drank her cocktail before saying, "I'm married too. I'll tell you what. Let's wife-swap." Her fingernails walked from my knee to my balls as she said with a smile, "You *are* going to let me slide down your pole."

"Dude, I swear. I wish I were you right now," the bartender said, salivating.

The short time Toya had worked for me keeping tabs on my wife, I thought the diamond infinity band on her ring finger was for show to keep the men away.

My dick throbbed in protest. *We're already in trouble. Put this nut with all the other ones we need forgiveness for.*

The bartender was right. I told him, "Man, we gotta go. Close us out."

"Nah, my bruh. Your entire bill is on me."

CHAPTER 2

Mercedes

I was naked from the waist down, my purple cotton undies dangling against the wall on a gold metal hook. As I reclined atop the cool examination table, the thin layer of tissue rustled beneath my butt. I secured my feet in stirrups, scooted to the edge, then pressed my knees together.

"Ready for your close-up?" my doctor asked.

"If I'm going to rejuvenate my sex drive," I exhaled, "I have to try something new."

Gently, she parted my thighs and pointed her camera at my vagina. "This way you can see the before and after."

"I've never had a photo taken of my 'good good,'" I said, watching her click several times. "Take a few before shots with my phone."

Returning my cell, she retrieved a bottle of lubricant from the metal cart beside her. After this procedure, I should upgrade to sexier panties to make my husband jealous.

Looking at my pink flesh, I saw that everything was neatly tucked under my labia majora. Didn't have anyone to compare myself to. Had never seen the innermost part of my sisters or any woman. Porn was disgusting. I refused to consider that entertainment, no matter how many times my husband asked me to watch it with him.

Slowly, my gaze lateraled from the lube to the gorgeous woman between my legs. Her glowing skin was more radiant than the precious onyx stone in the ring on my middle finger. Her lips were the same natural tone. Teeth snow white showed whenever she spoke.

"You okay?"

At least someone cared enough to ask.

"This is my body. I *don't* need my husband's permission. He made his decision. I'm making mine. Why do you think men cheat?"

"I keep asking myself the same question." Her tone was melancholy. "That's why I take pride in giving women a reason to love their vagina," Dr. Stephens said.

Hadn't meant to trigger sad memories for her. I'd done everything the right way. Well, almost. Gave myself credit for staying a virgin until the summer after graduating high school. Only had intercourse sixty-seven times. Outside of trying to conceive, sex once a month was enough.

My husband was the second man I'd shared my sacred spot with. Didn't want a third. If there'd be another, he'd lose his mind sniffing this fresh flower. Or maybe I'd try women. Find someone who valued companionship over orgasms.

"How long will it last?" I asked.

"You paid for all three sessions so after your third one you should be good for about seven years. Maybe longer."

The doctor shook the bottle, squeezed gel into her palms. "This is going to be cold," she warned, massaging it onto my vulva.

Instantly, I became aroused. "Oh, my, gosh. I haven't tingled that much in months." The stimulating sensation of human touch other than my own washing myself was the most contact I'd had since Benjamin started sleeping at his mistress's house three months ago.

A smile parted Dr. Stephens's lips. "This is nothing. Your libido will be through the roof when you're done. You are going to sex your husband crazy tonight."

Exhaling, I rolled my eyes. There went my thrill.

"Are you sure you want the procedure?" she questioned. "If you're not sure, it's not too late for me to stop."

With my doctor giving me an out, one would think I was having an abortion like my sister Alexis wanted. I was confused about my marriage. Not about enhancing my sex drive. This ThermiVa treatment was for me and if he got lucky, my husband.

Mother.

Daughter.

Entrepreneur.

Wife.

Adulteress was not going to be added to my confessions when I stood at the pearly gate before God. Every person was a sinner but everyone wasn't forgiving, especially men.

For a moment, I thought about my father. Who was he? Where was he? What was his name? I despised my mother for listing my dad as "unknown" on my birth certificate as though she had no idea whom she'd had sex with. If my father were in my life, I'd ask him for marital advice.

Quietly, I nodded at my doctor, then said, "I'm positive. Don't ask again."

The hardest thing I had to do was learn how to make myself a priority. No more my kids this, my husband that. Certainly my family would welcome hearing my calling Benjamin by his birth name.

"You ready to get started?" my gynecologist asked, holding what I considered the magic wand in her hand that was about to transform my womanhood.

Respect was earned. I kept it real with everyone. Did Mercedes always have to speak what I thought? Absolutely. I still loved Benjamin but as I lay on this table I didn't like him at all.

A contrived laugh preceded my reply. "You should've gone to law school. How many ways are you going to inquire about the same thing?"

My husband used to be there every minute for me, for us. He was my hero. I was his queen. There was not a more perfect union of man and wife that I knew of. Now I got it. Man and wife. Not husband and wife. He had a new life. Moving forward, I granted myself permission to have the same opportunity.

Giving Dr. Stephens an urgent nod, I tried convincing myself this procedure was best for me. I spread my thighs wide as I could.

The doctor sat between my legs on a round swivel stool. The unit that would change my life was in the air. Never imagined I'd be doing this at twenty-seven. She lowered the device with a long cord attached.

"Relax. If this gets too hot or uncomfortable at any point let me know immediately."

Taking a deep breath, I closed my eyes. My heart flooded with sorrow. No need to cry. In thirty minutes, it'll all be done and my husband, my children, my mother, my sisters, none of them would know my secret.

The flat surface of the wand slid against my outer labia. It was warm. With each stroke the temperature grew hotter. I gasped, stretched my eyes.

"You okay?" Dr. Stephens asked.

Nodding, I struggled not to embarrass myself while having an orgasm. The sensation was delightful.

Six minutes of stroking on my outer lips, then she slid the device up and down inside my lips next to my clit for the same amount of time.

"I'm getting ready to insert the wand into your vagina for eighteen minutes," she said. "I'll start at the entrance then gradually go deeper."

I managed to get through the outer part without losing complete control but when the tip of the hot wand entered my vagina, I screamed. Unexpectedly, I had my first orgasm from penetration.

I leaned forward. "I apologize," I said, admitting to myself that the receptionist up front was right. An apology to her was in order but she wasn't getting one. Hopefully she hadn't heard me climax.

Dr. Stephens said. "It happens to some women. Look at it this way. You've got a jump start on your husband. We're all done." She paused, looked at me. Trading the wand for tissue, she removed the excess gel. "Give me your camera."

First taking the after pics with her camera, then I scanned the photos she'd taken with my phone.

"Remarkable. I approve." Side by side, the differences between my old and new vagina were definitely noticeable.

"After you have intercourse, let me know if there's improvement."

No man had made me cum from penetration. Masturbation gave me satisfaction though it wasn't my preferred. Whenever Benjamin kissed my "good good," that was the best. The heat from the wand did what I doubted would happen again even if I were intimate.

Checking my cell, I saw that Dakota had messaged me a picture of a woman with stupid long hair, in a short pink dress, followed by, **Your husband hired Toya to spy on you.**

I replied, **She looks like a stripper to me.**

She is. Be careful. But you know I'm all over her. Will have their every move tracked, Dakota answered.

Studying every feature in the picture, I realized I'd never looked that hot.

A text registered from Benjamin. **I'll get the kids. Go to the grocery store. Get your favorite wine. Cook dinner. Let me know when you're headed home so I can draw a nice bath for you.**

Speechless, I stared at the screen.

"Everything okay?" my doctor asked.

Softly, I answered, "I'm not sure."

Another text from Dakota appeared. **Don't worry, honey. Every stripper has a price. I'm going to put her on my tab and our team.**

I wasn't stupid! My husband was feeling guilty. If Benjamin was fucking strippers now, it was time for me to leave him for good.

CHAPTER 3

Benjamin

Inch by inch my dick extended along my inner thigh. Toya's wife unfastened my belt, removed my shoes, socks, pants, and boxer briefs. At the same time, Toya unbuttoned then took off my shirt and undershirt.

"Stand here. Don't move," her wife said, blindfolding me. The raspy tone of Toya's wife's voice made my dick harder. Holding my arm, her wife led me down one, two, three . . . fifteen steps.

"Back him up a little," Toya instructed.

Click. Click. Click. Click. "What the hell?" My wrists and ankles were cuffed.

Toya uncovered my eyes. Standing up straight, I was strapped to a leather-covered board like a damn frog. A chill traveled from the nape of my neck, to my spine, to the crack of my ass. I looked down; my dick pointed up. My shit was excited about some shit we were clueless about.

"Which one of us do you want to fuck and which one do you want to suck?" Toya asked as she climbed the pole that was in what she called her honeycomb hideaway.

I'd seen her legs spread east and west before but that was at the club. This pole was in her basement. She flipped upside down. Midway on that pole she flipped right side up, descended to the floor, did a full split bouncing her pussy on the hardwood.

I was not ready for Toya's "good good" as Mercedes would call it. I was confident with my performance ability but what I'd witnessed Toya do might snap my shit in half.

Toya's wife rolled a barstool in front of me. Straddling the seat, she pressed the remote, elevated her pussy to my dick's level, aligned the opening of her vagina with my head.

"Please. Don't," I protested. The only woman I'd penetrated since standing at the altar was Mercedes.

Pressing the remote, she lowered the seat, opened her mouth, then drooled all over my knob. A strand of saliva stretched from my third eye to her lips. I watched her suction it in like spaghetti.

Toya rolled a stool behind me. "My turn," she said, flipping me in her direction.

"Oh, shit!" Suddenly I was upside down. Blood drained to my brain.

Snatching my shaft, Toya held me tight as she licked my balls, then tossed me back to her wife. This time I felt Toya's finger penetrate me.

"Hey. Hey! My ass is off-limits!" I'd felt the air against my back but didn't realize they had access to my ass until now.

Ignoring me, she inserted a butt plug. That shit started vibrating. I damn near came instantly. Had to focus on her wife's teabagging my nuts, then sliding her tongue to the tip of my head. Between the sucking, stroking, and buzzing, I shouted, "Yesss!" like a lil bitch as I came all over Toya's wife's breasts.

"If you still want to chill," Toya said, "my spouse can pick up your kids and take them to your house. She can also cook, clean, and do your wife. Whatever I tell her to do, consider it done."

My erection subsided like a wet noodle when I laughed. "Hell, no. Take these cuffs off. Y'all trying to kill me and get me killed in the same day."

I'd told Toya all about my situations before I'd hired her. I did not need her to be a side to the side I already had, especially since Toya already had her hands in my wallet. How was she going to do the job I'd paid her to do if she was sexing me?

I'd been here long enough. "We'd better get to work," I said, heading upstairs. Quickly, I put on my clothes. I'd shower soon as I got to Arizona's.

After I handed Toya her weekly five hundred, she unlocked her phone, showed me a picture of a small parking lot with one building. Mercedes's car was in a stall near the entrance. "This is why your wife couldn't pick up the kids today. She went to Newman."

Sarcastically, I replied, "She's there? Now?" I felt foolish. All the shit I was doing with Toya was for retaliation against my wife when my wife was partially right about my being a dog.

I couldn't let Mercedes win, especially if this was our last round as husband and wife. Things became worse between us because she took it upon herself to hire that smartass private investigator Dakota Justice to spy on me. I returned the favor by putting Toya on my team.

Reading the banner in the picture, I said, "Ciao Bella Medical Center. What kind of place is that?"

Toya looked into my eyes. "Your wife is having a vaginal procedure."

"Procedure? For her what?" The more I wondered why, the less I could breathe.

Felt as though my heart stopped, then fell into my lap where Toya's wife's hands were minutes ago. *Vaginal what?* "Is that some kind of new terminology? Do not say that's another way of telling me *my* wife is having an abortion!"

"Calm down, man." Toya placed her finger over my lips. I gripped her wrist, moved her hand.

"Don't tell me what to do! My wife is killing *my* baby." Rubbing my neck I felt my veins protruding. Was this my fault? I couldn't leave Mercedes if she was pregnant. But if she killed my unborn, I'd . . .

Toya's wife handed me a glass of ice water, then exited the room.

Our having another kid would make me do right by my wife. An abortion would make me hate her. I sucked on a cube, started crunching it.

The next photos Toya showed me were of a woman's vagina but that wasn't my wife's. I knew what my pussy looked like.

"I don't give a fuck about another woman's shit."

"Dude. Stop tripping."

Fuck that. Toya might have an artificial dick but I was a real man. I took care of mine.

"Benjamin. Your wife got a treatment called ThermiVa. It's like a facelift for her pussy. It makes a woman more beautiful and tighter inside and out." Toya laughed. "If your wife has never squirted, she might after today."

Say what? My jaw dropped. I stood in Toya's doorway. "There's nothing wrong with my wife's 'good good.' " If Toya was right, I wish I could convince Mercedes to sit her new pussy on my face tonight. Smother me with her, what if she had fat, juicy lips now?

She had a what? I thought, shaking my head. "You need to break the mechanics all the way down. How do you know my wife is really there if you're here with me? And how are you sure that's what she's really having done?"

Toya held the edges of a C-note. *Pop! Pop!* She patted me on the back.

"Dude, you hired me to find out everything. I don't have time to follow her. I have reliable sources everywhere. You want my wife to test drive your wife's new vagina? Seeing how blessed you are it's probably going to be too tight for you." She laughed.

Why did some lesbians think every woman was secretly on their team? "My wife doesn't get down like that."

Toya raised her brows, curved her lips sideways. "If you say so."

"So you're saying my wife is bisexual?"

"I'm not saying anything."

Now I had a reason to ditch going to Arizona's and making good on my earlier text to spoil Mercedes. I texted my wife, **Baby, I'm headed to pick up the twins. Meet me at home. We need to talk.**

CHAPTER 4

Benjamin

"Let's get it on."

Adjusting my Beats headphones, I uncovered my left ear, sang along with Marvin Gaye, Teddy P., Trey Songz, and screeched to Minnie Riperton's "Lovin' You." I was doing all the right shit to make sure my wife smeared all of that new pussy in my face tonight. Hadn't listened to our favorite romantic songs in, damn, in years.

Four o'clock. No response from Mercedes. That wasn't okay. I decided to get things cooking. Milk. Butter. Sauce. Turned up the flame. Stirred the pot.

I yelled from the kitchen, "Brandon! Brandy! Y'all take a shower, then do your homework." By six, I wanted them in their bed, watching television with the door shut.

What in the hell was a new vagina? Could I go somewhere to get shine on my dick? My shit was good in the girth and length departments but females getting "good good" enhancements on top of the fact they could outfuck us men wasn't fair. If my wife had upgraded my vagina, I'd best be the only man who'd penetrate it.

I texted Arizona the truth: **Can't make it tonight.** Anything more would be a lie.

My wife was only twenty-seven. The parts of her body that I saw nowadays looked fine to me. Why did she have to go get something enticing done right when I was torn between leaving her for my mistress? Probably to surprise me for my birthday! Yeah, that was it. I had to hold off on making an irrational decision. A part of me became excited that I didn't want the twins to notice if they entered the kitchen. Brandon believed in the three-minute shower.

Standing closer to the stove, I didn't realize I'd splashed Alfredo sauce on the burner until I heard the sizzle. Lowering the fire, I rubbed fresh basil in my palms, then slapped my hands together hard. Two tablespoons of pesto, then I dumped a jar of sundried tomatoes in before putting on the lid to let it all simmer.

I checked my phone. My wife really didn't want to play games with me. Where in the hell was Mercedes? Newman was only forty minutes out, give or take five.

Fresh broccoli spears, carrots, and snow peas were in a bowl. One by one, I trimmed, snipped, or diced each piece.

A light ring tone came from my cell indicating a new text message. I dried my hands on my apron, unlocked my phone. It was my side asking, **Are you sure? I just finished cooking your dinner.**

I'd been crashing at her place on the regular for the past two months. My wife had screwed up our happy home by hiring that damn detective to follow me every fucking where. Arizona was getting too emotionally attached. Eventually I'd planned on ending it with my side. Now I wasn't sure. Didn't want to be persuaded by new pussy if I weren't hitting it. Didn't want to see my wife and kids happy with another man.

"How much longer before we eat, Daddy?" Brandon asked with drooping eyes. "I'm hungry."

"Yeah, I'm starving," Brandy said, holding her stomach.

"Homework done, you two?" I inquired, checking the time. It was seven-fifteen.

Over three hours had passed since I'd left Toya and her wife at their home. I texted Toya, **Where's my wife?**

"Done," Brandy said.

"All done," Brandon commented, backing up his sister.

"We'll wait a few more minutes for your mother. Go wash your hands and set the table with silverware."

Toya texted back, **@ Haven@1411**

With whom?

I had to know if Toya was really on top of things or giving me false information. There was no reply. I wanted to go find out but I couldn't leave my kids home alone.

What if my wife was on a date? If she was, it definitely wouldn't be Mercedes's idea to cheat on me. Dakota probably set this arrangement up for my wife to get back at me for being at the strip club. I hated Dakota's ass for ruining my marriage. If it was going to end, we didn't need outside help.

"Aw, shit." What if Dakota followed me to Toya's and that nosy bitch had taken photos of me again to show my wife tonight? Fuck, Dakota.

After putting two portions of vegetables in the steamer, I blackened the shrimp in a separate skillet, then hand-shaped six crab cakes. My wife and daughter usually ate one each. Brandon and I always devoured two.

I pan seared three crab cakes, placed them on plates for the kids. I'd wait to eat with my wife. Drizzling Alfredo sauce over the pasta, I topped the fettuccine with three prawns. They were so big and juicy I had to eat one of Brandy's. A spoonful of vegetables completed each plate.

"Kids," I called out, placing their plates on the formal dining table.

Brandon and Brandy raced into the room, sat at their seats.

"Where's your plate?" Brandon asked.

"And Mom's," Brandy inquired. "Where is she?" Instantly my daughter became saddened. "Call her, Daddy?"

"Yeah, call her. We haven't eaten together in a long time," my son added.

"Mommy is with a client. I'll wait for her. You guys eat."

I watched our kids say grace. Brandon always ate all of his veggies first to get them out of the way. Brandy alternated broccoli, shrimp, carrot, a bite of crabmeat. I went to the kitchen to check my cell. No missed anything. I poured two glasses of fresh lemonade, no ice for Brandy, lots of ice for Brandon, and returned to the dining room.

"Thanks, Dad," Brandon said right before he chomped on his last shrimp.

"When are you going to stop traveling so much, Daddy?" Brandy asked.

Brandon followed with, "Yeah, you've been gone every night. Are you going to be here when we wake up?"

"Yeah. I miss you tucking me in, Daddy," Brandy said.

"Us," Brandon corrected. "He tucks me in, too, you know. And I'm his first born."

Brandy's eyes darted toward Brandon, then froze. Her fork stabbed the last mound of crabmeat on his plate. "This could be you," she told her brother.

Damn! When had my little princess become hardcore? "Apologize. Now," I told her.

The family values my father instilled in me . . . now I got it. My affair should've never started. Definitely not worth my sleeping under a different roof missing out on time with my kids. If my wife was with another man doing the things I'd done with my mistress every night, I'd have no choice but to leave her for good and take my kids.

There was no ring tone but I checked my cell. Not a single message from Toya or my wife. I prayed what I'd imagined was far worse than what Mercedes was actually doing. Couldn't leave the house without taking the kids with me. They'd never met my mistress. Never will.

"You okay, Daddy?" Brandy asked.

I didn't realize I was biting my bottom lip until she spoke.

"You disappointed him," Brandon added.

"Did not!"

"Did too!"

"Yes, baby. Daddy is fine. Who wants dessert? Homemade sweet potato pie à la mode."

"That's what I'm talking 'bout," Brandon said. "Mom does not cook like you, Dad. Hurry up and finish that business deal so we can keep getting your delicious meals."

I removed their plates, went to the kitchen. I'd made a half dozen individual small pies. After removing them from the foil pans, I topped Brandon's with ice cream. Brandy's ice cream was in a small clear dessert bowl next to her pie.

The swelling in my chest hurt like hell. I wanted to yell, *Where the fuck are you, Mercedes!* I placed the plates on the table before my kids, kissed them on their forehead, said, "When you guys finish, watch television in your room," then returned to the kitchen.

I'd done all this shit when I could be sitting at the table with—

I texted Arizona. **With the twins. See you in the morning before you go to work.**

I tossed the remaining crab cakes in the garbage disposal. Followed that with the shrimp, sauce, and vegetables. Turning on the water, I scooped the mouthwatering pies out of the pans. Let them plop on top of the food in the sink, then flipped the switch.

Watching everything go down the drain, that was how I was starting to feel about my marriage, especially if my wife was out there letting another man eat *my* new pussy.

CHAPTER 5

Devereaux

"**P**lease. Allow me."

I looked at a stranger dressed in a red, fitted, collarless, button-down, long-sleeved shirt, black slacks, and black, hard sole, polished-to-perfection shoes, as he held open the door.

Whoa. Wow. His simple gesture to wait until I was inside surpassed the consideration of my ex-fiancé. If my mental wasn't messed up about my man having fucked my employee, I wouldn't be in awe of what this six-foot-three, olive-complexioned giant with neatly trimmed black hair and dark brown eyes had done.

Acknowledging his chivalry, I gave a half smile. "Thanks."

Attraction to a man other than Phoenix hadn't happened since I'd stopped communicating with my former director. This guy with a squared chin and sleek cheekbones smelled amazing. Inhaling his masculine fresh scent I relaxed my shoulders. Not wanting to appear desperate or walk away, I employed a stall tactic my sister Alexis would use. I opened my purse in search of my cell. A side glimpse revealed that his manhood protruded farther than his stomach.

"I love your show, Mrs. Crystal." His Italian accent wasn't sexier than his physique yet both excited me inside and out.

After my television series started trending on social media, more people knew me than I them. Softly I answered, "Thanks."

Haven @1411 was in my neighborhood. I'd brunch here on Sundays the few times my schedule allowed. The mansion where I now resided, alone, was less than two miles away. I'd never invite a man over without his taking me out first, but I wasn't the type of woman who didn't need a man.

Hearing the title Mrs. almost made me cry wishing that were true. Getting involved with any man before having closure with my ex wasn't wise. A clean, emotional reset was what I wanted.

"I'm not married," I replied. Entering 582512 to unlock my phone, I redirected my attention to him.

Handsome stared at the engagement ring on my finger, then looked into my eyes. "If you're honestly available and would like to get together, here's my card. I'd love to take you out."

The Antonio Marino? Film producer extraordinaire, I thought, staring at his name. I wanted to hug him! He appeared taller and definitely more attractive than the photos on his IMDb page. My heartbeat quickened. I had to take a deep breath.

Composing myself, I said, "I'll have my assistant contact your office."

"My interest is personal. Use my direct number. Please."

What would my wild and crazy sister Alexis do? The fortune she'd inherited from her deceased father made that girl the worse millionaire I'd ever known. I didn't want to come across disinterested or disrespectful.

"Nice meeting you," I replied. "I'll text you my number." If he was really interested, he could contact me.

Success without a love interest wasn't what I wanted. I'd come here hoping to find the strength to make a final decision to call it quits with my daughter's father. Maybe unexpectedly meeting Antonio was the answer.

"Hey, darling. Glad you made it. How was your flight? We're seated in the private booth next to the chef's kitchen," a beautiful bubbly woman said, then escorted Antonio across the dining area while jiggling her booty.

Bright and bouncy wasn't my personality but when did I stop being happy? I questioned if I'd done the right thing by kicking my man out of my house. I was a Libra woman and my life was eighty percent work, twenty percent everything else, which included sleep.

Phoenix was supposed to be my balance. I tried to let him lead. That hadn't worked well with my Capricorn ex, who was full of get-rich-quick-the-easy-way ideas.

Silencing the monologue in my head, I could no longer ignore Mercedes frantically waving from across the room. She was seated in the corner at the bar. The only available stool was the one she'd reserved for me next to the crimson brick wall.

"Hey, Sis," I said, greeting her with open arms.

She hung her purse on the hook beneath the counter. Sliding out my chair, I placed my bag next to hers.

Touching my cheek, she commented, "Your skin needs moisture. Don't let yourself go. He's not worth it."

I hadn't seen my sister as much since the night her private detective drove me to the house of my star actress. From secretly duplicating every key on Phoenix's ring to discovering one of them fit the front door of his side's home, Dakota Justice was the best at tracking cheating men.

Exhaling, it felt good to sit still for a moment. I told my sister, "I'm glad you could meet on such short notice."

"Bartender." Mercedes snapped her fingers twice. "Two glasses of your best. Cayman cabernet. Make that a bottle." Facing me, she held my hand. "No need to ask how you're doing. You look a hot mess. Who was the guy you walked in with?"

Insults were not what I needed. I sniffled, then blinked repeatedly, fighting to keep a flood of tears from gushing onto my blouse. Telling Mercedes who Antonio was wouldn't remove the daggers she'd helped Dakota put in my heart.

"I'm no superwoman like you." That was the truth. I wanted my man to come back home. Sleep beside me at night. Wanted to put my family back together.

If I hadn't entered Ebony's house using the duplicate key Dakota had made, hadn't heard Ebony and my fiancé fucking upstairs, hadn't witnessed her shouting for my man to call her a bitch, hadn't heard him say it, hadn't found my baby Nya asleep downstairs in one of Ebony's bedrooms by herself . . . Lawd, Jesus!

"Oh, dear," Mercedes exclaimed. "Let's switch seats."

Hadn't realized the tears I struggled not to release were streaming down my cheeks as I faced all the patrons at the bar. Several sets of eyes were on me. Thank God, no one pointed their cell phone at me.

Not bothering to dry my face, I said, "Sure," now looking at the brick wall.

"I've been here since four because I didn't want to go home to Benjamin."

Four hours? Really? "I find that hard to believe."

"You shouldn't. You know I can relate," my sister said, meshing her side with the edge of the oak wood trim.

No, she could not. I'm forgiving. My sister wasn't. Phoenix Henry-Watson wasn't the perfect fiancé. Wish I didn't know now what I didn't know before hiring Dakota. Wish he wasn't my ex-fiancé. My sister's husband, Benjamin, had his faults but he took excellent care of his kids. Phoenix was a good dad, too, but sexing my star actress? Why? Shaking my head, I wondered how he could have done that to me after all I'd provided for him.

The bartender poured a splash in the wineglass, handed it to Mercedes. She sipped, gargled, swallowed, then nodded. He filled our glasses halfway.

A guy approached my sister, handed her a gift bag, then left. Sitting the shiny white bag on the counter next to a small wooden keg, Mercedes continued, "He's a dog, Devereaux. He needs to be neutered. Stop soaking, honey." Handing me a square paper napkin, she commanded, "Dry your face."

Was chastising me my sister's way of coping with her marital disaster? Mercedes refused to accept her husband having a mistress. Said she was teaching him a lesson by withholding sex. Gave him an ultimatum and where was he laying his heads at night? Not beside her.

The harsh realities of man-sharing in Atlanta made me want to go get my man from wherever he was. Picking up her gift bag, I inquired, "Who was that and what is this?"

The guy appeared to be about six feet. The short-sleeved, fitted shirt exposed his hard biceps. His stomach was flat, ass sat high. Flawless skin. I needed to get laid soon.

"That's my new personal assistant slash trainer. I'm about to get all the way fit." She winked at me. "Benjamin stepped out on his mistress today with a stripper."

Shaking my head, I couldn't believe it. "You're still having him followed?"

Mercedes nodded. "If he wants her, I'm taking every dime he's got. This is my husband's newest favorite perfume, Tory Burch. End of discussion."

Frowning, I asked, "Are you having—"

"Having an affair with the guy that left?" Leaning closer, Mercedes whispered, "Not yet," then licked her lips.

That was certainly a response Alexis would give. "Have you spoken with Mom?" I asked, wondering what Antonio looked like naked. He seemed hairy.

"When Mom isn't working, all she does is spend time with her new conquest, Bing, and that spoiled Yorkie, KingMaxB." Mercedes twirled the edges of her jumbo-spiraled Afro.

Normally her hair was smoothed, pulled back, and she'd have on black-framed glasses that didn't have a prescription. The neutral-colored lipstick was replaced by a peachy matte. There was something illuminating about her attitude.

In Mom's defense, I had to say, "I'm happy for her. After having to raise the four of us by herself, she deserves a mature man like Bing. He's more suited to her than Spencer."

"She needs to have Dakota do a background check on—"

I had to interrupt with, "Don't you dare ruin her life the way you've done mine."

The wine goblet hadn't rested five minutes before I picked mine up and dragged a long sip. My sister didn't touch hers.

"Hmm," was all she said.

Glancing to my left, I tried to shield my disgust with her forever interfering in other people's situations. "I haven't eaten all day. Bartender, let us have a Haven Truffled Potato Hay."

"Half order," Mercedes insisted.

"I—"

Interrupting me, Mercedes said, "I know that look." Sternly she gripped my hand again. "You'll be okay."

How did she know? This chick just didn't get it. I tried to wash away the lump in my throat. Swallowing the last mouthful of wine I glanced over my shoulder to see that Antonio was still at the private booth with bright and bubbly. His back was to me. She laughed in my direction. I scanned Haven's crystal wine rack that was filled with bottles from the ceiling to the floor. Facing Mercedes, I inhaled, leaning my elbow on the bar.

Mercedes's eyes darted around the room. I recognized that mask. Squinting, a single sympathetic tear fell from her left eye. She wasn't as tough as she portrayed. What she didn't know was I struggled to keep from telling her how I really felt fearing her insensitivity would make me erupt like a volcano.

Suppressing my emotions, I had to numb my pain. I asked, "Bartender, can you refill my glass? Please and thank you." I felt I'd been at the bar for hours yet I'd sat down less than thirty minutes ago.

Hot air escaped Mercedes's mouth. I held my breath. Fanned the space in front of me. "Stop that."

She laughed. I didn't understand what was funny. As I watched my sister lean closer, she lamented, "He's no good for you or to you, Devereaux. You've got to euthanize that lying, cheating, mangy mutt of yours. He fucked your lead actress while your daughter was in the bed downstairs, for God's sake."

"Nya was asleep. It wasn't at our house. I—"

Hissing again, I pinched her nose this time. "I don't want to inhale your frustrations. I have my own," I said, letting go.

I wanted to add that I'd gotten Nya out of Ebony's house before my daughter had awakened. What Nya didn't know hadn't hurt her.

"You will appreciate my help. My private detective is still on his trail. If you're thinking about taking him back, and I know you are, I'll have Dakota give you an update on Phoenix's indiscretions. He still has the key to Ebony's place. Bet you didn't know that."

Staring up at the flat screen above Mercedes's head, I should've asked, *Where's your husband?* Instead, I told her, "He's not a dog.

He's the father of my child. No matter how many keys or women he has, I can't change the fact that he'll always be around." If my sister wanted to waste her money spying on my ex, so be it.

"Stop pretending Phoenix did not . . ." She paused, then snapped her fingers twice and commanded the bartender, "Menus. Two. Now."

"Don't act as though you don't know why Benjamin is sleeping at his mistress's house every damn night. You're not only bossy. You're disrespectful. That man behind the bar is not your god-damn servant!"

People at the bar clapped, making me aware that my voice was above room tone. Mercedes's eyes scanned from the front door, along the entire bar, then locked with mine. I hated making a scene but Little Miss Perfect never knew when to take her foot off of any-one's neck. Thankfully, the lights at the bar dimmed. The softness of one of the acorn-shaped chandeliers glowed between us.

Placing both menus in front of me, the bartender said, "Thank you for telling her what I was about to."

I watched my sister's lips transform to a tight, sinister grin. Mer-cedes quietly picked up a menu but not before rolling her eyes at the bartender. Loud enough for nearby diners to hear, she re-torted, "He applied for a job taking orders. He shouldn't be of-fended when he's told what to do. Changing the conversation. You never answered me. Who's the man you walked in with?"

I'd asked *her* to meet *me.* That meant I wanted to discuss some-thing of importance in my life. Discomfort set in, as I turned side-ways in my seat wondering if Antonio would disassociate himself from me if he'd overheard Mercedes's last condescending com-ment. She'd already damaged one relationship.

Confronting my sister, I asked, "Why do you care whom I walked in with?" If I gave her a chance, she was sure to ruin my getting to know Antonio.

"Darling, his posture, designer suit, hairless face, rugged chest, speaks volumes. He's a man worth dating and bedding."

Shaking my head, I answered, "Maybe," then added, "I guess."

"You guess?"

"I'm considering consulting with him on my new project. It's a documentary with all women and I want all females to work on this."

Mercedes's eyes grew larger than I'd ever seen. She gasped. Anticipating her exhale, I held my breath. Her breasts thrust forward.

"Don't you dare," I said.

Pressing her lips together, I heard the breath escape her nostrils as she begged, "He's a man. Men are worthless. You know this. He can't be your consultant. You've got to include me on this project."

Back to Mercedes's world, I refused to concede on my masterpiece. "It's unlike anything on television. I'm praying this project elevates me to the big screen."

She popped her long, skinny fingers in the air back-to-back-to-back. "Champagne! Your best! Now!" was followed by two more snaps toward me. "Devereaux!" She hugged me. "See what you can accomplish when you don't have a deadbeat weighing you down. We don't have time to think about Phoenix what's-his-last-name. That's right . . . Hound Dog, Dirty Dog, Filthy Dog." Tilting her head back, she laughed as it bumped against the wall.

I didn't consider any of what she'd said humorous. My cell rang. Phoenix's photo appeared. Mercedes snatched my phone. Placed the call on speaker.

"Devereaux is busy coming up. Go poke a ho, you lying loser."

The room tone at the bar lowered. Embarrassed, I refused to turn around. Continuing the conversation, softly I said, "Hey, Phoenix. What's up?"

Normally I'd call him babe. Not anymore. He was what he'd become to me though I didn't want to admit it. My daughter's father was a real deadbeat.

"I want to see Nya tonight," he said.

"She has plans."

That was the truth. My baby was at my other sister Sandara's place.

Nya had recently turned three. I was hurting too much to let him come to her birthday party last week and watch him pretend he was the world's most amazing dad. His mom was there. Mrs.

Etta Henry-Watson pleaded with me to let her keep Nya while I worked.

Long as Phoenix was under his mama's roof, I couldn't let Nya visit. Teaching our daughter it was okay for a man to leech off of his mother was wrong. He was supposed to be our child's role model. Phoenix's poor judgment, sexing a woman while he was supposed to be watching our child, made me believe the second his mother left the house, he'd sex women while our daughter was with him. I refused to be the same fool twice.

"Don't make me beg. Dev, please," he whined.

"Please what? Nya isn't going to be home, you idiot. Try showing up at a decent hour." Mercedes said what I couldn't.

I took the call off speaker. My sister rolled her eyes toward the ceiling.

Phoenix didn't want to see our daughter. He wanted to get back in my good graces. He didn't value the lifestyle I'd afforded him when we were together in my five-thousand-square-foot five-bedroom home. His good dick didn't contribute to a single mortgage payment the three years he lived with me. Learning he'd been fucking Ebony Waterhouse aka Goldie Jackson the past two years made me want to end the call.

"What do you want from me?" I asked him.

"I've got to hear this," my sister said, leaning close to my ear.

Because he'd put a ring on my finger, I'd moved him in, paid all the bills while he regurgitated false promises heaped on top of more lies. Everything he'd told me was bait to keep me holding on to what? For what? Asking me to hire his fuck buddy hurt me the worst. When he brought that bitch to me on a silver platter, he'd already eaten her pussy.

The one opportunity I'd given him to manage the lead actress in my now number one television series, *Sophisticated Side Chicks ATL*, thanks to Mercedes I discovered that bastard was a dog.

"Dev–"

Cutting him off, I suctioned in my churning stomach. "My name is Devereaux."

Phoenix's voice escalated, "Please, Dev! Just hear me out. Let me come over tonight. It'll be like old times. Just the two of us and I can explain."

I wondered how many other women he'd sexed during our relationship. Had he used protection to protect me?

Mercedes took my hand, placed the microphone to her mouth, told Phoenix, "We'll see you at ten o'clock sharp. Leave the overnight bag at your mama's house," then ended the call.

I looked at my sister. "Thanks."

Mercedes said, "Bet he'll show up with an empty heart and a hard dick. He probably wants to knock you up again. Don't be like your lil sis."

Sandara had three babies and no husband.

"I'm telling you, Devereaux. Whatever you do, don't have sex with that pathetic excuse for a man. He's your kryptonite."

Sometimes I wish I was strong as her. What was Mercedes's weakness? I wanted to see Phoenix. Wondered if I would love or hate him when I stared into his eyes. Or if my heart would feel the way it felt now.

Numb.

CHAPTER 6

Sandara

"Nya, Tyrell, Ty, Tyson. It's bedtime, you guys." The kids were seated on the floor in my living room in front of the television.

Nya looked dead-on Phoenix but had her mother's long, curly hair. She skipped to the rear of my small two-bedroom apartment, returned, then handed me a purple silk scarf. "Tie me up," she said, turning her back to me.

Smoothing the edges of both braids, I felt sorry for my niece and her mom. After Devereaux put Phoenix out, poor Nya slept over with whatever family member could keep her and she had to stay on set with my sister during the day.

"I'm thirsty, Mama," my three-year-old whined. Tyrell had light brown skin like his father.

I wanted to have my tubes tied like my sister Mercedes told me but a part of me wanted to get married and have my husband's baby the way Mercedes had done.

Checking the time on my cell, it was eight thirty. Tyrell's bladder must've been the size of a golf ball. Any liquids after seven and that child would pee a puddle on my mattress by morning.

"It's too late," I told him, then added, "Go use the bathroom right this minute."

"I'm not sleepy," Tyson protested. "When are you getting Grandma's dog back from Remy?"

Lawd, why did I have to deal with this by myself every night? My kids, plus Nya, and my job were too much. KingMaxB was right across the street with my girlfriend and her kids. I'd get him whenever my mother got back.

Tyson was four, a year older than Nya. My daughter, Ty, was the same age as Nya. Ty gave me her favorite pink head wrap. I circled it, then tied a bow at the top.

"Tyson, don't make me tell you twice," I said, staring at him.

"Right this minute, boy," Ty scolded as though she were the mother. Taking the remote from Tyson, she powered off the flat screen.

I texted Devereaux, **Getting ready to tuck in the kids. I have a call-back so you need to pick Nya up by 8a.**

"Give the good Lord His praise for this day. When I open this door, anybody with their feet on the floor will need Jesus."

Nya knelt next to Ty, then laughed. "TeeDara funny."

"Don't try me, lil girl. You'd better ha-ha in your sleep," I warned.

The boys were side by side at their twin bed. I waited until they got under their sheet, then gave all of them a hug and a kiss. Nya sat up.

My younger son, Tyrell, shook his head. "Mama means it, Nya. Put your head on the pillow."

Nya cried, "I want my daddy."

Sitting on the bed, I held her. "I know, sweetheart. Maybe he can tuck you in at home tomorrow." By the time I'd finished the sentence she was asleep.

With glossy, almost teary eyes, Tyson slowly blinked. "My daddy probably had to work late. He coming to take me to school?"

Slowly, I exhaled. "I'll let you know in the morning," I answered, then turned off the light.

Never giving up hope that his father would one day make us a family, I left the door partially open, then went to the kitchen. I poured a glass of white wine, sat in the living room. Finally, the first moment of the day for myself.

Little Five Points was my neighborhood since I'd gotten pregnant and dropped out after my freshman year at Baylor. Mercedes told me to have an abortion, get my degree, meet a man who wanted to give me his last name, then give birth to my first child.

Section 8 had served me and my three kids well. The two hundred dollars I paid last month should've been the full rent of fifteen hundred based on my new income. Why should I do the right thing when the President didn't pay taxes?

Rubbing the black leather, I traced the split in my sofa, poked the yellow cushion that stuck out. The wall in front of me was covered with framed pictures of my babies, Nya, and Mercedes's twins. Soon my sister Alexis's newborn would be added to the wall. That was if she didn't take Mercedes's advice and terminate the pregnancy.

My mom's photo was centered. She was my everything. Wish I could say that about my dad, whoever he was. Tears clouded my eyes. The only time I cried was over my father and Tyson's father. Neither one of them loved me enough to claim me.

"Time for me to move out and move on."

I texted Tyson's dad, **I need you to keep your son for two weeks.**

Copying then pasting the same message to my other children's sperm donors, I heard, *Knock. Knock* followed by, "Sandara. Open the door."

Shaking my head, I hurried to let Blackstone in. Should've never let him give me that big black dick. Now I was stuck with him until Tyson graduated from high school.

"Hey, boo. You put the kids down?" he said, walking in.

"Yeah. A few minutes ago."

"What you sippin' on?" he questioned, drinking straight from my wine bottle. "I need a nightcap."

"Not tonight. I have a callback tomorrow with—" He opened his mouth and covered mine, smothering the words I was about to say.

"The only backing you need to do is on this," he said, unzipping his pants. "Don't start denying Daddy his pussy jus' 'cause yo' money flowin'."

Soon as he raised my dress above my hips, I pulled it down, backed away. "Not tonight, Black. I'm serious." Black's loads were heavy and I didn't want to take any chances on leaking while modeling expensive designer clothes.

He had the same last name as my mom's first boyfriend, Billy, and I was thankful there was no relation. One sister in my family with an incest situation was one too many.

"Since you got that lil modeling gig, you too big to fuck with your boi? You got one of those international muvphuckas with good hair and a accent and shit? This always gon' be mine, boo."

He cupped both holes between my thighs and butt real tight. I held my breath.

Grabbing my biceps, he turned my body toward the refrigerator, forced my braless tits against the stainless steel. I felt my nipples getting hard. I submitted the second he pressed the lever. Crushed ice fell into his hand and onto the floor. This scene replayed at least three times a week.

I turned an ear to the kids' bedroom. Listened intensely. The only sound I heard was my heavy breathing.

Black had to hurry up!

His hand slid on my clit. He penetrated me with his cold finger, then poked me several times shoving chips of ice in my pussy. I moaned as my muscles tightened to his movement. Kneeling behind me, he pulled my panties to the side and started licking my asshole real slow. His tongue slid along my anus. His mouth felt like one big ice cube.

Hated how my body naturally responded to him. Just when I was getting ready to cum, he stopped, stood, then opened the freezer.

Holding his wrist, I faced him, then whispered, "Those are for the kids when they get home tomorrow. I only have four. What if Nya comes back?"

Staring into my eyes, he lied effortlessly. "I'll get 'em some more."

I was accustomed to him not doing what he'd say more than he'd kept his word, especially when it came to our son. But I couldn't deny Black. Maybe one day he'd live with us.

Unwrapping the strawberry flavored Popsicle, he eased it in my pussy. I cringed as he pulled it out.

"Turn your ass back around," he commanded.

I felt the syrupy, frozen block begin to melt as he put it in my butt.

"Fuck this shit," he grunted. Yanking out what was left on the stick, he stuffed his engorged head and shaft in my ass.

Forcing him back, I looked over my shoulder, he lowered his pants to his knees, then shoved his dick in my syrupy ass again.

"I don't care how famous you become, you always gon' be my bitch," he said, jamming all of his dick inside of me. "Whose ass is this?"

Tears streamed down my face. I liked rough sex. Hated that he wasn't in love with me. "Why you don't want us to be a family?" I asked.

He fucked me harder. "We are a family. I'm here, ain't I?"

Opening the refrigerator door, I shielded my body from view should any of the kids come out of the bedroom. I slammed my butt into his crotch, concentrating on getting mine first.

"Make that ass clap for Daddy," he said, slapping me hard.

I grabbed his hand. "Stop. You gon' wake them up."

Black hissed, "Twerk, then, bitch, so I can bust this nut."

With three kids, three baby daddies, I'd stopped letting other men cum inside my pussy. A finger, dildo, a vibrator in my V-thang right now would get me off. Learned the hard way with my last one that birth control wasn't one hundred.

Fingering my clit, I came so hard my knees buckled.

He hiked my butt cheeks toward him, then grunted in my ear. "Take all this cum for Daddy."

The side of my face was flat against the lemonade container. Grunting in my ear, he came inside my hot ass. Semen saturated my crack, streamed down my thighs, plopped to the floor.

All of this was my fault. I kept letting Black come back. Success didn't make me love him any less. I wanted him to be proud of me. Maybe if I knew who my father was I'd have one man who loved me for me . . . maybe. There was also a chance that I'd never meet my dad.

Black shuffled his feet to the counter, unrolled a fistful of paper towels, wet them, then scrubbed his dick and balls. He handed the soiled mound to me, got a fresh bunch of paper, dried himself, handed it to me, then pulled up his pants.

"I was just about to text you when you knocked." Filling a bucket with hot water, I added bleach. Cleaning up his mess, I told Black, "I need you to watch your son for two weeks. I have a big runway show coming up."

He shook his head. "Can't."

"Why?"

"You gon' let me hold a hundred?"

"To keep *your* son?"

"Now that you the man you need to pay me for this." He grabbed his dick.

Mopping the floor, I started crying. "Never mind. We're moving anyway and I'm not giving you the address. You ain't never gon' do right by us. I'ma get me one of those fine men with wavy hair and an accent."

He rubbed his hand over his mouth. "Okay, boo. I got you." His hand cupped my neck.

"Ahh!" I dropped the mop.

He was jealous? I always wanted to role-play but not with his being angry. Black's grip became tight. I held his wrist. "Ba—"

Tried to call him "baby." The thickness of his fingers curled. I couldn't exhale. Inhale. Digging my pointed nails into his triceps, I dragged his flesh.

His other hand rose eye-level. As I watched Black make a fist, my eyelids grew wider. As he drew back his arm, he thrust forward. Stopped inches from my nose.

Loosening his touch enough for me to choke, he whispered in my ear, "Bitch, don't make me mess up that pretty little face."

I saw his rage. Imagining how helpless my mother must've felt when Fortune beat her, I was terrified of what would happen if I'd scratched him again. I closed my eyes and prayed, "Please, let me go."

"Daddy?"

Oh God. I hadn't heard Tyson get out of bed.

Black kissed me, then released his grip with a shove. "I love you. Let me know when you need me," he said. "I'll see if my mom can help you out."

I picked up Tyson, held him close. "Baby, your daddy has to leave. Mommy will tuck you back in."

"You're red, Mommy," my son cried, softly touching my neck.

Checking his little hand, I was relieved there was no blood on his fingers.

"No, you won't," Black said, taking Tyson from me. "This one here is my boy. I'll put him back to bed." Kissing my ear, he mumbled, "I'll keep him but you coming up off of some of that bank you stashin'. Or I'm taking you to court."

Tyson leaned his head on Black's shoulder. "Night, Mommy." There was joy in our son's voice.

Shaking my head as Black took Tyson into the bedroom, I became scared all over again. He was going to act a fool when he saw that the flesh I'd ripped away from his biceps left gashes in his tattoos.

I went to the bathroom, locked the door, glanced in the mirror. Stretching my neck, I knew it would take more than a few hours for the deep red bruises to fade from my light skin.

I got my cell, raced into my bedroom, locked the door, pushed the back of a chair under the knob, then texted my girlfriend Remy, **Can you keep my kids and Nya tomorrow?**

Remy replied, **Sure. I need three hundred to pay my car note. It's late.**

CHAPTER 7

Devereaux

"Geez." I barely recognized the man standing in my doorway. A beard coiled like Berber carpet spanned Phoenix's face ear to ear. The length of his mustache hid his upper lip. There was no skullcap covering his once ultra-low fade. An inch-high, unlined, matted Afro had taken its place.

"Well. Well," Mercedes said. "Your new mommy can't afford to give you an allowance to clean yourself up? As I recall, you were always in a barber's chair on Devereaux's dime. You don't need to cross the threshold because your daughter isn't here."

Interrupting, I told my sister, "Mercedes, please. Not now," then invited my ex into my home.

Phoenix had done me wrong. Me. Not her. I didn't take pleasure in stomping on any person when they were down. Seeing my ex appear homeless was a heart-wrenching first.

"Aw, give me a break," Mercedes lamented. "That despicable look is to play you like a fool. Don't forget he doesn't care about Nya." She redirected her words to Phoenix. "Just because you couldn't come to your daughter's party did not excuse you from getting her a gift."

Phoenix scratched his beard, stared at me, tilted his head toward Mercedes. His eyes shifted to my sister, back in my direction.

I shook my head. Obviously, he wanted to come in and wanted Mercedes to get out.

"She's right," I said. "A card. A text wishing Nya happy birthday would've been nice."

Cautiously, he took one step. I was quiet. He took another. The heaviness of Phoenix's hands caressed my hips. Instantly I became weak. Wanted him to take me right here on my living room floor. I touched his matted afro. I didn't care about that he looked unkempt. One trip back to the barbershop could restore his sexiness.

"I love you, Dev. I can't live without you."

Mercedes yelling, "Call me a bitch!" startled me. "Sounds familiar? You still love her too?"

I shouldn't have given her all the details of Phoenix's infidelity. "Please. Respect the father of my child."

"Yeah, bitch!" Phoenix stood tall. "Where's your man? Why you so fucking bitter? Learn to suck dick and your man might keep his ass at home."

His shade was accurate. I needed to stop revealing my intimate details but I hadn't shared Mercedes's business with anyone, including our sisters, my ex, or my mother.

Gently touching Phoenix's chest, I said, "Close the door," feeling bad for him. The hem of his light-blue wrinkled polo stopped short of covering the bulge protruding from the front of his gray cotton sweats. The waistband sagged around his butt. "Are you hungry?"

I'd never seen him this casual unless he was headed to the gym.

"Something hot to eat would be nice, babe," he said. Lounging on my sofa, he picked up my remote, turned on my television.

The thought of not sleeping alone tonight, I'd already considered letting him stay.

Mercedes approached Phoenix. "Don't you mean some*one* to eat?"

Ignoring her, he said, "Let me get a Hennessy straight up, Dev."

Mercedes stood over my ex, snatched the remote control. "He's only here because Ebony wouldn't let him move in with her and I refused to let you let this bum move back into your house." She folded her arms, tapped her foot, checked her cell. "I'm staying the night."

Bypassing Mercedes, Phoenix came to me. Pulled me into a strong embrace. "Baby, I'm sorry. I'll never disrespect you again. I need you, Dev. I'm nothing without you."

"You were nothing with her. You'll never be anything. And her name is Devereaux." If Mercedes stood closer to Phoenix, to us, we could group hug.

"Get that." Phoenix paused, exhaled, let me go, then walked away. "Because of you, Dev, I'm trying really hard to be respectful to her ass."

I watched my sister follow Phoenix back to the sofa and block him from sitting down. This time she stared up at him, placed her hand on her hip.

"Other than a second chance to fuck up Devereaux's life, why are you here, Phoenix? Huh? She's successful! You're nothing! A real man would love to marry her. She begged you to set a date and you thought you were the one settling."

Phoenix towered a half foot over Mercedes. "I'm not gon' tell you twice. Bitch! Back up off of me."

Aw hell no! He'd crossed the line with the "b" word. My heart pounded. "Phoenix, you need to leave," I said. Not that I agreed with Mercedes but tolerating his calling my sister out of her name wasn't happening.

Slapping Phoenix's face, Mercedes said, "You heard Devereaux. Out! You vagabond." She shoved his chest twice.

"Mercedes, stop it!"

"He shouldn't have called me a—"

Phoenix grabbed Mercedes's biceps, picked her up. Her feet dangled as she tried to kick him in the balls. "I ain't no punk nigga like your husband." He tossed her on the sofa. As he drew back his fist, his eyes were cold. "Open your mouth again."

"No!" I cried, grabbing him. "Both of you stop it, please."

Phoenix dropped his hand to his side. Shook his head.

My sister kicked him in the groin. He grabbed his nuts. I shielded Mercedes's body with mine, then snatched the home cordless phone off the sofa table.

"Move out the way, Dev. I'ma beat that bitch's—" Bending over, he cupped his dick. "Fuck!" He fell to his knees. His forehead banged against the area rug.

I didn't care if he crawled to the BMW I'd bought him that was in my driveway. "Get out of my house, Phoenix. Now!" The situation escalated beyond my control. I dialed 9-1-1. I'd seen black eyes and a busted lip on our mother. I'd get my gun and . . . Shit! He knew where we kept two loaded guns on the shelf by the front door.

Don't look at the box, I told myself. None of this was supposed to happen.

"Nine-one-one operator."

Mercedes screamed, "Get the hell out!"

"He won't leave," I said. "Please, just send someone to get him out of my house before somebody gets hurt." I ended the call. Begged Phoenix, "Leave before the police gets here. We can talk later. Just the two of us. I promise." I'd say anything to get him out. There was no way I'd allow Phoenix back in my place.

He stood as though he'd regained his strength. "We can talk now. She's the one that has to go." Grabbing my arms, he started to pull me off of Mercedes. "Since Mercedes wants to act like a man, I'ma show that bitch how it feels to get kicked in the nuts."

I didn't want to do a repeat of what Mercedes had just done. I had to. Letting me go, he stumbled, bit his bottom lip, then backed away.

Bam! Bam! Bam! "Police! Open up!"

I whispered at Phoenix, "Go upstairs to the bedroom and lock the door." I motioned for him to go now.

Hands clamped over his genitals, he grunted. Shook his head. "Why, Dev? You kicked me. You called them. I ain't do nothing wrong. Let 'em in."

Mercedes opened my front door. "There he is."

I told the officer, "We have it under control. He's leaving now."

The cop entered without my permission. His partner followed. The first officer questioned, "What's the problem here?"

Mercedes spoke to him, "Things got out of hand for a moment." Pointing at Phoenix, she said, "Escort him outta here. We're good."

I was pleasantly surprised with her response. That was exactly what I was going to say.

Phoenix complained, "That's a goddamn lie."

Shaking my head, I stared at my ex. He removed his hand from between his legs. I warned him, "You don't want to do this."

The second officer directed her comment to Phoenix. "Tell us what happened."

"She started it," he said, pointing at Mercedes. "First, she slapped me in the face. Twice. That's how I got this," he whined, then flipped his bottom lip. "Then her crazy ass kicked me in my private."

Shifting her eyes from one side of my heaving breasts to the other, the second officer said, "Is that true?"

If I confirmed Phoenix's story, Mercedes was going to jail. Staring at my sister, this time I noticed her biceps had blue fingerprints. Scanning myself. The marks on my arms were darker than hers. Phoenix's lip was slightly swollen. Mercedes had hit him pretty hard.

"Did she assault him first?" the female officer questioned.

Nodding, Phoenix said, "Tell the truth, Dev. You know she did."

I wished he'd let it go so all of us could sleep in our beds tonight. This was not a moment for revenge. I loved my daughter's father.

"Ms.," the first officer said, directing his attention toward me. "Is that true? If you don't say something, everyone is getting arrested."

My sister sat on the sofa. That was the quietest she'd been since we'd met at the restaurant earlier.

"Tell the truth, baby," Phoenix insisted, standing beside me.

The hardest decision of my life tore me between two people I loved. This wasn't about telling the truth. In honor of our mother, Blake Crystal, I had to do what I'd done all my life.

Pray.

CHAPTER 8

Blake

Bing Sterling sat beside me at our favorite place in Paris, Café de la Nouvelle Mairie.

An empty bottle of their red natural wine was on our table. *Lord, let this be the one I've waited for,* I prayed, smiling at my new man. He was one of our financial institution's wealthiest clients. I'd known him for years, as a customer. Turned down three offers by him to take me out before saying yes.

Knowing he could have practically any woman he desired, I still couldn't understand what attracted him to me. My promotion from branch president, in Atlanta, to corporate, in Charlotte, allowed me to go from servicing his accounts to catering to his personal needs.

"I love you, Blake," he said, placing his hand on my thigh.

The left side of his body was fleshed against my right. Covering his hand with mine, I confessed, "I love you more."

Sidewalk seats were positioned for intimacy—kissing, touching, feeding didn't require leaning over an appetizer, cocktail, or a meal. Couples near us looked into each other's eyes when speaking. Observing them inspired me to be present in the moment with my man.

Fabulous, the world can wait. I need you here with me. My last guy, Spencer Domino, those were his words when requesting my undivided attention. He'd take my cell out of my hand. Sometimes he'd power it off.

A small island divided the quiet street. More travelers graced the *rue* than cars.

"You felt that?" Bing asked, as a warm summer breeze fluffed our hair, carried a few falling leaves a short distance. I watched the foliage float until each one gently lay on the grass beneath a chestnut tree.

"Where do you think she's going?" Bing asked, picking up a leaf that had made its way inches from his brown, well-polished Italian shoes.

"To make her presence known to those who take time to appreciate her."

He nodded.

This man made me notice many things that I'd taken for granted. Strolls through Jardin des Plantes, a tour of Josephine Baker's estate, or shopping for others brought him joy. He didn't have kids of his own but I liked that he cared for my girls.

Something simple as breathing fresh air, I no longer took for granted.

The dozen chairs, handful of square, wooden tables lining the storefront all faced the same direction toward the curb. Watching people in Paris was one of my favorite things to do. At home I barely sat still long enough to notice my surroundings.

"Take Me to the King," the text tone for all my daughters, played. Checking the message, I saw it was from my youngest, Sandara. **Now that I've got bank Black told me last night he's taking me to court! I know you're on vacay but Mama can you believe this? I need to talk to you. I need to find my father. Call me.**

Not that again. Truth was, I wished her father were dead like Alexis's. Wouldn't care if Mercedes's and Devereaux's were sitting somewhere in an urn.

For once in my life I deserved not to be on-call for mommy duty. I placed my cell on the square, wooden table to my left. Placed my hand on Bing's thigh. Before dating my man, I'd never experienced Paris. This was our third trip, a monthly getaway I looked forward to.

"Could you live here?" he asked in the deep, masculine, articulate tone I'd come to crave penetrating my eardrums.

Hell yeah! I thought as moisture saturated my panties. That was the selfish side of me screaming my truth. Honestly, I'd welcome an extended stay anywhere, long as I was with him.

His elbow lay on the table to his right. The remainder of his wine, a half-full goblet rested in his large hand. He raised the rim to his thick, chocolate lips. The crispness of his lavender shirt opened three buttons down exposed the innermost area of his chest, making me undress him with my imagination.

He kissed me, then said, "I love your vibe."

Ten years my junior. I'd done well two times in a row. My ex, Spencer, was twenty-three years younger. What did I do to attract this man? Forty looked great on his six-foot eight-inch frame. He slid his fingers over his black, wavy hair.

Speaking with my daughters in mind, I answered, "Paris is a lovely place to visit but it's too far away from my girls and grandkids. Where would I work? I know many of the natives speak English, but I don't speak their language. Sounds nice, though."

Bing pointed directly in front of us. "What do you see?"

Focusing on his manicure first, I trailed an invisible line. Softly, I replied, "Leaves."

"Darling." He pressed his mouth to mine. A hint of wine lingered. "A tree grows wherever you plant it. Learn to speak French. Your children reside in America. We can visit them anytime we'd like."

Nodding, I thought, *Focus on the forest, not the—*

Another text with the same intro distracted me. This one was from Mercedes. **You're going to have to come off of sabbatical with that man and start babysitting Brandy and Brandon. I need your help. If I knew who my father was . . . call me right now, Mother.**

Since she was a child, Mercedes never pleaded for anything. My listening to whatever her problems were wasn't going to help either of us. I'd learned family couldn't always be there. My time off wasn't going to be cut short for them.

Placing my phone in my lap, I said, "True. But where would I work?"

"Everything okay?" he asked, staring into my eyes.

Had never lied to Bing. Wasn't going to start. "No. But it can wait."

"Wanna talk about it?"

I shook my head. I really didn't.

"This is living," Bing said. "Don't take our time together for granted. We work for three basic reasons, my darling. Self-gratification. A greater humanitarian purpose. And let's be honest, for the money. You can have the first two without money. You can have money without the first two. Blake, hear what I'm about to ask you. Are you happy with the way you're living? Lots of folks put emphasis on material things while neglecting their own health and happiness. No matter how hard we work to acquire possessions, we can't take it with us, Blake. With that said . . ." He paused, reached into his pocket, pulled out a piece of paper, then placed it in my hand. "For you. No strings attached."

I unfolded a cashier's check drawn on his United States bank account. Wow. He'd given this thought before we boarded his private jet. Staring in disbelief, I was speechless. The amount was totally negotiable based on my knowledge of his balance. If I cashed it, there had to be a caveat regardless of what he'd said.

Clearing my throat, I closed my eyes, savored the richness of my life. Slowly opening them, I looked into his. "Fifty million dollars." Staring at the check again, it was made payable to Blake Crystal.

"Free and clear. Blake, I need you to quit your job. And I'm going to make you comfortable doing so."

Handing him the check, I insisted, "Hold on to it for me."

He placed the check back where he'd gotten it. A white carriage trimmed in bright lights, drawn by two white horses, commanded my attention. "Look, babe. Isn't that gorgeous?"

The driver had on all white, slacks, shoes, shirt, jacket, and a top hat. He stopped in front of us.

Bing stood, extended his hand. "Shall we?"

Was he serious?

Scanning my surroundings, my eyes moved in every direction. Why was I resisting this fairy-tale life? I stood, stared at him. He extended his hand, helped me step into the carriage. I sat on the plush, white, spotless, leather seat.

Bing cuddled beside me, then rested his arm on the cushion behind my back. "You like?"

I did not feel worthy of this man. My tears spoke for me.

"Where you sit, what you stand up for, and who you lie with determines how you view yourself," he told me, then added, "Your decisions also dictate the things you will never experience."

The fifty million was where it belonged. In his pocket. Maybe what I did with the money was some sort of a pass-or-fail test. Leaning my back against his body, I chose to enjoy the view.

Part of me didn't feel deserving of his consideration. Never married. Reared four girls by myself. Busted my butt to pay for their college education. Wasn't my fault Sandara only completed her freshman year. They were all grown. I was accustomed to giving. Not receiving.

Two messages registered back-to-back.

Devereaux sent, **Phoenix is in jail. Mercedes is staying at my house. Long story. Can I add you to my reserve list to start helping out with Nya? I need to give Sandara a break.**

Alexis, my one child who challenged me on everything, texted, **I can't have this baby. Can you take me to have an abortion? My appointment is in the morning.**

Really? They knew I was on vacation. They didn't know where. I refused to end my getaway early. Sandara was twenty-five. Alexis a year older than Sandara. Mercedes was a year ahead of Alexis. Devereaux was twenty-eight.

"My girls act as though they're helpless when I'm not home." Grow the hell up, damn it! It was my turn to get spoiled.

"Blake, do we need to go to Atlanta and check on our girls? I always wanted a daughter. Now I have four and knowing their fathers are not in their lives, I want to fill that void, if you'll let me. I can text my assistant. We can leave in the morning."

The problems my girls had, near or far, I nor Bing could solve. By the time we got to Hartsfield, they'd have new issues. I wasn't going to sit here with my man and start a text marathon with *my* daughters regarding problems I couldn't solve.

Brandon, the gay love of my life, could check on the girls. That was if he was in the States. I texted him, **Where are you?**

He replied right away, **Bitch, since I introduce you to the dick I should've had I can't find your ass. Where are you!**

Not that I'd missed a call or text from him but I did groom him for taking over my position as president of the bank. He'd demand, and I'd give him, full details when I returned.

I'm in Paris with Bing, I let Brandon know. **Cocktails on me when I get back**.

Yes, bitch . . . and the CockTales are on me. An emoji with the tongue sticking out was followed by three bananas.

Trying not to feel guilty for not meeting my girls' expectations of me, I texted my oldest sister, Ruby, **Remember what we discussed? I'm going to need you to cover for me.**

I powered off my cell, then gazed at my man.

"Let's enjoy our moment. Everything will be all right."

CHAPTER 9

Alexis

Filthy men undressed me all the time with their lustful, roaming eyes.

The old, unsavory guys made me want to lose my lunch in their lap. I knew the more beautiful a woman was, the more lies she'd be told, perverts she'd have to put down, bullshit dicks her pussy had to dodge. I dogged men out, one, 'cause they enjoyed it, two, 'cause they deserved it.

Tonight would be no exception. A text registered from my brother. Spencer made himself my Plan B with, **dude! where r u? got a sec?**

Going live on my social page, I turned up the audio in my Ferrari, I masterminded my own song. "I went from being that bitch. To being a rich bitch. Beat the lames at their damn game."

Exiting the freeway, I glanced up at the new football stadium. Pointed. "I own a suite up in that bitch. The wind won't blow through my hair. Fuck the haters I don't care. Beatin' lames at their own damn game.

"Pussy made most things possible. Good pussy made niggas do the impossible. Having seven figures in the bank, I'd increased my opportunity to meet a man like my mom's, my future billionaire husband was out there . . . somewhere.

"Mariah, Janet, I was on that flow. Ballers, y'all beneath me. Drop to your knees when you see me. Eat me! Sike. I like Sykes. Not bitch-ass niggas that are dykes. Yikes! I'm beating lames at their own damn game."

Sitting at a red light, I bounced in my seat, kept flowin'. "Money can't boss AC. You full of tricks. Nigga, I'll snatch *all* your damn treats. Eat 'em better than you. Treat 'em just like you." I slayed my hook. "Beatin' lames at their own, damn, game."

I stared back at the dude in the car next to me, laughed aloud, tossed my head back, gunned my engine, then left his ass on that automatic shit. "Bitch!"

Parking my whip in the last available of the ten spaces in the front lot, I hit finish on my video. I wasn't ready to let my door up. I chilled in my car. The second the first tear fell, I refused to let another roll down my breast.

I whispered, "Did anyone love me . . . for me?"

Not for my naturally bodacious booty, voluptuous tits, wicked-tongue bedroom skills, strap-ons, dildos, or the flawless dark chocolate skin I was blessed with. After my inheritance, all of my sisters practically stopped talking to me. Didn't think I'd miss Mercedes's insults.

I did.

I'd rather hear Mercedes tell me how I should stop using people or say again how she agreed with my having an abortion. Some communication was better than having my mother and my sisters ignore my calls. My texts.

I'd be okay.

The kick in my stomach reminded me the baby was there. Had been growing for five and a half months and ticking. No more wearing tight clothes. Could probably look like one of those Greek women with a sexy belly for another few weeks.

Keeping it real, Mercedes was jealous of my ability to make my lovers beg me not to dump them, Devereaux too. She did the most for Phoenix and he still cheated on her. Nobody had agreed to go with me during my first trimester. All of my sisters had at least one kid; I think they wanted me to join in their misery.

I had plans for my future and they didn't include a dependent. I was determined to get on Devereaux's reality show. Had to find a way to get in her graces to showcase my raw talent. I wouldn't have to act in front of the camera. I was about to become the ultimate side chick bitch that fans loved and hated at the same time. Sandara, I let her hold keys to my Porsche and she'd put me on mute too. Wow. My family wasn't shit right now.

I called my on-again, now-off, ex-fiancé, James Wilcox, to meet me for a drink at Tom, Dick & Hank. Really just needed the companionship. Going through pregnancy alone was fucked up.

"How's my baby doing?" he answered.

He'd know if we were living under the same roof. The tone of his voice indicated there was a smile on his face. My lips curved up. "We're good. Thanks for asking. You wanna meet me at—"

"Baby, you ready?" resonated through the phone. "We don't want to be late."

I didn't want James back but the chick in the background sounded extremely familiar. "I know that's not who I think it is."

"Great. Glad you're cool. You had me concerned the other night when you kept crying. What's up?" he asked, going from all cheery and shit to being proper.

"Answer the fucking question, James, before I come over there!"

"Ba-beee." Her whining ass confirmed my belief.

My ex-girlfriend, Chanel, that passive-aggressive ho who allegedly didn't like real dicks, knew he was talking to me. She needed to take her ass to Hollywood with James's other ho and audition for a straight man.

"Fuck her! Fuck you!" I ended the call. Whatever I wanted to say didn't matter anymore. I should give back the lil Lexus James bought me and his engagement ring so that wannabe-me bitch could get off the stripper pole and come up, then raise up off of my fiancé. That nigga always gonna be mine!

Checking my surroundings twice, I unlocked the armrest compartment, removed my gun, put it in my purse. Fools in the ATL were on some dumb shit nowadays. They'd blast a bullet for a lot less than a two-hundred-thousand-dollar luxury vehicle.

I'd pretend things were copacetic until I knocked my ex-girlfriend back on a vibrator, then I'd screw James's scheming no-good ass in the ass to remind him of what I knew he was missing.

My door slid up. I shook my long, dark, wavy hair behind my shoulders, eased on my shades, let my black-and-white checkered stilettoes kiss the asphalt. Standing tall, I adjusted my blazin' fuchsia halter minidress that flared out from the band under my boobs. I entered through the side door, then went directly upstairs to the rooftop.

CHAPTER 10

Alexis

I didn't want to be in this place or any other joint, but I couldn't bear being alone in that huge house my father had left me. Found myself at the bar again. Not caring about a man, woman, the baby inside of me, and myself, I was prepared to turn up.

Life was fucked up. Every day I struggled not to let my situation consume my mental. The baby was a full human being . . . yet, I rationalized that terminating my pregnancy was like eating scrambled eggs. Almost every one digested unborn chickens.

Tom, Dick & Hank was buzzing with laughter, loud people. A few notable celebs were in here. That was the norm. R&B boomed through the patio speakers. Chicks on fleet wearing designer everything flaunted their assets for well-dressed men.

Heads turned toward me. The eyes of dudes with girls shifted in my direction trying to make a connection. Keeping it moving, I gave a few dudes my two-second stare with a quick wink. Two made them watch me. A three second glance meant the chick might be worthy of pursuit but she was probably thirsty and no longer a challenge.

My hook replayed in my head, "Beatin' lames at their own damn game." Men really were shallow. I didn't understand why women took these niggas seriously.

Undoubtedly, I was the baddest female in this spot.

Sitting on the wicker barstool, I noticed my feet were swelling. This pregnancy had already started changing my body. In another month I wouldn't be able to camouflage my stomach. Under no circumstance was I kicking off my five inches. If I had to be a mom, I was giving birth in heels.

"What would you like, sweetie?" the mixologist asked.

Oh, snap! Consumed with my situation, I'd forgotten my brother needed me. I typed, **U bartending at Cheesecake tonight, chick?**

"I'll come back to get your order. Here's a menu," she said, placing the single, laminated sheet on the counter.

Soon as I pressed send to Spencer, I said, "Goddamn!" Julio Jones had just walked in. If I weren't with child, the cute female he was with would have to hitch a ride home. Real women were grown and sexy. Cute was for kids.

"Excuse me?" the mixologist said, placing her hand on the counter.

Bitch, the triple X flick in my head is not about you. I'd undressed that player and was doing the unimaginable. Pointing at my cell, I sent my brother a follow-up, **Meet me at Tom, Dick & Hank now**, then told the mixologist, "Let me have a mai tai."

Spencer replied, **CUN 30 flat**

Gulping half of my drink, I scanned my social pages. Wanted to get that instant buzz, take a woman home and sex her, but I needed a man to fulfill my mission. My jaw dropped as I read, EBONY WATERHOUSE LEAVES THE CAST OF *SOPHISTICATED SIDE CHICKS ATL.*

Praying it wasn't a rumor, immediately I called the person who could confirm. One ring, then I heard, *"This is Devereaux. Leave a message."* "Sis, don't give away my part. Please. I am Ebony Waterhouse. I can do this. Call me back," I said, then pressed end. I should've had that role all along. Devereaux knew that though she refused to hire me. No personal invite from the casting director. This was my time! Had to reinvent myself as Ebony's replacement.

A very pregnant waitress set a plate of wings, greens, mac and cheese, and a second order of fried shrimp, baked beans, and French fries in front of the couple to my left. I had to handle my unfinished baby business before it was too late for me to maintain my spotlight.

Fighting back tears again, I gazed at the Museum Bar across the parking lot. The external structure had all the original features of the Baptist church where people once worshipped God.

Church.

Couldn't remember the last time I'd been. Oh yeah, that was when Spencer sat between my mother and me. Prayer could solve my problem. A part of me didn't feel deserving of anyone saving me, including God. I hadn't earned the mercy and riches the Lord had recently bestowed upon me. People who lived by the Bible, I did not envy. They were sinners too.

A shadow hovered in my peripheral. I didn't shift my gaze when I heard a masculine voice say, "Hey, beautiful. Let me refresh your drink." If a female had said the same, we'd be locking eyes. There was plenty of time for me to home in on a dickatunity.

"Sure," I said, looking at the club, lounge, eatery across the parking lot. Real wine had replaced communion grape juice; appetizers fed sinners instead of the bread of Jesus. Lounge sofas and chairs were more comfortable than the old wooden pews that had been removed.

Not many people in the world were holy.

Ho-ly? Definitely. The guy offering me a drink was no different from the random men I'd invited to my house lately. Taking home a stranger wasn't my concern when I was at home. Although I'd never killed anyone, I wouldn't hesitate to pull the trigger if a dude went left. Guns were in every room of my mansion and that included the bathrooms.

I already knew the man to my right wanted me to stroke his salami. All these ATL losers wanted to do was cum and go home to their woman, man, husband, wife. I had no pleasantries for the guy standing beside me. The sound of his voice indicated he wasn't Spencer. Soon as my brother got here, we were walking across the parking lot for a change of venue. I was tired of seeing the big-belly waitress rub her stomach every time she dropped off a check.

The bartender picked up my drink, gave me a fresh one.

I told the guy next to me, "Thanks."

"Am I that ugly you can't look up?" he joked.

Whateva. I wasn't laughing. I'd already made up my mind that I wasn't spreading for him. It was too early to make a dickcision. Shifting my eyes up and to my right, I froze. Wow!

"I'm West-Léon," he said, not needing an intro.

It was *the* West-Léon, the lead actor in Devereaux's television series *Sophisticated Side Chicks ATL.* My heart raced. Pussy damn near did a somersault.

Extending a smile, then my hand, I said, "I'm Alexis," withholding my surname.

He smiled with his eyes. "You're gorgeous," he said as though he was interested in more than a one-night stand.

A guy's intentions were masked in his tone, mannerisms, and his words.

There was the above-normal pitch "you're gorgeous" that implied his dick was interested in not being acquainted with my pussy, just dropping a load or two, *any ho would do but I'd prefer you.*

Then there was the crackling "you're gorgeous" that clearly displayed his low self-esteem. *I know you'd never date a dude like me but I'm out to get lucky.*

And I despised the deep throat, "you're gorgeous" fake-ass nigga that was more impressed with himself than he'd ever be with me. Those were the ones I rough-fucked in their ass.

"You married?" I asked West-Léon, already knowing he hadn't claimed a wife on social.

Practically showing all of his super-white teeth, he shook his head.

"I need you to say yes or no." Men in Atlanta did that nonverbal shit, then when the Mrs. started calling and texting, or he couldn't answer or return a weeknight call, dudes fell back on that I-never-said-I-wasn't-married drama-king bullshit.

"No. I'm not married," West-Léon said, then bit his bottom lip.

Hesitating to tell him I was Devereaux's sister, I inquired. "Are you cohabitating, in a relationship, or gay? I did say 'or' not 'and.'"

"I like you," was his answer. "But I'm not on set. That means I'm not here in an entertainment capacity."

Yeah, yeah, right. Soon as I unlocked my cell to see if I had any texts or missed calls, my jaw dropped. To my dismay, Chanel and James strolled in. Covering my drink with a napkin, I told West-

Léon, "Excuse me. I see someone I need to say hello to," then picked up my purse.

This was the first time I'd seen them together since our three-some at my old apartment.

"Hi, Alexis," James said, placing his hand on Chanel's lower back. "Don't start a scene. Please. We can dis—"

Slap! Slap! Wham! My hand found its way to Chanel's face and James's. Two for her stupid ass and a hard one for his dumb ass.

"Ah!" Chanel grabbed her face, stood behind James. "Don't just stand there. Protect me," she cried.

"Get that bitch outta here!" I demanded, reaching into my purse.

James grabbed my hand. He knew what I was reaching for. I snatched my arm away.

"Don't touch me, you deadbeat!" I yelled at James. "You have the audacity to prance that bitch in front of me while I'm pregnant with your baby! Bitch, you'd better get and stay behind his ass *every* time you see me!"

By the time the crowd realized what was happening, the show was over. Too late for live video posts.

I didn't care that both of them had placed an engagement ring on my finger. Doing an about-face, I strutted to my seat as though nothing that shouldn't have happened, happened.

The two years I'd dated James, he had reason to, yet he'd never popped up on me. How fucking coincidental now that Chanel was his main, they were going to be late getting to *my* destination. Now his bitch, my ex-bitch, knew what she was up against for real. She got exactly what she deserved for hawking my social media pages. She had another smackdown coming if he didn't get her outta here in sixty seconds.

I sat. Texted my mother, **I'm not going to be like you! This baby has got to go!**

Why the hell were James and Chanel still on the rooftop? I stood. Took a step in their direction.

West-Léon firmly placed his arm around my waist, handed me a fresh drink, then said, "You ever thought about acting?"

Either he hadn't heard me say I was pregnant, he didn't care, or he was like a lot of men. Anxious to fuck hot, pregnant pussy.

I liked this guy. I was definitely taking West-Léon home . . . right now.

Firmly, I told West-Léon, "Close the tab. Let's go."

Dropping a fifty on the bar, he said, "Right behind you. Ladies first."

CHAPTER 11

Blake

Awakening to birds chirping at sunrise, I eased from under the soft white linen, opened the French double doors, then walked onto the spacious balcony of Bing's chateau overlooking a valley of rolling green hills. A picturesque backdrop of Douglas fir stood over 150 feet in the distance.

I could live here with him. Forever was a long time.

The first man to genuinely worship me was on the other side of the closed, white, double doors that led into the bedroom where our naked bodies intertwined in saliva, sweat, and tears well beyond midnight.

No man had cried while making love to me. Last night was a first.

Thought he was going to propose during our horse and carriage ride yesterday through Buttes-Chaumont Park. No man had ever asked for my hand in marriage. Perhaps this relationship would culminate with an all-too-familiar ending. I had an uncanny way of screwing things up even when I wasn't trying.

The closed doors opened wide. The most handsome man in the world stood before me. Seeing Bing completely nude, recalling the sensation of him cumming inside of me—my body tingled all over.

"Cappuccino or mimosa?" he asked, welcoming me into his arms.

One long kiss followed another, and another. Our tongues danced.

Learning it was okay for me to have it all, I smiled, then said, "Both." Needed my caffeine fix. The cocktail would help take me to a place of promiscuity. That and help take my mind off of my girls.

"Both it is," he said, gesturing for a hug. Holding me close, he pressed his lips to mine several times, then slid out his tongue.

I never tired of sharing affection. Mother's instincts surfaced. Something was seriously wrong with one of my girls. Trying to relax the tension in my mouth, I touched his chest, then stepped back.

"I'll be in in a minute." My frown should've been a smile.

"Stay here. I'll bring everything to you," he said, then asked, "You okay?"

Had to stop worrying about what was happening in Atlanta. My feeling bad for not responding to anyone's texts, churned in the pit of my stomach. Access to the world was splendid but what were Bing's long-term intentions?

This time I answered, "I'm good." Lie number one had escaped my lips.

A lingering stare from him preceded, "We'll talk later, sweetheart, about what's bothering you."

Quietly, I did an about-face. I touched the rail, then jerked my hand away as though I'd been shocked. Removing my robe, I let it fall to the white travertine tiles. Inhaling all the fresh air that I could, I filled my lungs to capacity causing my chest to hurt. Bing was right. Paris was spectacular. Living here would require adjustments, especially since I was his woman, not his wife. A part of me wanted to respond to my daughters. This was a great time to resist and see if they could depend on one another if I moved here. My worst fear was they'd abandon one another the day I left the country or the day I died. Whichever came first.

"Here's your mimosa, sweetheart," Bing said, placing the flute in my hand. "I'll be back shortly with our cappuccinos."

"Thanks," I said, then softly kissed his cheek.

As I sipped my beverage, all the messages from my girls both-

ered me but not enough to reply. Holding back tears, I refused to
let them steal my joy. They were definitely aware of where I was
and whom I was with. I'd appreciate a "Have a great time in the
'city of love,' Mama" text, or a simple "I love you, Mama" message
would've made me feel they cared about my happiness.

Alexis. She was the darkest of my children in every way. Let her
tell it, we treated her like the black sheep. That was a damn lie. I
loved all my children equally. She was the one who demanded
more. No matter how much I gave her, how much any person did
for her, she was never satisfied. Maybe having a life dependent
upon her to survive would make her compassionate.

My fingers tightened around the rail. I flinched. Remembering
how Alexis had fucked Spencer, I sipped my mimosa. That little
girl didn't respect the fact that even though Spencer was a year
older than her, he was my man. Mine! Was. She'd destroyed what
could've been good for me. Now I'd never know. I didn't want
Spencer back. I simply hated why and how our love for each other
ended. I pleaded with the wobbling in my legs not to let me down
the way my daughter had.

Alexis could get rid of her baby the way I'd done with my first
and last. Ruby, my eldest sister, was the only one who held all my secrets. She'd gone with me both times. Fourteen was too young to
be a mom and our mother was already struggling to feed us. Plus,
I couldn't tell my mom that I had been raped by . . .

The second termination, I was too damn old to be the same fool
a fifth, make that sixth time. I blamed myself for sneaking downstairs in the middle of the night to steal a glass of milk. When I
closed the door, there he stood, in our kitchen, naked.

Gazing over beautiful terrain, I thought, *Don't do what I hadn't
done to you, little girl.* Supporting Alexis's termination would make
me relive memories of two of the worst men I'd encountered. Not
that any of the other deadbeats I'd gotten pregnant for were much
better.

Aborting her child at this point would be murder and possibly illegal. That little girl was the devil's best friend. I could never trust
her. She didn't want to see anyone happy. Even if my ex had begged
to lick her pussy, out of respect for me! She . . .

I sipped my mimosa, which was still half full. I hung my head questioning, was I a horrible mother? All of my girls needed me and all I wanted to do was to enjoy time with my man.

The countless messages that I suspected were on my cell would not ruin my last day in this glorious paradise. I hadn't powered on my phone since the carriage ride. Last night I'd buried that device in my purse where it would stay until I was ready to respond.

I was glad this was our last night in France. I was ready to get back, not to Atlanta, but to Charlotte. Had to talk to Ruby. Needed to return to work, sit in my corporate office at the bank, and address our customers' financial concerns before my arch nemesis coworker stabbed me in the back.

I thought, *When Spencer sees how happy I am without him, he'll regret that he cheated on me.* If he'd never crossed the line with my daughter, I wouldn't have had to give him back his relationship ring, and I could've maintained my dignity. Bing was exactly what I needed. A mature man, a gentleman, and a businessman.

"Listen to the birds. That's the sweetest music," he said.

I glanced over my shoulder. Bing placed two cappuccinos on the white, round, wrought-iron table, then embraced me from behind. Pressing his lips to the nape of my neck, he continued, "You know man learned to whistle by mimicking birds," then blew a seductive tune into my ear. His hands settled on my naked hips.

Shivering as a small orgasm pleasured my vulva, I embraced his energy.

My man exhaled a sweet, "Nice," to me, acknowledging he liked the way I moved.

"Like the invention of planes," I commented, then suggested, "Let's have a seat. I want to soak in every remaining second of our trip."

I'd learned late in life that there were other ways to reach a climax than penetration and oral copulation. Trading my mimosa for my morning caffeinated beverage, I said, "Thanks for loving me the way I've never been loved before."

"Cheers to you. Those other men were fools. The second I laid eyes on you I realized you were the one. I like that you made me wait. That you weren't impressed with my net worth."

I'd heard other men say they could tell right away when a woman was *the one*. Of course they'd never mentioned that to me. Bing was a first. I inhaled, switched to my flute. Let the next taste of champagne and orange juice glide onto my palate. Savoring the liquid for a few seconds, I swallowed, let the nectar consume my senses.

"This is living, Blake. I'm not ready to leave. Let's stay an extra week," he said as though he wasn't asking.

Unlike Mr. Sterling, I couldn't be a no-show and risk losing my job. "I have to get back to work."

"Obviously, you need more than money. What will it take for me to convince you to quit?"

Corporate had overlooked me ten consecutive times for a position they knew I deserved. Walking away for a man when I'd never had a man provide for me wasn't wise. I was still getting acclimated to my new Consumer Retention Management Analyst title. Had the ear of my supervisor to create an interoffice cross-departmental position specifically for me. That way I could acquire skills from various areas while preparing myself for advancement. She was a thirty-year-old millennial who embraced innovators. My counterpart, Herman, a guy who felt my presentation of fresh ideas was stealing his spotlight, wanted me gone!

Admiring Bing's beautiful birthday suit, I touched his thigh. I was no Cinderella charity case but he was definitely Prince Charming. My mind flashed to the urgent conversation I needed to have with Ruby, just as Bing said, "I don't want my wife to work."

That was more of a statement than a proposal. Wasn't sure what to say. Had my own agenda. "I'm going to text you my sister Ruby's contact before we leave." Should've given him a number for emergency purposes a while ago, but I had an ulterior motive for this decision.

He nodded. "Text me the girls' contacts too," he insisted, then followed with, "I'm not in the habit of repeating myself."

Giving him Devereaux's, Mercedes's, and Sandara's numbers might happen. Sharing Alexis's contact info was out of the question. Slightly annoyed, I pressed the rim of the flute to my lips, tossed back my head, and gulped the remainder of my cocktail.

Bing grabbed my flute. "Wait! I didn't expect you to do that. Don't—"

Coughing, I covered my mouth, heaved, then spat the largest pink diamond solitaire I'd seen into my palm. Tears from my esophagus being scratched and those of disbelief chased one behind the other. I was glad I hadn't swallowed.

Standing in front of me, Bing took the ring. His dick swaying in front of my face was not a distraction as he decorated my finger.

His eyes softened as he stared into mine. Passionately, he said, "Marry me, Blake."

Again, his tone wasn't in the form of a question. There was nothing to ponder. If God allowed me to live another fifty years, I doubted I'd find a love and a lover like this.

"I accept."

"Then I insist we stay a week longer," he said, wiping my fingers with a napkin. "No worries. The jeweler will be here momentarily to properly clean her up."

Her? Hmm. I liked that. Yes. Just decided to name my alter ego after the shine on my rock . . . Blaze.

Stains and all, I was not taking this precious gem off. I countered, "Three days." That way I could call in sick for a few days.

"Deal. I'll reserve my private jet to Hartsfield in three days, then I'll meet you in Charlotte on day four," he said.

Day what? Holding my bling up to eye level, reluctantly I smiled, then nodded.

My fiancé suctioned my tongue into his mouth. I hadn't realized my lips were tight until Bing held my face, then asked, "What's wrong, sweetheart?"

If I lied about something this small, our entire relationship would be ruined. "Can we leave as planned tomorrow? I really need to get back to work."

"No problem. Don't want you to be late," he said, then added, "You can leave now. I'll have my assistant charter you a jet and pack your bags."

"Bing, please don't take it the wrong way. I didn't mean to upset you."

"I ask you to marry me. Gave you a pink, seven-karat solitaire, flawless, I might add. And you can't enjoy our engagementmoon? You have your priorities confused," he said, walking away.

Watching the sunrise beam to a blinding shine, memories of how fast the most beautiful moments with my ex had instantly become the worst. I felt stupid. I wanted to take the ring off 'cause as usual, I didn't deserve it.

I'd learned that time and silence were the best resolutions to my conflicts. Nothing at home was so pressing that it couldn't wait a few more days. My fear of losing control of my welfare made me cling to employment situation.

Sitting at the table, I held up my hand, admired that . . . it was on my hand, and he'd put it there. I loved this man. Three days. Seven. I wasn't going anywhere until *my* fiancé was ready.

Truth was, I'd give him my last. But I was scared to let him love all of me.

CHAPTER 12

Mercedes

Icouldn't stay at Devereaux's house forever, nor did I want to. Propping a purple-beaded, square pillow with bold splashes of red behind my back, I reached for my phone, then read the morning texts from my children's father. The smile on my face grew wider with each message.

Babe, are you okay?

Call me when you get this message to let me know you're safe.

I cooked for you again tonight. Putting the kids to bed. Want to talk?

What time are you coming home tonight?

Mercedes. I get it! I'm sorry. Let's talk.

I'm not your manny! I'm your husband!!

Where are you? Who are you with?

It's cool. You want to be an unfit mother. An adulteress. A whore. A slut. Shack up with another man. Fine! He can have you!!

I know what you did!

If you're not home tonight, stay gone! I'll file for divorce!

Laughing hard, I refused to reply. He didn't know anything. I'd sworn my other two sisters and my mother to secrecy via text. They replied but no one had called to check on me. My car was where I'd parked it the night Phoenix was arrested. I hadn't left Devereaux's house in three days.

"Benjamin. Benjamin," I said softly, then took a selfie below my waist.

ThermiVa was more amazing than I'd ever imagined. I sent Dr. Stephens an e-mail, Haven't tried out my new "good good" yet. Maybe tonight.

The sexual energy circulating in my womb made me want to entertain myself. I got out of bed, went to the bathroom. Gathering my light brown, wooly hair under a zebra-print cap, I stared into my greenish-gray eyes.

Was my father white? Did his complexion and my mother's dark tone create my creamy skin? Did he know I was alive? Did my mother know who my father was?

Not wanting to break my own heart questioning the unknown, I turned on the water, stepped into the shower, adjusted the temperature hot as I could enjoy it, then I removed the handheld wand. Water sputtered against my vulva. I switched to a rapid pulsation. Alternated back and forth, then twisted the knob all the way to the blue side to icy cold.

Closing my eyes, I exhaled my sexual frustrations, relaxed my shoulders, stretched my neck side to side. "Thank you, Jesus." I deserved this total body pleasure even if I had to give it to myself. My new pussy was my little secret from my man. Opening my eyes, knowing he was sexing his mistress, I might not ever let him lick this again.

Benjamin's communication was his guilty conscience for cheating making him worry if I was doing the same. Not a single text from my husband was about me. If I was home, he'd be with her. My husband was more pissed over not being able to cuddle up with his mistress the last few nights. That, or he was lonely in our bed.

Welcome to my world, honey!

"Oh, my, God." My "good good" felt like ice chips were bouncing off of my clit as I came.

Soon as I was alone at my place, I was going to cum as many times as I could and scream loud as I desired, then enjoy a fine glass of red wine. Drying my body, I flinched when I grazed my kitty.

The scent of fresh-brewed coffee crept into my sister's guest bedroom where I'd peacefully slept. I'd borrowed everything of hers, from the red nightie I'd slipped on to her clothes and natural hair-care products.

Placing the plastic cap on the vanity, I stared into the mirror, then fingered my spirally afro. "I really need to take off an inch or two," I said, patting the edges almost a foot away from my scalp. I brushed my teeth.

God could not have created a more perfect being. Observing my mother's passive behavior taught me what not to do. My work here at my sister's was done. Time to let her thank me and return to my home front.

Trotting down a flight of stairs, I was in awe of how Devereaux's mansion was fit for royalty. The double en-suites in her master bedroom, three guest rooms, Nya's princess palace, Devereaux's private office, the waterfall in her living room were sheer paradise. Bet the cot Phoenix was curled up on in a cell made him regret he'd got caught fucking Ebony.

Devereaux was at her darling nook, sipping from her #SSCATL mug. I glanced at her papers. She was going over her script for film the way I'd seen her start each day.

Dawn's light peeped through the uncovered bay windows. Her lifestyle was foreign to me. I'd gone from living with Alexis and Sandara in our mother's house, to having a roommate at Spelman for four years, to marrying Benjamin, his buying us a home and my giving birth to twins. Had lots of lonely nights. Never lived a night alone.

Each day Devereaux departed by seven in the morning, I had her home to myself.

"Morning," I whispered. Helping myself to a cup of Colombian dark roast, I joined my sister at the table. "I'll pick up Nya from Sandara's for you today and keep her long as you'd like."

Witnessing how hard Devereaux worked, I had to make sure she didn't slip back to her ex by allowing him or his mother to babysit my niece.

She muttered, "Nya's good. Sandara cancelled another go-see."

"What?" I raced upstairs, sent a text on my way down, **Why are you a No-Show again?**

baby daddies drama something you can't relate to, she replied.

Once upon a time that was true. She knew my current situation wasn't peachy. All my family did.

Reclaiming my seat, I decided not to respond to my baby sister right away. I'd call her after Devereaux left.

Our mother had done a few things appropriately. Just a few. Blake requested that despite our dysfunctions and differences, we'd unite when necessary. Didn't always work. Devereaux took me everywhere with her until she went to college. Then I'd get an occasional invite to a campus party. A year later, I was at Spelman and we were closer. After she started dating Phoenix her senior year while she was at Clark-Atlanta . . . I lost my best friend. We went from talking all the time to my seldom hearing her voice.

"Good morning, Mercedes," she said, placing the paper in her hand on top of the stack. "We need to talk." Sliding her black-rimmed glasses to the top of her head, she continued, "I've wanted to say this for three days. I—"

"I know. You don't have to say it. I appreciate your letting me stay. I'll be gone by the time you get back."

Devereaux took a deep breath. "I—"

"Trust me. I get that you need your space. I want you to focus on your television series. I'll give Sandara a break and get Nya and I—"

This time she interrupted me. "Mercedes, shut the hell up. And listen!"

I stretched my neck backward and my eyelids widened. I heaved hot air toward her face. "How dare—"

"Do it again and you'll have to call the police on me." The tip of her finger was less than an inch from my nose.

The strain of my eyes focusing on her nail hurt. What was her problem? I'd been exhaling since I was a kid. Obviously, her passive-aggression had kicked in and she was ready to dominate my conversation. Folding my arms under my breasts, I leaned back in my seat.

Here she goes.

"I don't care how you take this and I mean it. I asked you to meet me the other day at Haven because Mother was busy, and I wouldn't dare ask for advice from Alexis or Sandara. For once, I needed you to listen to me."

Well, I agreed with her in part. Alexis had been quiet. Hadn't heard from her since I'd been here. Hopefully, she'd had that abortion. Sandara, if she kept letting the lowlifes keep her on her back, she'd better stay put and hold on to that Section 8 certificate. I was not going to waste my precious time on them, but the last person I'd accept relationship advice from was our mother.

Snapping her fingers in front of my face, Devereaux commanded, "Stay focused on me. I came to you to share, I'm—"

Aw, hell no! I had to interject, "Don't snap at me again and you'd better not be pregnant with that loser's baby. He's—"

Slam! My sister's hand hit the table so hard, both cups of coffee splashed, staining her papers. She needed to get laid soon. I did too. Devereaux was not going to ruin my self-love high. I had two more ThermiVa treatments to go. My husband wasn't seeing my new pussy until he came to his damn senses.

Devereaux popping her little fingers again, it was old. I thought, *Oh, well.* They were her soggy papers. She could trash them, clean up her mess, and start all over. I was nobody's maid. Not even my husband's. I sat waiting for the next act.

"You are about the rudest bitch I know, Mercedes! If you don't want to hear me out . . ." She paused. "You know what. This is my damn house and I don't have to accept your demonic behavior. Get! Out!"

Tears flooded my gown.

Devereaux became quiet.

Demonic? Would Benjamin agree? Embarrassed, I covered my face. Crying was a sign of weakness. Told myself, *Get yourself together.*

My sister didn't move to console me or apologize.

Fine. I put my tears on halt, initiated a peace offering to hug her. She pushed me away, the same way she'd done the other night after the cops handcuffed her leeching man and removed him from her house. A thank-you from her to me was warranted. But I supposed I deserved this . . . according to her.

"I'm listening. For real this time. And I apologize." I never had said or would say "I'm sorry." That was reserved for losers like Phoenix. He was beyond redemption. That man was pathetic.

"I swear, if you interrupt me, I'm getting up from this table and I will never speak to you again."

Never? That was harsh, I thought, staring into her eyes. I heard her say that before. Devereaux couldn't throw out an old, worn pair of shoes, end a toxic relationship with Phoenix, or stay mad at anybody, especially me. Wasn't her fault. Libras required balance. My sister was the most forgiving person in our family.

She'd adjust. She always did.

"I know you don't care for Phoenix, and trust me, the feeling is mutual. I wanted to open up to you. Tell you how much my heart aches every night when I sleep in my bed alone. Find out how you deal with Benjamin practically living with Arizona since you confirmed, then confronted him about cheating. Sis, I struggle to look like I've got it all together but I'm falling apart."

I watched the tears roll down her face. I wanted to hug her but I wasn't foolish enough to initiate that again. My birthday was April first. Aries were sensitive, but we could turn on a person without their ever knowing. Exhaling through my nostrils, I listened as she'd requested.

"Are you aware that Sandara's court date is coming up soon? Blackstone convinced the others to join him and all three of her children's fathers are taking her to court for child support."

A half smile spread toward my left cheek, my eyes shined a little, as I remained silent, shaking my head. Guess Sandara wished she could change her mind about taking my advice. Told her to empty her babies' daddies' pockets, snatch their tax refunds, make them pay.

Those trifling deadbeats wanted to cash in on Sandara's modeling contract. They'd omitted the most pertinent aspect: custody. Obviously, they didn't want to see their kids. If they did, they didn't need money for that. No worries, I'd tell Sandara how to handle those dirty bastards. The kids go with the check. If I divorced Benjamin, I'd gladly pay him to raise our children.

Devereaux continued, "Alexis wants to abort the baby and she's asked me to go with her. I stopped responding to her messages days ago because I can't support her on this. She knows I'm pro-life. Maybe you can take her."

Was that a plea for me to step in? I wanted to comment that she needs to exercise her pro-choice rights, do the right thing, and terminate the pregnancy but at almost six months, I wasn't going to take her because she'd waited too long. I kept my mouth shut. That girl can't take care of herself. What was she going to do with a dependent?

"We're all messed up, Mercedes. You think it's because we don't know who our fathers are? Alexis was the only one to meet her dad and now he's dead. I pray mine is still alive. I want to find my father. I want to know my father. Doesn't it bother you not knowing yours?" she asked with watery eyes.

Was this her way of granting me permission to say something? I nodded once, remained quiet.

Devereaux said, "I'm not going to take Phoenix back."

I had to say, "Good."

"But I can't lie and say I don't want to. If he'll sleep with my cast member."

My eyes stretched, causing her to pause. *Sleep? Honey, he had a full-blown dick-all-down-her-throat relationship with Ebony Waterhouse.* Hell, she was the main and you were his side. *There was no equality here.*

She read me. "I hear you. But hear this. I love you with all my heart. But don't you ever again put me in a position to choose between you and Phoenix. He went to jail when you're the one that should've been arrested."

What the hell! She could save the entertainment for one of her scripts. Trifling-ass Phoenix. Yes, he did deserve to be behind bars for leeching off of my sister and if she was too blind to see it, I was no longer going to convince her otherwise. I may have gotten the cuffs slapped on but his failures to appear got him thrown in the backseat of the patrol car. He should blame his mother for not raising him. When a man's mother didn't want him . . . damn.

I had my own problems to deal with. I stood, then pranced away.

Not a single word surfacing in my head, if it had escaped my mouth, would've kept my sister from making good on her promise to beat my ass.

Devereaux knew not to let my one-hundred-fifty-pound, five-eight, size eight, give her the wrong impression. I could and would fight a female.

Sis hadn't forgotten. I was sure of it.

CHAPTER 13

Benjamin

"Hey, Mr. Bannister," my kids' teacher jovially greeted. "Your wife picked up the twins early today. How are you?"

Whatever game my wife was playing, I wasn't going to become her foe. Not wanting my marital issues to become apparent, I matched the teacher's enthusiasm with a smile. Thumping my palm to my forehead, I lied, "That's right. I forgot she was picking them up," then checked my cell. No new messages from Mercedes.

Bright eyes beamed as the teacher kept watching me.

"Oh, I'm great. How long ago did she leave?"

"I'm fine. Thanks for asking," she said with a cute tilt of her head.

I was the parent, not her student. Had no interest in apologizing for not minding my manners at the moment. I explained, "I have a lot on my mind. How long?"

"It's okay. About an hour ago. Oh, I mentioned to her Brandon's grades are starting to decline. Just a little but we should address it now. Enjoy the rest of your day," she said cheerfully, then redirected her attention to a kid tapping on her thigh. "Hey, sweetie. Next time say, 'excuse me.'"

Getting in my car, I typed, **Where are you?**

Deleting the text, I decided it was best to confront her in person. I headed to the strip club hoping to see Toya "You Ain't No

Real Detective" Johnson. Hadn't heard from her since I'd left her house. If she knew so much, she'd know I was on my way.

Entering the half-full room, I was relieved and pissed at the same time. Toya was at the bar, laughing over her copper mug. The bartender was equally as loud with his ha-has. The seat to her right, which I'd vacated to do my fatherly duty, was occupied by some young dude.

I posted up on her left, greeted Toya, "What's up?"

"You saw her?" she asked.

This was not fuck-with-Benjamin-Bannister day. Sternly, I asked, "Saw whom?"

"Your wife? I thought you'd run into her at the school."

Squinting, I stared at Toya. "Your timing was off. All the way off. How was I supposed to know if you didn't give me a heads up?"

"Oh, you missed her. I wanted you to be surprised. She's at home now."

"You're fired," I said.

Toya snapped her fingers twice. "No problem. Cash me out."

Her palm was two inches in front of my chin. I wanted to bite off her pinkie. How the fuck she and her wife gon' freak me now Toya was acting all fresh? The bartender handed me a cognac.

"On the house, man," he said.

"Thanks." I dug into my pocket for the last time.

The bartender added, "You need to step back from Toya, bruh, and pay her. You not coming up in here and doing what you're not man enough to do in your house. If I come from behind this counter, I ain't asking and I'm not telling you twice. Show some respect." He never raised his voice.

Toya was real chill. "The threesome encore still stands. No charge."

It was five hundred a month, not a week. Didn't need any problems like I'd heard about my boy Phoenix. I put my drink on the bar, tossed five C-notes on the counter, then exited to the parking lot. Had to sit in my car for a moment to regroup. What the hell was I doing? It wasn't the information Toya gave me about Mercedes that made me angry. It was what she wasn't saying. Driving to my other house, I kept going until I reached my preferred destination.

Walking up her steps, I dialed Arizona.

Opening the door before I put my key in the hole, she said. "Hey, I saw you pull up. Perfect timing. I just finished cooking for myself. I'll blacken a breast for you. Won't take long, baby."

The biggest smile, accompanied by a warm, inviting hug and a passionate kiss, greeted me. She held me close. The aroma of sandalwood oil and sage filled the living area. I inhaled the lingering scent of Tori Burch behind her ear. Appreciated the way she stayed presentable. That was why I'd started taking her out more than I did my wife.

Mercedes had a long list of reasons for why we couldn't go to dinner, see a movie, or hang out and listen to jazz on a Sunday afternoon. It was too late notice to ask any of her sisters to watch the twins, or she didn't feel like doing her hair, makeup, changing her clothes. Let some other man deal with her after our divorce was final.

"I miss you, Ben. Haven't heard from you in a few days. Are you okay?" Arizona asked.

Not "Is everything okay?" No Q&A marathon, interrogation, or backlash. My mistress inquired about me. Why couldn't my wife care about me this way?

"I'm good, babe. Needed to spend time with my kids. Brandon's grades are slipping."

Nodding, she became quiet. I kissed her lips, then trailed her to the kitchen.

"I know. You don't want to meet my kids."

"Yet," she said. "You served her the papers?"

"Not yet. But I will." Maybe. It wasn't that simple. I was in position to stay with Mercedes or move in with Arizona. I was practically living here.

"I'm not going to be your mistress forever. It's time for you to take care of me full-time. And make sure you ask for every other weekend with your kids. I love you." She added, "After dinner we can soak in the tub and catch up." What she said about my family never bothered me. Her voice was soothing.

"I love you, too." Even with her demands, Arizona was easygoing.

Her standards dictated no intercourse before engagement. I had similar restrictions, so I didn't mind not fucking her long as she got me off. Dinner was nicely presented as always. Baked chicken for her, blackened for me, mashed potatoes, and spinach. Shitake mushrooms, her favorite, topped everything.

"How was your day?" she asked, smiling.

Staring at her pretty, dark chocolate skin, I ate a forkful of everything on my plate. Toned biceps, firm thighs, a tight butt, and a flat stomach with vertical and horizontal definition were one-hundred-percent natural. Her eyes shined with joy one couldn't fake.

I mumbled, "This is delicious, babe," then replied, "Interesting," wondering what my wife was doing with her new vagina. I should go home.

Arizona picked up my plate. "I can see you're not hungry." Resting her hand on my shoulder, she said, "I want our own children. I'm not raising hers. Don't respond. I'll put your plate in the microwave in case you feel like eating later."

I'd kept a vow not taken at the altar. A value instilled in me as a young man would not be broken; long as I wore my wedding band, I'd never stick my dick in another woman's vagina. Unless I was positive my marriage was over, I was not risking fathering an illegitimate child. Arizona enjoyed my company, conversation, and we were content with fondling and oral copulation.

I checked my cell. No texts or missed calls from Mercedes. What was she doing with her newfound womanhood? Was another man at my house with my children? Was she on a date?

I made my way to the bathroom and removed my clothes. Settling into the hot, steamy water eased the tension in my body, but not my mind. Fuck! I punched the suds. This shit wasn't right.

Arizona entered. "You need a vacation. What do you think about our going to Italy for two weeks? My treat and I can make all of the arrangements," she suggested.

This woman deserved a man worthy of her unselfishness. "Let me know the dates. I'll check my schedule," I said, knowing I wasn't going but not wanting to reject her idea.

Why shouldn't I go? My wife didn't want me. Arizona had my

pertinent travel info from prior trips. I needed to hand my wife those papers and stop holding on to disappointment.

"Let's do it," I said, leaning my head back on the tub pillow.

Despite all that had happened in my marriage, I loved my kids. And much as I wanted to deny it, I was in love with my wife. Otherwise, I would've made this situation with Arizona permanent.

Getting out of the tub, I dried off, then said, "I have to make a run. I'll be back in a few hours."

"Sure. Let yourself in. I might be asleep," she said, stepping into the tub.

Arizona was different from every woman I'd dated. She never raised her voice. Not once. I'd never seen her mad or even upset. Whatever I suggested or did was okay with her.

I parked in my driveway, as my wife's car was in the garage. I quietly entered my house. The only light came from our bedroom. After tiptoeing upstairs, I pushed the door.

Mercedes lifted her head. She looked at me, turned her back, then rested on the pillow.

I removed my clothes. Sat on my side of the bed. "First you disappear for several days. You couldn't tell me you were picking up the kids?" I asked.

"I do not owe you anything. Not even an explanation. They're my kids too."

My wife looked beautiful. Her radiant light skin was flawless. The scarf tied around the edges of her hair was silky soft. Blood flowed to my dick. Sliding under the cover, I got close. Poked her with the hardest erection I'd had in months.

Mercedes scooted to the edge. If she sneezed, she'd fall to the floor. "Save it for your mistress."

"Can we just talk? I don't want to continue living this way," I pleaded.

"And I'd appreciate it if you'd get out of my bed, out of my bedroom, and out of my house. But we don't always get what we want, do we, Benjamin?"

If I went back to Arizona's tonight, this would be the night I'd leave my ring on the nightstand and make love to every part of my mistress.

My wife was hurting and I was partially to blame. Rolling onto my side, I tucked the pillow underneath my head and shoulder. Hopefully, Mercedes would have a change of heart come morning. I closed my eyes.

"Oh, my, God . . . Yes."

At first I thought I was dreaming.

"Haa. Haa. Haa. Haa." Her sharp moaning became louder each time she exhaled.

Who was this woman with her hand between her legs, her knees bent and spread wide? I turned on the light. She closed her eyes, continued stroking her clit.

I sat at the foot of our bed, stared between her thighs. My tongue and dick hardened. Saliva coated the inside of my mouth. I could almost taste her.

Her breaths grew closer together. The pace of her middle finger rotating in tiny circles stopped.

What? No. Keep going.

My dick could not be denied. I started jacking off.

Her hand cupped her vulva. Tightly, she pressed her thighs together until her hand disappeared. Slowly, she opened her eyes. Stared at me. I released my dick to let her see his standing ovation and how much he wanted her.

Gradually, she parted her legs. Her pink pussy was prettier, plumper. My chest heaved with anticipation of discovering if my shit was tighter.

As she curled her pointing finger at me, not wanting to appear desperate, I touched her ankles. She closed her eyes. She wanted me to take her. My dick was so damn hard. I didn't want to hurt her.

I stroked myself. About to bust, I had to massage the opening of her vagina with my precum. She was hot. Wet . . . and damn!

"Are you serious?" I whispered, ejaculating sooner than I'd wanted.

My wife's pussy was so tight, my head could not get in.

CHAPTER 14

Blake

Bing picked up his cell off the nightstand. My phone stayed at the bottom of my purse all day yesterday and this morning.

"Sweetheart, change of plans. We have to depart tomorrow. I have an urgent meeting in Charlotte that I have to conduct in person."

Making my fiancé feel bad about putting a beautiful engagement ring on my finger was never my intent. We'd been at his chateau an extra day of the three we'd agreed upon. To maintain harmony, I extended a tear-dropping apology—essentially for being myself. Small effort to exert in exchange for peace.

"Today?" I repeated. My tone was absent of excitement yet underneath I was thrilled. Our naked bodies intertwined, arms cuddling, legs overlapping.

Bing gently tucked my hair behind my ear. Kissing my forehead, temple, cheek, chin, opposite cheek, nose, he navigated his way to my breasts, then sucked my nipple. I took a deep breath, rubbed my fingers through his slick hair.

"You e-mailed your boss your resignation?" he asked, peeling away the white sheet from our bodies.

I let him know, "I'm going to request an additional week off for a family emergency," wanting to tell him, *I may not be a billionaire but I fought years for my banking position at corporate in Charlotte.* He owned an empire. He knew etiquette was more about being able to get rehired. Resigning through an e-mail was unprofessional and not how I was going out, if I was leaving.

"If you have to lie to keep a job, is it worth it? I need for you to stand up for yourself, sweetheart."

For myself or for him? This time I kissed him. "I love you. I'm not you."

"This isn't about me. It's us. We are a team. One. Remember that I'll never suggest anything that's bad for you. I've been following our girls on social media. Alexis and Mercedes would be a perfect fit for Bing Sterling Enterprises. Wouldn't you agree?"

Our girls? Alexis? When hell froze over! No reply warranted. My daughters were not his until my last name was the same as his.

He headed toward the kitchen. "Mimosa? You hungry?" he asked.

Struggling to let this man lead me, if it was going to be, he was the right guy to set the pace. "Yes. Yes. Please and thanks." Needing a damn drink, I dug into my purse, powered on my cell, group messaged my girls, **Bing and I are heading back to Charlotte from Paris tomorrow**, went to the bathroom, emptied my bladder, then squatted over the bidet.

I joined him near the refrigerator, pressed my breasts against his back as he placed his cell on speaker, then ordered, "Top of the morning, Chef! Let us have eggs Benedict, fresh lump crabmeat, shrimp cocktail, caviar, and foie gras." Facing me he asked, "Did I miss anything, sweetheart?"

Fresh cut pineapples and mangos were standard. Most of what was being prepared would not be consumed. Neither of us ate much. No need to be extra wasteful. "That covers it."

"That'll do. I appreciate you, Chef," he said, ending the call. Bing mixed two mimosas, handed me one. "A toast to our love."

I tapped my flute to his, followed him outside on the balcony. I was going to miss this view. What would it have been like to share this moment with Spencer? He was the first guy to make me squirt. Bing was the second. I missed Spencer's youthfulness, not his lies and deception.

Bing was the intellectually clear choice for me. Spencer tapped into an uncensored side of me, making me feel whatever I wanted to do wouldn't be judged.

"Why the sudden change of plans, babe?" I inquired, tilting my face to the sun. From my vagina to the crack of my butt, this was truly the first even tan I'd had.

"North Carolina just passed a law that allows discrimination against the LGBTQ community. I'm withdrawing my project to break ground on twelve new restaurants. I can't support an economy that legally discriminates against anyone. If you truly love and want to be my wife, I hope you feel the same."

Wow. Alexis would love to operate a restaurant chain. I wouldn't approve of her doing so for Bing. He'd have to be in constant contact with her. Mercedes was a better fit.

Knowing my fiancé, *legally* was the operative word. We understood that biases and racism were prevalent everywhere.

"I agree with you, but there are LGBTQ people in North Carolina that were depending on your jobs. What about them?"

"Strike two," he said, then entered the French doors.

As I trailed him, Bing looked at me. "Blake, I love you but I can't marry a woman who doesn't understand the significance of economic power. The NBA has pulled the plug on their All-Star Game. Moved it to New Orleans. Maybe Louisiana is where I'll open my establishments. When North Carolina goes bankrupt, businesses fold, companies pull out, conferences cancel, tourists vacation elsewhere, and residents relocate, North Carolina will sink or die trying to stay afloat. Either way, I will not be the one throwing a life preserver to anyone who takes pride in emotionally lynching innocent people."

Hold up. Rewind. Strike what? Honestly, I didn't realize Bing was deeply passionate about human rights. Now wasn't a good time to reveal that I had a deep, dark secret that would bond us closer or rip us apart. Had to speak with my sister Ruby soon.

This was not the time for a pissing match. "I'll send the e-mail today," I said, not wanting to lose the first man who volunteered to be a father figure to my children.

"Obviously, you need time to think this through. Come wash my back for me," he said, heading to the bathroom.

Bing had earned the right to have the best. I was starting to see that included the woman who'd take his last name. No need to inquire about brunch getting cold. His chef would re-prepare everything upon notice.

If I refused to wash his back, would that be strike three?

Facing me in the spacious Jacuzzi, he asked, "Is the water to your liking?"

Lathering a sponge, I straddled him, wrapped my legs around his waist. "Yes, it is," I replied, squeezing avocado oil body wash on a loofah. Gently I scrubbed while moving my hips in a circular motion.

He reached around me, stroked my back. "This is how I want our marriage to be. You wash my back. I do the same for you. Two people with the same goals can accomplish more than one who worked twice as hard. I need a woman in my life. I want you to be my wife. We'll be okay," he said, holding me close.

Tears streamed from my eyes. Was this how married couples vibe? I struggled to let go of being the strong, black, do-it-all-by-myself woman.

I guess I'd have to try harder.

CHAPTER 15

Devereaux

Trending on social media, my panty-dripping sex scenes and jaw-dropping drama ranked number one. Probably the only person on set who wasn't getting laid was me.

Watching Emerald's sex scene with her guy had me sweating between my thighs. Her lover eased the red lace bra down until her nipple popped out. Tilting her head back as he bestowed feathery fluttering strokes upon her breasts, she opened her mouth. His middle finger slid along her tongue. Slow. Steady. I watched her lips suction him in up to his knuckle. When he pulled out, with baited breath, soon as I saw his cuticle, I clinched the walls of my vagina from the opening, up to my G-spot, and didn't stop until I couldn't squeeze any higher.

Desperately, I wanted to take over my director's role and yell, *Cut!*

What I really needed to emotionally rid myself of was my ex, move on, and let a new guy fill my void. In hindsight, I was relieved Phoenix hadn't stayed the night that night he went to jail. My sister was looking out for me, couldn't hate her for doing what I wasn't brave enough to do. I would've given in to Phoenix. Mercedes knew it. He knew it. He'd be in my house right now while I was at work. I'd worry the entire time I was here, who he was calling a bitch in my bed.

I exhaled. Ebony Waterhouse no longer being on my payroll was a relief. Would memories of my ex cheating ever fade to black? Could I trust him again? Should I?

The director said, "Everyone take fifteen."

My panties were moist. Motioning to stand, I needed to freshen up before the next scene.

West-Léon swooped in from my left, sat beside me dressed from the waist down. I stared into his eyes. My peripheral soaked in his nakedness. When I had a man, lust never lingered. I'd never, nor would I ever cross the line of professionalism but Lawd this man was salacious. And he did not come packaged with off-set sexcapades.

"Devereaux," he said, touching my thigh. "Don't hire anyone to replace the role of Ebony. I met someone that's a perfect fit for me. This chick is super-bad, drop-dead gorgeous, all the way turnt up. I want you to give her a shot."

His brown skin embodied strong, broad shoulders, lean protruding biceps, a well-defined chest with areolas the size of a nickel. I had the director make sure the camera angles kissed all of West-Léon's body, especially his protruding massive groin area that drove women, and men, in Atlanta insane.

West-Léon's stomach abs rippled down to the smooth pubic hairs above his belt. I knew more than I should because I'd seen him nude during a wardrobe change for one of his bedroom scenes with Phoenix's ex-side. Feeling West-Léon's hand on me made me hotter than filming him coming out of the water on the beach in Puerto Rico. Waves crashing against his dangling—

Pausing mid-exhale, I'd refrained from exhibiting one of Mercedes's habits. "I know you're concerned about your character but trust me, your fans' momentum is unwavering. In fact, it's growing with anticipation. We'll select someone soon."

Anxiously, he asked, "Are you open to my recommending this person? Please, Devereaux."

Wouldn't hurt. My casting director hadn't found the right fit thus far. If this actress was his smash piece, both of them could forget about it. I nodded. "Like you guys, she has to be a fresh face to television."

"She's brand-new," West-Léon said, standing.

"Wait. Before you refer her, know that your reputation is on the line. If you blow it, you cannot bring anyone else to me. I need a woman who looks the part and she's ready to work immediately. And don't bring me your cousin, sister, friend, or ex. Agreed?"

"Cool. Thanks," he said. "You can check out her social pages. Her name is—"

"Dev! Dev!" A familiar voice shouting from outside interrupted.

West-Léon laughed. "You want me to get rid of him, again?"

"I'll do it." Sighing heavily, I told West-Léon, "Excuse me," getting up from my seat. How many no's would it take to keep my baby's daddy away?

I opened the door to beautiful sunshine, and eighty degrees warmed my face. Beneath a clear blue sky, there stood my ex.

"Dev!" Phoenix yelled as though I were still inside.

Approaching him, I said, "Please stop. Don't come on my set embarrassing me. Time is money and right now you're wasting both, again."

"So you don't care about me, the father of your child. I can't even see my baby. I know you don't want me to let your crew know you're a deadbeat mom. Where's Nya?"

I prayed for a strong breeze to carry the stench oozing from Phoenix's body in the opposite direction. He had on the same shirt and sweats when he was arrested almost a week ago.

Sighing heavily, I asked, "What do you want?"

"I want to come home where I belong, Dev. Please. Just one more chance."

His breath smelled like week-old garbage. I stepped backward across the threshold. "You made things this way. Not me. I gotta get back on set."

"No, you're covering for that bitch Mercedes! Watching me be cuffed, then stuffed in the back of a police—"

That bitch as he'd called her was watching our daughter. I'd heard enough. "You never accept responsibility for your actions. You had an FTA on your record. That's the real reason the cops took you to county."

He should be grateful he was out. The BMW I'd paid for, I noticed he'd parked it next to my car. He could sell it, pawn it, do something to generate enough cash to wash his ass.

"That was a bullshit traffic ticket. My mama didn't tell me I had a court date," he complained. "I—"

Why hadn't he used our address? No doubt he was someplace inappropriate when the police stopped him. Interrupting his pitch with, "I've got to get back to work," I began closing the door.

Walking toward me, Phoenix would not let the conversation end. "My mom said I can't stay at her place. She won't even take my calls since you bailed me out." The closer he came, the louder he became. "All I have is the clothes on my back! Let me come by and get some of my stuff, Dev! At least let me wash my ass! I smell like shit."

The last thing I heard Phoenix say was, "I'll be out here when you're done!"

I could have him arrested for trespassing but it wasn't worth it if I was the only one who'd get him out. Undoubtedly, I loved Phoenix.

West-Léon said, "Time is up," then closed the door.

Getting pussy was the least of West-Léon's problems. Having my vagina stroked would be nice. Foreplay. Penetration. Inviting my employee to my home tonight would be my biggest mistake.

I knew that, yet I was torn.

CHAPTER 16

Sandara

I wasn't in the habit of turning down paid jobs.
Black had no idea how much more I could've lost. His bruising my neck almost cost me thirty thousand dollars on the runway, fifteen in catalog ads, and an additional ten for an appearance at Baylor University

One thing stayed with me when Fortune battered my mother. Witch hazel helps get rid of passion marks and bruises. I wrapped soaked gauze from my ears to my collarbone, chilled at home while Remy kept the kids. Now I was in the Big Apple doing what I loved.

Getting hair and makeup done, I smiled. Stared at myself in the mirror thinking, *You've done good for yourself, chicka-chick.* I bet my dad would be proud of me if he were here. Glad my mommy was coming back from Paris sometime today, I prayed I'd made her proud despite that I'd given birth one less time than her in the same manner. Well, not exactly, my kids knew of their daddy.

A call from Black registered. I curled the left side of my lips, then took the deepest breath before answering on my Bluetooth, "Hey, what's up?"

"Where you at?" he said with urgency as though we were married and I was late walking in the door.

Proudly, I looked at my reflection. "Getting prepped for my show."

"Show? You need to start telling me your schedule. Where's Tyson? When you gon' be done? It's almost eight. I need you to suck my shit in two hours. Lay them kids down soon as y'all hit the do' so I can lay this pipe. Get some strawberry ice cream for Daddy. Be ready."

Black had feelings? The curves of my mouth stretched to the max. "I'm in New York. I can't."

If I were home, I'd stop at the grocery store. Get some marshmallows and chocolate syrup, too. But ice cubes never got old. Sexing Black had to wait. I wouldn't be back for a few days.

"Stop lying. You know you in the A. I was knee-deep in it less than forty-eight."

Yeah, where was his dick last night? After Black choked me out, I hadn't heard from him until now. Mercedes had advised me to stop telling my baby daddies when and where I had a show. I didn't need Black; he didn't want me. I wanted him. He needed my money. We were both messed up. Four years of fornication and, I paused. Listened.

Guy chatter was in the background. One boasted, "Boy, you my nig'. You got that pussy on pause." Another chimed in, "And he 'bout to snatch that purse." The first one followed with, "Man, you got that ho on a fashion stroll. Straight beast mode, bruh. Let me hold a c."

Black laughed. "This dick is an animal, man. Can't none of my bitches tame me. Here you go, bruh. That's a fuckin' loan, nigga."

Did he just hand his boy a hundred dollars? I haven't got that much outta Black in four years for Tyson. I ended the call. Read a text from my girlfriend, **The kids are good. How's it going? I'ma need help with my car note when you get back.**

I just gave you three hundred to make a payment, I texted back.

That was month before last payment. I'm still six hundred behind.

Remy was the only person I trusted with my babies other than my sisters and my mom. Alexis gifted me her Porsche. I could pay it forward. I typed, **How much to pay it off?**

She sent an emoji with a teardrop.

Done with makeup, the stylist spritzed my hair.

"Wardrobe, Sandara!" the coordinator announced.

$7,321.16, Remy texted.

Was that all? I thought. Months ago that would've been a lot of money. It still was. Pre-modeling, three kids and no child support coming in taught me financial responsibility. I had too much pride to ask my family to support my mistakes. Tyrell, Ty, and Tyson were blessings. Getting pregnant for Black and the other two deadbeats was my downfall.

A call came in. I hit end. He dialed again. I answered, "Not now, Black."

"I got these papers and this dick waitin' for yo' ass when you get back," he said all loud, then hung up on me.

Setting my cell and Bluetooth on a table, the assistants lowered my garment over my head. I stepped into my shoes. Tears welled, clinging to my bottom lids.

"You'd better not mess up my work," the artist said. Dashing off, she returned with a tissue. "Honey, I don't know what you're cryin' for," she said in her Jamaican accent. "You've got the pick of the litter of men. Every man wants to date and marry a model. Give it some time. You'll see."

"But he's taking me to court for child support."

Gently placing the tissue at the base of my lash, she said, "Don't you dare give him one thin dime. You got them children. You got them bills. You got the money and you keep all of it. Now get out on that runway and strut your butt off, Mz. Sandara."

If I had my dad in my life, I imagined he would've cautioned me not to have children before graduating from Baylor. Thanks to my mother I had an all-expenses-paid chance to earn my degree. A real father would have a sit-down with all my children's sperm donors. Tell them to do right by their kids. But how could my mystery dad make demands when he hadn't done right by me?

Holding my head high, I was in an all-white halter gown with a plunging neckline, and a split from my waist to the floor. Stomp. Twitch left. Stomp. Twitch right. I marched to the edge of the runway, did a three-sixty turn on six-inch heels, brief eye contact with the most handsome man I noticed seated in row one. His shadow beard, thick brows, and juicy lips made me wonder if he was a model too.

One-eighty, one-eighty, eye contact with him again, one-eighty, then I strutted off stage for a fast wardrobe change. Back on the runway, I avoided locking eyes with him.

What guy would want a twenty-five-year-old with three children?

The six digits in my bank account still didn't feel real. I always wanted to model, took a chance and went to an agency, and here I was, little Sandara Crystal, all dressed up in designer fashion.

I knew I didn't have my daddy but I thanked God for my mother.

CHAPTER 17

Mercedes

"What do you want from me, Mercedes? Child support? Alimony? Blood? A rib?" my husband questioned.

Draining his veins would not suffice. He was forever indebted for the pain and suffering he'd caused me. A few moments of passion did not void years of his infidelity.

"I want my family more than anything and you know this, Benjamin. But—"

Digressing into thought, I didn't want to appear desperate in public. He knew I was certainly capable of ripping off his pants, covering his face with the crotch, tying the legs around his neck, and exposing him to all the people who were convinced he was the perfect husband. No matter how hard his mistress tried, she was not becoming my problem or his wife.

Wasn't my fault he hadn't cum earlier before I had to meet with a client. Well. Honestly. There was no appointment. I climaxed every time he tried to but failed to penetrate my tight "good good." Stopped counting after orgasm number nine. Had to call Dr. Stephens, let her know the procedure was working well after one treatment.

"You got off real good but no satisfaction for me. Sucking my dick would've been nice."

I despised performing fellatio. He knew that. Tired of arguing about my not putting his dick in my mouth, I remained silent.

I hated him right now. At the same time I loved Benjamin more than I'd admit.

My husband stared at me without blinking. An emotionless tone penetrated my ears. "Hiring a private detective to follow me is your way of?" A chilling stare glazed with disdain lingered in my direction.

We were never going to move forward if he kept highlighting what I'd done.

Benjamin reverting to forming incomplete sentences when he didn't want to concede didn't matter. My middle name, if I had one, could be Victorious. I'd been with that man long enough to complete his thoughts.

Making things better. Nah. Nah. Hell, nah! That investment was justifiable! I pushed my spine to the cushioned seat. Waited for his next complaint.

Playing all the cards in my hand at once would be callous. I'd learned to do the opposite of what I'd seen my mother do. She'd lied to me—*"I'm all right"*—to keep from crying over breaking up with man after man. Despicable could not begin to describe her actions. The fake smiles and empty hugs for me pretending she was all right when I felt her sadness. As a little girl, her pain became my pain. I'd cry for her.

The tip of his liquor-saturated tongue glazed his milk chocolate–colored lips, then disappeared into his mouth. His hair, beard, and mustache were freshly trimmed to a shadow. The faded scar between his arched brows made him appear sexy yet tough.

A woman told the host, "We'd like to sit there, please," pointing to the empty table next to us.

Really, bitch? Who does that?

With the exception of another couple on the farthest side of the patio, everything else was wide open. The woman with her sat adjacent to me on the long bench. The bold one sat in the seat near my husband then softly said, "Hi," to him.

I knew of who she was. Wasn't sure why she was here or if Dakota or Benjamin had written Toya a check.

In slow motion Benjamin gave her an upward nod, closed his downward slanted eyes, then slowly opened them looking at me.

Matching my husband's nonchalant attitude, I sipped my cabernet, then said, "Keep disrespecting me if you want. Consider yourself warned. I will not allow you to blame me for your infidelity. What Dakota uncovered were facts. Funny how you communicate with me all the time but somehow you overtly omitted mentioning you had a side bitch for two years. Two whole years."

The stripper, double-agent spy closest to him stared at me. She knew who the hell I was. I was sure of it. I returned the favor. I wished her dark-skinned, fake-horsetail-wearing, big booty behind would open her mouth. I'd toss my wine in it, then drag her ass to the curb where she belonged. I knew where she lived and my husband had been to her house.

"What would you like to drink?" their waiter asked them.

My husband hunched his shoulder, nodded to his left. I didn't give a damn what the woman sitting next to him heard. Or what game he was trying to win.

Seductively, she responded, "I'll have a Moscow mule and a pomegranate martini for my wife."

Had to give them a twice-over. Dakota hadn't mentioned Toya had a wife. Neither of them appeared butch. Noticed that their diamond infinity bands matched. Benjamin gave me that mind-your-own-business mug-face, then looked away as he watched the cars drive by on Peachtree Street.

He hunched the broad, muscular shoulders I barely embraced anymore. Benjamin flexed his biceps until the movement beneath the pale blue shirt I'd gotten him from the Tom Ford store across the street was apparent. Casually, he unfastened the first two buttons, massaged the nape of his neck, then propped his ankle atop his opposite knee. Black Kenneth Cole shoes shined to perfection dazzled in the sunset. The next thing he did that annoyed me was scoot back. Both of the women had a clear view of the navy pants with light blue pinstripes gathering along his inner thighs showcasing his well-endowed manhood.

Benjamin taking care of me was never optional. It was mandatory. I was nobody's pushover. Mother had passed the gullible gene to my baby sister. Not me.

Sandara had consummated relationships that resulted in three offspring, an equal number of trifling baby daddies trying to dig into her purse now that it was heavy, and recently there was females that wanted to fight her over worthless dicks.

Guys didn't mind busting a nut inside any of Sis's holes 'cause she'd let them. Despite all her shortcomings, she'd done one better than our mom. At least her children knew who their father was.

Benjamin nodded. Tugged his chin. Remained silent. Swirled the cognac in his snifter.

I hissed at him. "I did not put your dick inside her. You did that."

Shaking his head, he smirked. "You should get your money back for."

"Being stupid." When he was the adulterer. Taking another sip from my glass, I gave him a tight smile.

The twisted-lip response meant he was frustrated. I knew that already. My mother passed the lie-with-a-straight-face gene to my spoiled sister. Not me.

Alexis was a pathological liar and a tyrant. Mauled every man (and woman) who slept with her. I couldn't understand why her lovers begged her not to leave them. If James had an ounce of intellect, he'd stay away from my heart-slaying sister instead of circling back for her to decapitate him and his unborn.

"I refuse to play Russian roulette," was all I said, wondering how we'd gotten to this unhappy place in our picturesque marriage. Had to admit: Benjamin was once a reliable man for keeping his family first.

Interlocking his fingers, he rested his chin on his thumbs. "That's your problem if you want to take."

"Someone else's word." What the hell? "Finish a damn sentence. Photos don't lie." Mother had passed the believe-everything-your-man-says gene to my oldest sister. Not me.

Devereaux had the spine of a rag doll. Believed every tale Phoenix fabricated. I was vindicated that he'd slept in a cell. Wish he'd done more time for his ridickulousness. Dragging my two-year-old niece to his side's house while my sister worked her behind off to support him. Devereaux had better not take him back. If I could eventually raise twins on my own, she could do the same with the one daughter of hers. Us mothers had to bond together.

Going parenthood alone was never my plan. The possibility hit me hard. "When I'm done making you pay, she'll have to keep a roof over your heads."

The woman sitting next to my husband inserted a "Humph. He can move in with us tonight" into her conversation with her spouse across from him, then slowly inserted the tip of her fingernail into her mouth.

Shifting my attention to her, I didn't blink. Wanted to tell her, there was a pole out there waiting for her to slide down. I didn't know a lot about Toya, nor was any stripper worth my time. I narrowed my eyes, then scrolled my stare back to Benjamin.

He stretched his arms above his head, winked at the woman next to me, then replied, "If that's what it takes to provide for my kids, at least they'll have a place to visit me. I know you wouldn't want them to."

This time the bitch diagonally from me laughed. The veins in my temples swelled. Home-wreckers in the ATL derived pleasure from making another female's skin crawl. I refused to let that amateur belittle me. She was trash. I was sure of it.

Five trophies with "Father of the Year" were displayed on the mantel in the family room of our Buckhead mansion. I'd given— make that he'd earned—them all. So why'd he cheat on me with a less attractive, W-2–earning witch? It would take all of her government coins to cover Brandon's and Brandy's tuition.

Focusing on the purple and lavender asters, I wondered if this was a place he'd dined with his mistress. Based on the images in my phone he was obviously comfortable showcasing his side in public. Bones. Houston's. Chops. BRIO. Seasons 52. Hudson Grille. Hell, he dated her more than he dined with me!

"Hiring my resource was my way of discovering what I knew you'd never tell me. How long have you been . . ."

Words transitioned into visuals of him kissing his mistress's "good good." My only regret for viewing the evidence was the scenes were etched in my mind. Maybe letting Arizona devour his privates was some sort of sadistic revenge for my not getting on bended knees.

Realizing I was slumping, I sat up straight. *Get it together, Mercedes.* Why my husband when there were tons of dudes in Atlanta who would gladly do her? Thirsty chicks were uncouth. If Arizona didn't stop seeing my husband, I'd crush her to dust fine enough to sprinkle over the Atlantic Ocean.

I mumbled, "If you don't care anymore." Sighing, I stared at the blooming asters again. Was his side worth my time too?

"Repeat that. I want to hear what," Benjamin insisted.

"What do you have to say, Benjamin?"

"How do you know what I would've told you? You never asked. But you're right about one thing. You talk to me all right. You talk down to me. At me." He dragged my name. "Mercedes's," then snapped, "Monologues. I barely get to say a word when you're upset. Let me make myself crystal clear."

Oh, really. The ridicule was not called for. Normally, I wouldn't place my elbow on the table. Shielding my expression from the romantic chick flick to my right, I greeted Mr. Magnificent with a tight smile. I despised his coating the name of my consulting firm, Crystal Clear, with sarcasm.

Staring at my husband, I wondered, Were his mistress's juices on his genitals and his lips? Had he left her to meet me? Or was he looking forward to sexing her tonight?

Legally taking on the surname of a financially secure Morehouse man was my main objective while at Spelman. No man had exceeded my expectations. Ever. But I had to admit. Compared to other men I'd dated, Benjamin was spectacular.

I had been determined to have it all and, unlike my mother, I did. Now I had doubt. Should I forgive him when he'd shown no remorse? God, please. I didn't want to follow in my mother's footsteps. My family would humiliate me to my face.

Where'd he meet Arizona? Did she come on to him? Him to her? The woman next to my husband stared at me. Obviously, she was no real private investigator. What was he really paying her to do?

"Bitch, you'd have to stand in line. He already has a mistress."

Benjamin stood. "I have to go to the restroom."

She stood, then followed him. Her wife smiled at me.

"Hi," she said, seductively sipping her martini.

For the first time, I noticed her entire face was plastered with makeup. Wish I could say she resembled a clown. Scanning her up and down, I saw her dress was short, heels high.

Inhaling her sweet floral perfume, I opened my mouth, then exhaled in her face.

I refused to do all the extra to get attention. Didn't help Alexis and sure as hell it hadn't helped my mother.

CHAPTER 18

Blake

CLOTHING PROHIBITED

"That's cute," I laughed. Silently, I read the sign again as the door to Bing's jet closed behind us.

"Remove everything," Bing said, unfastening his tie. "We don't have much time."

He hung his navy designer jacket, crisp white shirt, and his pants on hangers inside a closet. Placed his shoes on a top shelf. Tossing his undershirt, socks, and boxer briefs into a hamper, Bing lifted his balls then let them go.

Peering into the cockpit I noticed the pilot and copilot fully dressed. "What if they come out and see me?"

"I don't have time to undress you, sweetheart," he said. "You'll miss showering before departure if you don't hurry. I'll see you in a few." Bing exited toward the back.

A woman appeared from the rear of the plane. Stood where he was seconds ago. The red, sheer robe covered a gold thong. Her stilettoes were too high for anything professional.

"Who? What? I don't understand," I exclaimed.

"No worries. I'm Mr. Sterling's certified in-flight personal assistant," she said. "Let me show you to the master suite."

Yeah, but was she trained to save our lives? It was apparent I'd be on my own if she had to choose.

Trailing the sexy woman, I saw her body appeared smooth and tight all over. Envying her firm ass made me wonder if she'd seduced my man to get this job.

She bent over. The hem of the robe slid between the crack of her ass. Her labia was engorged.

"Oh, my, God," I said before I'd realized I'd spoken aloud.

"Excuse me," she stated, standing up. No effort was made to readjust the wedge.

I hadn't seen many vaginas in my lifetime. Of course my girls' until they were old enough to maintain their personal hygiene. Then there was my mother. My sisters and I had taken turns bathing her during her last days as she was too weak to care for herself.

What I just saw, there was no way Bing's relationship with her wasn't beneficial. She picked up a tiny piece of paper, giving me scenic vulva visual snapshots. I confirmed in my mind that she indeed had the prettiest, plumpest pussy I'd ever seen and I was no lesbian. She wasn't under forty. I could only guess from her face.

Thoughts raced. She really needed to stop bending over like that. Would Bing have sex with this woman if I wasn't on this flight? What type of man had I agreed to marry? I prayed he didn't intend for us to have a threesome. I'd never done and I'd never do that.

Why me? Why did he ask me to be his wife? One thing was certain: unlike my daughters' fathers, Bing did not need or want my money.

Continuing our journey, we bypassed a dining room with a table large enough for four. A pornographic video silently played on a fifty-inch flat-screen television mounted above.

"Everything you need is in the shower. You have to hurry. The water will automatically shut off in five minutes."

The bed inside the master suite was wide. I glided my fingers along the sheet. Smooth Egyptian cotton. There was a stocked wet bar, a different X-rated movie on this screen. Removing my clothes, I turned on the water, stepped inside the shower.

I had time to wash my ass, vagina, brush my teeth, and that was exactly what I'd done. I dried off. Hung the towel on the rack. The escort, now completely nude, with the exception of her heels, led the way to my fiancé.

"We'll take a more thorough cleansing together after we're airborne. Here," Bing said, handing me a glass of champagne from the table between our armrests. "Isn't life grand? Cheers."

I'd been on his jet before and this was not the same one. Was not going to inquire if it were chartered or if he owned several planes.

We were still on the ground. The alternative, I could put on my clothes and leave him sitting here. Then I'd have to book a regular flight from Paris to Atlanta, go through security and customs, and make a reservation or drive from Atlanta to Charlotte.

Soft butterscotch leather comforted my neck, back, butt, thighs, and arms. Sipping my drink, I tried to relax.

The woman appeared again. This time fastening the seat belt across my bare hips, she said, "Whatever you want, let me know," then headed toward the rear.

Bing said, "Wait. Bring my lovely fiancée the ruby heels I had made for her in Paris."

This wasn't normal. I stared at Bing's limp dick resting in the crevice of his thighs. The woman returned, strapped the stilettoes to my feet.

I said, "Thank—"

Bing shook his head. Quietly, she left.

He was right. Mercedes would fit in well at his company but only the ability to dictate clothed would suit her. Bing's not saying "please" or "thank you" was the same as Mercedes's. He was firm yet polite. Definitely a man accustomed to giving orders. My daughter, she was rude.

I raised my flute and brows at the same time. "Cheers."

"Cheers, darling. And yes. The rubies are real."

All of this was brand-new. Chill bumps covered my body. I shivered. "Can she turn up the heat?"

"That's my department," Bing said, leaning in for a kiss.

The moment our lips parted, I said, "I really am very cold."

"Good. Drink up."

After swallowing every bubble in my glass, I requested a refill.

The champagne made me colder. I slid my hands up and down, then sandwiched them between my thighs.

"It's good to experience being outside of your comfort zone," Bing said. "Sacrifice, struggles, and failures build tolerance and character. Extremes teach us to adapt to our environment. If you can't handle this, how would you survive if you were stranded in the snow? No pain. No progress. I don't want a mediocre wife, Blake." He slid his flute up my hard nipple.

And I don't want to catch pneumonia.

My skin layered in bumps like sandpaper. The second cocktail made me feel worse. What if we had to deplane with no clothes on? I'd lose my job for sure if anyone videotaped us and posted it on social. Closing my eyes, I prayed for a hot flash.

From the moment we'd left the chateau, the only bag my hands carried was my purse and that was optional.

"Okay, this is different. I get your point. Is there a robe I can wear?"

"Yes. And, no. Why cover up your sexiness? Being free is what life is all about. If the plane goes down, I want my last memories to be my best memories. For the next eight hours, let yourself be free as those birds we saw in Paris."

"They had feathers," I said, making both of us laugh during takeoff.

As we leveled at thirty thousand feet, hot water beading against my body never felt this good. Bing's fingertips danced on my vulva.

Penetrating me with his middle finger, he pressed deep as he could, swirled several times, then quickly pulled out.

"Look at your thick cream." He licked it off like it was the last of the butter frosting that was left in the bowl. Guiding my hand to his erection, he moaned. "Mmmm. Jack my dick, baby. Not too hard."

Massaging his shaft, I teased the head, then rubbed his dick on my clit. My body shivered. Muffling, I wanted to scream with pleasure.

"Let it out. No one cares. The pilot and copilot are on my payroll."

"Yes, God," I grunted. "Put it in."

"You do the honors," he said, smoothing back my slick hair.

I could hardly breathe. Wait. He hadn't mentioned his personal assistant. Was she an employee or was she on his personal payroll?

"Here, let me help you." His strong arms lifted me above his thighs.

I wrapped my legs around his waist. Hadn't had sex in this position since . . . "Damn," I exhaled, holding him tighter as he lowered me onto his erection. The walls of my vagina suctioned like shrink wrap to every inch of his shaft each time he lifted me.

"Sit all the way down on this dick," he commanded, then whispered, "Don't ever deny me. I'll never tell you no. You're so beautiful. Can't wait to see you walk down the aisle to me."

Bing turned off the shower, carried me to the bed. "Hold my sweet pussy open."

Kneeling beside the bed, his personal assistant planted kisses on my clit. It felt good. I felt dirty.

Lifting my head and shoulders from the mattress, I watched Bing place his hands on my breasts. "Relax. Every woman should experience the pleasure of another woman."

Closing my eyes, I wanted to pretend a woman wasn't doing me.

She alternated between the softest kisses, to gently stroking my clit with her finger. Something whisked across my body. I opened my eyes, and Bing was teasing my body with a long, white feather.

"Stop overthinking everything or you'll lose the pleasure of this moment. Let go, Blake."

It was hard knowing a woman was down there. At least she hadn't . . . I'd thought it too soon. She inserted her finger into my vagina. Now her mouth and finger pleasured me.

She sucked my clit while stroking my G-spot. Stroked and sucked while Bing teased my nipples and French kissed.

I felt my eyes scroll toward the top of my head. My entire body was on fire. I'd give anything to have colder air blowing all over me right now.

The woman continuously tugged her fingers inside of me, occasionally pressing to my left. Her mouth covered my vulva, inner and outer lips. Her tongue slid up, down, and round. Clockwise. Counterclockwise.

The intensity of Bing's biting one nipple while squeezing the other transcended me into a zone I'd never experienced. Turbulence reminded me we were in the air.

Suddenly, everything stopped. The next thing I felt was Bing's dick slowly sliding inside my vagina. He resumed kissing me. As I started climaxing, I felt the woman's finger going in my ass.

"Ahhh!" I screamed. First I was shocked. Little by little the probing turned to pleasure for what was a great three minutes until she pulled out. Now what was she going to do?

The woman brought hot towels, cleancd us up, layered a warm sheet over our bodies, then left.

Bing lay my head on his chest, held me in his arms, then said, "Darling, if you like her, she flies wherever we fly. If you don't like her, we'll find her replacement. Get some rest. I love you."

CHAPTER 19

Benjamin

All that brilliance beautifully packaged, my wife still hadn't learned how to suck my dick properly. That may sound degrading to some but show me a man who didn't desire seeing his woman wrap her lips around his corona. I didn't personally know of any.

My wife should thank my mistress.

Standing inside King + Duke near the restrooms, I told Toya, "Your other half is looking scrumptious. You wanna hook up later?" I added, "The three of us," to make myself clear.

Shaking her head, Toya said, "Your wife is extremely attractive. It's that bitter personality that makes her a monster. She's a real piece of work, dude. Give that angry bitch her hunting papers," Toya said, laughing. "Your request for a threesome is good only if you slinging dick. See ya back at the table."

Maybe Toya was on point. Why was I holding out on sharing my dick? Had to consider, should I continue to let my wife sink her fangs deeper into my neck and suffer the consequences? Or do what my father taught me? Be a man and keep my wife and kids first?

Heading toward the patio, I stopped inside the door, texted my mistress, **wyd** while I watched Toya squash Mercedes's dyad with the Mrs.

If my wife would've fought for instead of against me, we might have lovers' quarrels in place of bouts of marital remorse. Falling in love with Arizona wasn't what I wanted but it was better than being alone. That wasn't happening.

My father told me man was not meant to live alone but women were different. Some would stay single claiming they were happy. Fewer would marry. Others would never trust any man due to too many men breaking their heart.

Had I made a vow to the latter type of woman?

I returned to the table, and my ass wasn't settled in the seat before Mercedes's eyelids narrowed at Toya, then at me. "So you no longer want to be the patriarch of this family. Just say it." The clench of her molars was evident when her jaws suctioned inward.

I didn't care what Toya might have told my wife.

Arizona replied, **@home**

"Handcuffs or silk scarves?" Toya asked her wife, then raised her hand toward the waiter motioning a down and then up mark in midair.

Mercedes snapped her fingers twice. "Waiter, we'll have a fresh round of drinks, the charcuterie, artisan cheeses, and avocado toast."

No "please" or "thank you." That was my wife's modus operandi. The only thing I had an appetite for was getting far away from my wife. Toya was right. Mercedes was not going to change.

Taking a long, deep breath, I paused then exhaled into the warm wind, eager to hear handcuffs. The onset of fall welcomed us with a pleasant clear sky and seventy-three degrees. Romance breezed by our table.

Firmly, I lamented, "You put me out of the house I paid for, remember?"

Mercedes laughed. "Correction. You started sleeping out. That was your decision."

I messaged Arizona a pindrop of my location, then typed, **Meet me for a drink and wear something sexy!**

Mercedes refocused my attention with a stern stare. At this point I didn't give a damn. I was tired of her shit!

Providing shelter for my family did not warrant accolades. It was my obligation, but bouts of gratitude would've been nice. No matter where I lay my heads, I loved my kids enough to file for full custody. Arizona would learn to like them.

Scooting back, I turned my chair to Toya. I adjusted my pants, propped my ankle atop my knee. Slowly wetting the tip of my tongue with cognac, I glazed my upper, then lower lip. Letting the liquor linger beneath my nostrils was a habit I enjoyed. Plus, taking my time made my drink last longer.

Toya thrust her breasts forward, stared at my lap, then smiled at me.

"He's not packing your type of equipment, honey," my wife told my private investigator.

I shook my head.

"You're right. He's packing mine," Toya's wife confirmed, making me damn near drop my drink.

"You're not going to appreciate him until some other woman does," Toya added.

I nodded. Toya winked at me before resuming her conversation with her wife.

Mercedes hissed, "I'm not going there with you, you, or you. You hear me. Nod at her again and see what happens."

Looking at my wife, I turned my back to Toya, faced the street. I didn't want to see Arizona walking in. Needed a pleasant surprise.

ATL promiscuous females lured a lot of do-right men into extracurricular situations. For the first time in six years of marriage I had a mistress—the past two. As my determination to be all Mercedes wanted in a man, in a husband, faded, I was getting closer to penetrating Arizona. Maybe tonight.

"You know I've never met my father. I don't want our kids to grow up not knowing you." My wife's tone was melancholy as she spoke to my left ear. Refusing to face her, I remained silent.

"You guys have a good evening," Toya said, then I heard, "Handcuffs. Definitely."

Instantly, my dick got hard as I visualized my locking their wrists to each other.

The daddy card was worn so thin I could see the ace of spades in Mercedes's hand. "Your mom messed you up. I'm tired of you using this as justification for your inability to reciprocate my affection. If you want to find your dad, do like your sister Alexis and demand that your mother tell you what she knows and start there."

"Easy for you to say. You grew up in a loving two-parent household."

Staring at her, I banged my fist on the table. The water in our glasses spilled onto the white tablecloth as I told her, "I'll never apologize for that! I wish I would've listened to my dad and never married your ass!"

My wife's chin, cheeks, and lips dropped at the same time. I'd have to squeeze between the tables to comfort her. Not this time. Either she wanted me or she didn't but this control game had to end.

"So you want me to come home?" I asked, hoping she'd say yes.

She shook her head. The response didn't shock me. Then what the fuck did she want?

Feeling dejected, I said, "My kids know me. You're the one who don't know me."

Exhaling heavily, my wife reached for my hand. I interlocked my fingers with hers wondering what the hell we were doing.

My wife confessed, "I know you better than you know yourself. You—"

I interrupted with a headshake. "If you know me so well, then tell me why I'm having an affair."

"I'm not defending your infidelity, Benjamin."

Wow! Another woman could have me just like that!

Mercedes heisted, then said, "If I forgive you without your begging for my forgiveness, I might as well invite Arizona into our bedroom."

The scent of Tori Burch hovered in the wind. Mercedes's eyes scrolled up and down. I felt a gentle touch on my shoulder. Knew it was her.

"Hey, babe," Arizona said. "I'll be inside at the bar. I'll order you a fresh cocktail. Take your time."

Not responding or turning around, I watched tears fill my wife's eyes.

"I'm so not impressed. Her photos are more flattering. Her titties look like your chest. Broad shoulders. Masculine muscles in her biceps and thighs, she could easily suit up for a football team. What's the problem? You're not man enough to date a man."

"She is a man." That comment was intended to humor the both of us. "Before I go—"

"This is an all-new low, Benjamin."

"No, you're a new low. I hold you in my arms every night. Well, I used to. When was the last time you held me?"

Slowly pushing back my chair, I glanced at my wife. She wasn't strong right now. Took all I had not to break her all the way down.

Walking away, I unlocked my cell, joined the finest linebacker I'd ever seen at the bar, then texted Toya, **Rain check please!**

Arizona hugged me. Closing my eyes, I held her. I needed to feel her in my arms. Sipping my cognac, I said, "Thanks for meeting me."

"So that's her?" Arizona asked.

"Let's not talk about her. Let's focus on . . . us."

CHAPTER 20

Alexis

"I don't recommend your terminating your pregnancy almost six months in but the decision is yours, Alexis," the doctor said. "I can't do it but I can give you the name of a specialist outside of Georgia."

She wasn't my OB/GYN. I wasn't brave enough to let my physician know my head's desire. This doctor had given me a response that was not to my satisfaction. She made me feel like I wasn't shit. I didn't want to run all over the country, maybe the world, in search of an abortionist.

"What about the bleeding I told you I had from my emergency visit? I thought my body was rejecting the baby?"

Truth was, I hadn't gone to emergency. If I were losing my baby, I didn't want to get help that might've saved it. I was trying to save myself from motherhood.

A miscarriage would be God's will. He could relieve my guilt. Being pregnant was messing up my once-perfect figure. Then there was a chance I'd have stretch marks like Devereaux and Mercedes. The twins had messed up my sister's stomach. Sandara had three kids and her body was fit for runway bikini modeling. I might not be that lucky. Her dad's side of the family must've had those awesome skin elasticity genes.

"You, my dear, may have experienced a little spotting but you are healthy and so is your baby boy, Ms. Crystal."

"But the blood. I really was bleeding." How could nothing be wrong? I wanted to cry until I looked at West-Léon. His eyes shined as though he were the father of my son instead of James.

"If you've been sexually active, some men ejaculate blood with their semen if they have prostatitis. It could be caused by an enlarged prostate, a male bacterial infection, something simple as a UTI, or as serious as cancer. If that's the case, your partner should have an examination and use a condom. Be straightforward and ask him," she said, giving West-Léon a split-second glance.

Ask him my ass. To blast him on my socials meant everyone would know he'd been hitting it. I didn't owe West-Léon an explanation but he might need to explain some things when we left here.

"I'll give you a moment to decide what you want to do," she said, exiting the exam room.

For the first time in my life, I did not want to be an alpha female in control.

"You have my support either way," West-Léon said. "If you keep it, I promise you I'll be here for both of you. And to ease your mind, I recently had an exam. I'm good head to toe and don't mind showing you my results."

If he was fishing for information about my sex life, I wasn't volunteering shit. The random dudes I'd let bang me didn't always wrap it up. I knew I should but I didn't care anymore. Men always casually promised shit they didn't deliver! A lead role in a film, extra hours on set with my sister, a spin-off show of his own and West-Léon would forget my name.

"Promise?" I asked.

He nodded, then hugged me. "You're not that tough. You've got to let somebody care for you. Can I be that man?"

Dudes who were easy to conquer had an ulterior motive. I didn't need his or anybody else's help. Opening the door, I called for the doctor.

"You've made a decision?" she asked.

"I want to make my appointment to see the specialist," I told her.

Touching my belly, I said, "Forgive Mommy," to my son. God knew I didn't want to make this decision. Life was so fucking hard. One day I'd have to accept responsibility for sacrificing my son's life to enjoy mine. If what the Bible said was true, I could repent.

A few clicks on the keyboard, and the doctor handed me a sheet of paper from the printer. "Good luck," she said, then exited the room.

West-Léon stared at me. "Do you realize that if you gave birth today there's a chance he'd make it? I bet he's a fighter. Thought you were too. Guess I was wrong. The more I think about him, I can't support your taking his life."

That was because his ass couldn't carry a baby for nine months. That right there was the bullshit I expected. Two minutes ago West-Léon was down with Alexis Crystal. The kid wasn't here and West-Léon had already abandoned us. Men, like my father, had walked away from me for twenty-seven years then showed up like . . . what's up?

I was used to this bullshit!

"Go!" I yelled in his face. "You're like all the rest. I'll take care of myself!" I refused to cry.

West-Léon didn't move. Shoving him out of my way, I went straight to my Benz, called the specialist, made my appointment, and drove to Spencer's job.

Pissed, I sat at the bar.

"Hey, dude. This is a surprise," he said.

"Let me have a mai tai. Be generous with the alcohol." I needed something strong.

"Not on my watch," he said. "Give me ten minutes. I'ma take a lunch break. I'm overdue."

Watching him leave the bar area, I ordered a mai tai from the other mixologist. What difference did it make? If one drink would've ended it all, I would've had a double.

Happy people were seated to my right. The laughter of females smiling in the face of guys, that was once me. Fuck James and Chanel! Carrying this kid was weighing me down.

I texted James, **I have an appointment for an abortion.**

WTF!!!!!, he replied, then commented, **Give my child to me.**

I hit him back with, **You mean give him to y'all?**

I'd be damned if Chanel raised my son. Maybe this was her get-back way to make me suffer for hurting her. Chanel was wasting her time.

Alexis, WTF is wrong with you? Where are you?

Not responding, I gulped half of my cocktail. I complimented the mixologist, "This is really good."

As I raised the glass to finish the rest, Spencer snatched it from me. Damn near spilled the cocktail on my lavender halter dress.

"I told you not to drink this shit!" He poured the remainder in the sink. "Let's go."

Casually, we strolled Lenox Square mall. My brother held my hand. We passed by Bebe, Coach, and Guess.

"Life is a bitch," I said, breaking our silence. "Less than a year ago, we fucked like rabbits in heat."

Remorse wasn't in our DNA. If I made a decision, I was cool with it. Spencer was the same. Wasn't as though anything done could be undone.

"Yeah, then we found out we had the same dad." Spencer let out a lightweight laugh.

"Then he died. Funny how I didn't give a damn about Conner before or after. Not really. When he passed, I buried a stranger. Don't miss him a bit. Appreciate his house, wheels, and the mils though."

Whenever I did have a kid, 'cause two would never come out of my vagina, I sure hoped they didn't hate their father. What was my mom thinking repeating the same mistake four times over?

"You should drop Cheesecake and open your own bar and restaurant," I told my brother.

"Dad left you everything, me . . . nothing." His tone was bitter.

I hunched my shoulders. "Venus left you stacked on seven figures."

Spencer's mom meant the world to him. She'd built a small empire. He was her only child and inherited it all. Bartending kept him occupied. Everybody didn't want to be an entrepreneur. I got that.

"I miss Blake. That was my gurl," he said.

Where'd that come from? "She's engaged, chick, but I'm sure you know she's moved on. You need to pick up your pace. Get back on your ho stroll."

Spencer stopped walking, let go of my hand. "To that old dude?"

I stared at him. "Uh, yeah. Old dude with crusty bank. And he's only forty. He's just my kind."

"Yeah, if anybody can *fuck* up a relay, dude, it's you," my brother said.

What was fucked up was his comment. I started to check him, but I let chick slide on his feelings.

Spencer's tight lips relaxed into a curve to the side as he nodded. "Blake shoulda stayed with me. He probably can't make my gurl squirt."

I did a Mercedes, snapping my fingers twice in front of his face. "I wasn't finished," I said, fucking with his emotions. "Bing is wealthy. They're somewhere on another vacation. I think. Or maybe they're back from Paris. I'm not sure. All I know is my mom, like *every*one else, is dodging me." I grabbed his hand; we rode the escalator down one level to Steve's and Marjorie's Garrett Popcorn. Got my favorite, a small Chicago mix—caramel and cheese.

"I fucked that relay up," he said as though talking to himself. "Never shoulda smashed you."

Of course he had. He was a man. That's what they were great at. Had to remind him, "You fuck up all your relays, chick. Remember Charlotte's crazy ass?"

"True dat. But tell the truth. Where Blake at though? Atlanta or Charlotte?"

Enough about her. I ignored his last question. "You can say we did things we shouldn't have that hurt my mom. But you don't mean it." I didn't care where they were. She hadn't replied to any of my pleas. Guess, as usual, her man was more important. "I dropped by because I want you to take me to my abortion appointment," I said, sitting on a black leather couch in the middle of the mall.

Spencer squatted beside me. "Solid."

"You don't mind?" I contained my excitement. He was my only yes.

"If you don't care, I don't mind, Sis. Your body. Not mine. You get the last word. Just keep my shit about our old man under wraps and I got you."

"Hashtag real talk," I said, second-guessing my decision to kill my son.

"Been thinking about turning myself in," he confessed.

"What the hell for? He can't come back. I'll never tell anyone." I held up my pinkie finger. He locked his with mine. Gave me a firm hug.

A strange man with a lady by his side walked up to us. Spencer stood, looked at me. "You know them?"

"No harm intended, man," the guy said.

The woman politely added, "Excuse me, but did I overhear you say you're having . . ." She paused, then whispered to me, "An abortion?"

Staring her up and down, I told her nosy ass, "No." If they'd heard that, then they overheard what came after that. Never knew who was an undercover agent in the ATL.

The man stated, "I'm sure that's what we heard. We've been trying to get pregnant for over five years. Please," he begged. "Name your price and give the child to us."

Creepy creeps. Tears streamed down my face. I dried them immediately. Spencer inched closer to me. Held my hand slightly tugging. I felt his flow. These bitches were up to no good. Had my piece ready to pop both of them if need be.

"What else you got to say?" Spencer questioned.

The guy hunched his shoulder. The woman answered, "Nothing."

I wasn't giving either of them my personals. "What are your names? Full names?" I needed to know what they were up to and they'd better not hesitate.

"Paul and Karen Ramsey," he answered.

How could I have been so careless with my conversation with Spencer in a public place? Folks in the ATL were straight hustlers and that included ear hustling.

Saving their info in my phone, the details could be bogus. A background was going down. I told them, "I'll think about it, Mr. and Mrs. Ramsey."

"Oh, please do!" Paul said.

"Do you know what you're having?" Karen inquired.

Rubbing my stomach, I lied, "Not yet."

Their faces lit up. They hugged each other. What the fuck were they embracing for? They didn't know it was a boy.

"No more questions. I have your number," I said. Redirecting my attention to Spencer, I stood. "Let's go."

Retracing our steps back to my brother's gig, I wondered if that couple was God's way of giving me an out. What was West-Léon up to? Hadn't heard from him, but I needed to have sex tonight.

"Your lunch break should be over. Here, take my popcorn."

"You forgot where I work?" my brother said, then gave me a hug. His voice trembled. "Text me those weirdoes' particulars. And pay extra attention to your surroundings when you leave here.

"A carjacking recently went down in this parking lot in broad daylight. Two dudes with black hoodies approached a guy with a Benz. Didn't know what ole boy was focusing on but any bitch sportin' a hoodie in eighty-degree weather was automatic suspect. One put the barrel of a .45 in the dude's chest, demanded the keys. Punk-ass robber drove off. Other asshole took off running."

"Bet they can't outrun this." I dug in my purse, put my finger on the trigger. If Paul, Karen, or any other fool tried to lay claim to my Maybach S600, they wouldn't live to do it to anybody else.

Spencer's secret was safe. Our dad used to beat Spencer's mother really bad. Sent her to an early grave. Some shit people couldn't bounce back from. Some people didn't deserve to live. Even the Bible said, an eye for an eye.

As I headed to my car, the feel of a man's hands caressing my naked body was what I wanted. I seriously had to catch up to West-Léon or some other man was taking his spot.

CHAPTER 21

Devereaux

"Quiet on the set! Take eight!" the director said, then snapped the clipboard.

West-Léon, dressed in a fitted, black designer suit, greeted his side chick, Emerald, with a kiss, slapped her ass, then stood at the kitchen counter. Emerald was in a white, long tank top and a thong. She put away a few dishes, telling him, "I have to renege on taking you to the screening tonight."

"Why? What's up?"

"Not what. Who. I'm going with someone else."

"But I've already told my wife I'm going to be out of town. I'll chill here until you get back." West-Léon sat on the sofa. Reclined.

His side shook her head. "You need to make other arrangements. I have plans afterward, babe."

"We have plans," he protested.

"Had," she said. Snapping a cap off a bottle of beer, she gave it to him.

West-Léon pushed her hand away. "What's the real situation here?"

"Nothing. Stop tripping."

"You're fucking somebody else?" he questioned.

"How's your wife?" Emerald asked.

"Fuck her! We're talking about you."

"Let yourself out. Be gone when I get out the shower." She gave him a passionate kiss, then added, "Please." Emerald exited the kitchen.

"Cut!" the director said.

Approaching me, the director commented, "We need to do it again. I need to see West-Léon go from happy to see her, to frustrated with her decision, to pissed the fuck off like he's not going anywhere when she walks away. Emerald needs to tease and pull him in with her seduction while crushing him with her every word."

Either I wanted my pride or I wanted my show to be number one again. Ratings were declining since I'd released Phoenix's side from her contract. New shows were premiering this season. I knew the solution. I needed to get over what happened with my ex and rehire Ebony Waterhouse aka Goldie Jackson.

West-Léon's problem wasn't with Emerald. His energy fed off of Ebony's.

"We need to make a change," I told the director.

"But what about—"

Interrupting, I said, "I'll have my assistant work out what I should have done sooner. We need Ebony back."

Goldie got what she deserved at that time. I'd exposed a secret she wasn't aware of. Her marriage to Buster Jackson wasn't legal. Buster Jackson had married his husband first. My attempt to have Goldie deported was out of anger. I'd prayed she'd lose the home she owned in my neighborhood where my ex had a key to her front door. Her inability to get a role on any other show was my satisfaction. I'd locked her ass out of television and film.

"You sure you want to do that?" the director asked.

"Positive. This is a business decision." Goldie needed me but more importantly, I needed her.

West-Léon approached us. "Devereaux." He gestured with his hands. "You have to find my Ebony. Please, set up an audition for my gurl."

"Your gurl?" I told him no relatives. That included females he'd sexed. As I shook my head, West-Léon placed his large hands on my shoulders. "She's not related to me, but I think she might be your family. Her name is Alexis Crystal."

Laughing, I replied, "You must be kidding." His response did not shock me. Alexis had her way of getting the job done. "I'm not sure you or I am ready for her. My show is *Sophisticated Side Chicks ATL*, not *Sophisticated Side Chicks with Guns and Dicks*."

An unexpected uneasy laugh came from West-Léon. "Aw, man. Are you serious?"

I frowned. "You must not know my sister well. Besides, she's pregnant. She a definite no for that reason. I'm going to offer Gold—"

"What! What! Goldie?" West-Léon jumped high and higher. Soon as he shouted, "Yes!"

Nodding, I heard, "Dev! Dev! Dev!"

My director shook his head, told West-Léon, "Let's do the scene again."

"Dev! I know you hear me!"

I told my director, "How about we wrap up now?"

"Time is money. We're on a budget. We need to do this until it's right. Why do you let your ex keep showing up here?"

It was my damn money! "Wrap it up. Now," I insisted, then walked away.

He wasn't on my payroll to dictate to me outside the scope of his contractual responsibilities. I agreed with my director in that I had to find a way to make sure this was Phoenix's last time acting a fool. Opening the door, I yelled, "Phoenix, what do you want?"

"My family," he cried, dropping to his knees. "My fiancée. My baby girl. I apologize, Dev. I'm sorry. Please, take me back. I'll never cheat on you again."

Phoenix looked worse than before. I used to love that man. Two years of cheating on me with the same woman? Picturing Mercedes's face, I shook my head. A Ferrari cruised onto the parking lot. The doors went up. Alexis stepped out sporting wide-lens sunglasses, a red and purple halter minidress that covered her cute baby bump. I wished she'd retire the stilettoes.

Bypassing Phoenix, Alexis said, "Hey, Sis. I came to audition for my part."

"Girl, you are not going to be on my . . ." I paused. *Hmm, maybe I should write her in instead of bringing Goldie back.* "I'll think about it."

Her eyes lit up. Alexis was too cool to scream or jump up and down the way West-Léon had done. She gave me a hug that was tighter than usual.

"You heard from Mom?" I asked.

The excitement dissipated from her face. She whispered, "I have an appointment tomorrow," touching her stomach. "Spencer is going to take me."

With that statement, Alexis suctioned the life out of me.

A text registered on my cell. It was from Antonio. **Meet me for dinner tonight. I need to see your beautiful face.**

Whoa. I thought he'd either forgotten about me or he wasn't serious. My spirit danced in the midst of adversity.

"How's my baby girl?" Phoenix asked, redirecting my attention.

I'd forgotten he was on the ground. "Get up and get off of my property. Now!"

The man I used to spoon with at night. The thought of him touching me made me cringe.

Alexis added, "And don't bring your nasty, dirty stank ass back here again."

"I'm homeless, Dev. Please. Just let me shower and get a change of clothes, and something to eat and I'll be gone. I promise I won't take long."

My eyes and heart softened.

"Fuck that bitch-ass nigga," Alexis said.

I wasn't sure which one treated Phoenix worse, Alexis or Mercedes.

"He didn't give a damn about you when he was fucking Ebony aka Goldie Jackson's nasty ass. Go shower at her house, ho. You got the address. You still got the key? Oh, that's right. Oops. Boop. Her ass was deployed."

His brows grew close, almost touching, as though he didn't know Goldie's whereabouts. I didn't either but I'd have my assistant find her. Phoenix stood. His jaws and fists were tight.

Eyes filled with hatred, he asked, "You gon' let her disrespect me like that?"

Pitted again between respecting my ex or my sister, I told Phoenix, "Put your hands on my pregnant sister and you will do serious jail time."

"Let a nigga leap. You know how I roll," Alexis said, patting her purse. "You heard from Mom?"

"She got into Atlanta today but I'm not sure if she's continuing to Charlotte. I don't know where she gets off acting like it's okay to abandon us for a man. We've dealt with that all our lives." I didn't want to relive this moment longing for my father with my only sister that had met hers.

"Yeah," Alexis agreed. "We need to let her know we're not having her neglect us."

I told my sister, "I have an idea. I'll confirm where Mother is, then I'll let you know, and I'll call Mercedes and Sandara. If she's home, we're all going to surprise her."

I texted Antonio, **9pm okay?**

Great, I know you've had a long day and an early start. I'll choose something in Brookhaven close to your place.

I smiled. Men always made assumptions. That was cool. He didn't need to know everything. I texted, **Looking forward to seeing you.**

"What you grinning for? Who you texting, Dev? You gon' let me sleep in my car while another man take my spot in our bed? Dev, please. Have a heart."

I'd forgotten again that he was here. Maybe ignoring Phoenix would work. I didn't want to call the police and have him arrested for trespassing.

West-Léon opened the door. His face lit up. I looked at my sister. Her eyes shined, lips spread wide. Their chemistry was undeniable. I'd never seen Alexis shine for James, Chanel, or any of her conquests.

Pairing these two on set could work well. Knowing my sister, it was just a matter of time before the real-life off-set drama with West-Léon began. He had no idea what he was in for.

Goldie Jackson or Alexis Crystal?

Either way my ratings would definitely soar.

Maybe I should hire both.

CHAPTER 22

Blake

The moment we stepped off the jet, Bing told our flight attendant, "Thank you, sweetheart."

As I recalled what she'd done to me, my vulva tingled. I nodded at her.

"You're released from on-call. I'll have your last compensation in your account by noon tomorrow," he told her.

Released? Last? What happened to if I liked her we'd keep her?

"Thanks for the opportunity," she told him, then said to me, "The pleasure was mine." I watched her walk away. She got into the back of a black SUV with tinted windows.

"I could tell you were uncomfortable even though you wouldn't say it."

No, I wasn't.

Bing continued, "Repeats could potentially lead to ties if you're not accustomed to this type of entertainment. Plus, women are smarter, shrewder, and sexier than men. My assistant will find her replacement. She knows what I like."

I felt my forehead shrink. *What* you *like?*

Pulling me close, he commented, "All work and no play makes Bing a very naughty man."

Hmm. "I hear you."

As we approached his driver, the man opened the back door. I wondered if we'd ever have a threesome with a guy or would it always be a woman of his choice.

"After you, sweetheart," Bing said.

Although he laughed as he let me go, I knew he was serious about that all work statement he'd made earlier. Playfully he rocked me side to side. Minutes later we were in his town car on Interstate 75, headed north to my home in Buckhead. Traffic was congested as usual. I was in no hurry to be home alone. Nor was I enthused to resign as he'd requested.

As I thought of my, make that our, girls, guilt attached itself to my conscience. I knew my children needed me while I was away and I'd abandoned them.

"Give me a second," I said, powering on my cell. Soon as it started chiming nonstop, I put it on do not disturb. I had 101 missed texts. Glancing at the last one, I responded to Devereaux, **I'll be at my Buckhead home shortly.**

I missed my Yorkie. Decided not to ask about Max yet. Got a glimpse of Devereaux's previous message. Nya's name stood out. *No. Their burdens are not yours.* I dropped my phone in my purse, then quickly regrouped.

"Sweetheart, you are a trouper. Since you're quitting your job," Bing said, holding me, "I'll be in North Carolina for a while working long hours terminating contracts and finding suitable new locations for my restaurants. I want you completely available to me in seventy-two hours. Get KingMaxB from Sandara and bring him with you. I'll arrange a walker and sitter for him. And he'll have a room suited to his name. Leave that stuffed animal at Sandara's and buy my boy a real girlfriend."

Max might be okay with having a female companion. My concern was after he was done humping and shooting blanks would he be okay with sharing his territory with her?

"You sure you can't stay with me tonight?" I asked, enjoying the ride. "We can get an early start and leave together in the morning."

Considering our eight-hour on-and-off mile-high rendezvous that I could only share with my friend Brandon, I better understood why my daughter Alexis enjoyed being with women and men. That episode did not convince me to cross over. Nor was I planting my lips on any part of a female's genitals again.

"If I told you my schedule for tomorrow, you'd think I was crazy for escorting you home from the airport. Now if you want to go back to Hartsfield, we can go to Charlotte together. Tonight.

"Here we are," Bing said, waiting for his driver to open our doors. "Take all of Mrs. Crystal's luggage upstairs. I'll have someone come to unpack everything. All you need to bring to me is you."

Exiting his car, I asked myself if this was the future I wanted. Would I be happy or content being a well-kept wife?

Settling into my Buckhead home felt odd. I didn't want to be alone tonight. Had to admit I'd been spoiled beyond my imagination. Resigning wasn't happening until I legally had the title Mrs. Blake Sterling. I wanted to jump the broom, not the gun.

Initiating another hug, I shivered against his abs, hoping he'd make time for a quickie.

"I need you to get the ball rolling on the wedding. Don't fire the planner. Remember, she works for us, not the other way."

Whoever she was, she was going to have a *he* assistant. Brandon was going to be my liaison and personal consultant. He'd keep everyone in check.

Bing held my face in his palms. I placed my hands on his sides, slid them up and down his spine, then embraced his broad shoulders. His chest pressed against my breasts, making my entire body trimmer. I was too seasoned to let this or any man turn me into a freak.

"Hold on to those sparks," he said. "I have a surprise that's going to ignite a wildfire in you. You'll learn to ask for what you want. I prefer that you take it. Nice women don't always get what they deserve or what they expect."

Accustomed to taking care of my exes, my children, I wanted to relax. At fifty, I welcomed opportunities to experience the unknown with a man that I loved and trusted, but I didn't want to take charge in my relationship.

Why not? Why me? Hard to stop questioning my reality. Bing was a confident gentleman that no woman—including my daughter Alexis—could take from me no matter how hard they'd try.

"I'll call my boss tomorrow." That was true.

"I hear you," he replied. His tone was filled with doubt.

Dreading checking my e-mails, texts, and voice mails. I wasn't concerned about my supervisor. My crazy coworker Herman, and the four girls I'd given birth to were my immediate worry.

Bing reassured, "My travel agent is yours, too, sweetheart. There's no need to call and let me know you're coming."

This man would land his jet on my roof if he could. The driver was parked out front waiting to take Bing back to Hartsfield for his flight to Charlotte.

"Okay. I'll make arrangements in the morning."

First, I had to rescue my Yorkie from Sandara and my grandbabies. I wondered if they'd pampered Max the way they used to or if he was being neglected.

"I gotta go, sweetheart. Tell our girls I'm looking forward to seeing them soon."

Between our dates and trips abroad, I hadn't formally introduced Bing. Honestly, I was stalling. I didn't want Bing to leave. Didn't want to give my girls complete access to my fiancé.

Escorting Bing to the door, I couldn't stand to watch him walk away. I turned the lock, went to the kitchen, opened a bottle of champagne, and chilled.

I was alone. Not lonely. Felt good.

CHAPTER 23

Alexis

In the nick of time, I blocked that black luxury town car parked in our mother's driveway, unlocked my Ferrari door.

Bing was not getting away until I gave him permission.

Marching on my four-inch stilettoes, I confronted Mr. Bing, bang, sexy hot damn! Up close, he was too sharp for my mother, and a few years too old for me, but I'd make an exception. What did Spencer and Bing see in my mom? Blake was boring.

"So you can take my mother from me, not let her return my calls or reply to my texts. It was an emergency, man. I almost died."

"You must be Alexis," he said with a smile. "Cute."

Dogs were cute. I gave him the down, up, two-second once-over. His shoes revealed he had real long bank. Spencer's seven figures net worth was lunch money in comparison. I was already feeling Bing's love.

Devereaux hurried to me. "Alexis, leave this man alone. Hi, Mr. Sterling. We came to talk to our mom, not you. No disrespect intended."

By the time I was done blasting this dude, he'd be Team Alexis. Real bitches kept bands. Having my own wasn't enough. Just upped my game to become a billionaire or marry one. Devereaux would beg to hire me after this off-script episode.

"He owes me an explanation," I told her before redirecting my attention to Bing. "You know my mother has four daughters or did you forget about me," I said, placing my pointing finger near my cleavage.

Mercedes and Sandara joined the party in time to hear me say, "Are you that rich and insensitive guy that only cares about himself? I'm having an abortion tomorrow and thanks to you my mother didn't have time to respond to my text asking her to go with me."

Impressed that Bing was a good listener, I wasn't done firing ammo at him. My sisters had to wait their turn. My mom's Yorkie, cradled in Sandara's arm, stared up at me, then barked several times. "Bet if something was wrong with him"—I gestured toward Max—"she—"

"Lil girl, you are being very inappropriate," Mercedes scolded.

So? And her ass was rude to the tenth power all her life. She'd better not make me unleash on her. This was my platform and I had no problem knocking her off of it.

Staring at each of my siblings, I told them the truth. "What's inappropriate is you bitches leaving me to bleed out. Especially my mom."

Bing spoke directly to me. "Alexis, if you have to curse to make your point, I'm going to have to reconsider thinking about asking you to work for me. I understand that you're angry but there are better ways to express yourself."

I didn't need his handout and sure as hell didn't need a j.o.b. My daddy left me extremely well off. He didn't understand a damn thing about Alexis Crystal. "You're not accustomed to polishing your own shoes. How are you going—"

Mercedes grabbed my bicep. Devereaux shook her head at Mercedes.

"No. Let her speak. I like that. I'm listening, Alexis," Bing said. "Continue."

"You've been privileged all your life. I barely knew my father before he died. They never met theirs. So the woman you're flying all over the world is the only father we know—"

Bing interrupted, "You mean my fiancée."

His what? He put a ring on our mother's finger? My sisters and I stared at one another. I mean, Spencer had done the same except his was a relationship ring, not an engagement ring.

"I get where you're coming from. But you don't know anything about me. Everything I have, I earned. No one gave me a dime. Let me tell you girls a true story. My mother was a maid for this wealthy couple. The couple had three rich, entitled kids. Their father is my father. This well-known politician raped my mother. Told her she'd better not tell anyone and that included me.

"I was not allowed to eat, play, or go to school with my brothers. The youngest and I are the same age. Our resemblance is so close we could pass for twins. The secret and shame eventually killed my mother. She died on my eighteenth birthday. Before she took her last breath, she told me the truth. She told me everything. She'd saved most of her money for me to attend college. After her funeral I went to Harvard. Freshman year, some days I had nothing to eat. Other times I could afford noodles. Sophomore through graduation, I studied hard and earned my degree."

Bing looked at me, then said, "Alexis, you have to start earning, instead of taking."

The authoritative tone silenced me. All my sisters stared at me. I was dramatic but I was no fool. I returned their empathetic expressions.

"I understand," I told him, wondering if having your father disown you, or if not knowing your father was harder for Bing or us.

"Intelligent people have discussions. Every problem has at least one solution. Tell me your concerns. And we can work it out. Disrespect any one of us, and I'll disown you," Bing firmly stated.

Blah. Blah. Blah. Wonk. Wonk. Wonk.

All of a sudden, since Bing gave them the opportunity, Devereaux, Mercedes, and Sandara couldn't shut the hell up and let me respond. When they were done spilling their issues into Bing's ears, I said, "I apologize. It won't happen again."

Mercedes taught me never to say, "I'm sorry."

This time my sisters gave me wide-eyed looks. Alexis Crystal was no fool.

"Apology accepted, baby girl. Now that we know one another better, if you'd allow me, I'd like to be the best father I know how to you. Your mom and I are getting married and I already consider you my daughters. Let's go have a talk with your mother."

"What about your flight?" Sandara asked.

Too late, Lil Sis. I was already locked in as his baby girl and I'd make sure there'd never be enough space for two. If Mom wasn't careful, there'd be barely room for her.

CHAPTER 24

Blake

"Lawd. Lawd. Lawd. Thank you."

The words escaped my mouth as I added a Grand Marnier floater to my third mimosa. I raised my glass. Took a sip, placed my drink on a coaster. Feeling good, I reclined on my chaise, crossed my ankles, then closed my eyes.

If Jesus would've told me my love for Spencer would've been replaced with a man who could give me the world along with unimaginable sexcapades, I would've doubted Him. *Thank you, Jesus, for allowing me to release and let go of the man who I thought was my destiny.*

"Lord, forgive me for fornicating." I questioned whether I should've said that knowing I'd never had marital sex . . . but not much longer.

An incoming call disrupted my relaxation. Hadn't heard that tone in a while. I pressed send to voice mail. He called back. Annoyed, I answered, "What?"

"Blake, you can't marry dude," Spencer exclaimed.

The devil was an angel, too. Busy as Satan may be, I told my ex, "Please don't call me again," ending the call.

Our season was over. When I was with Spencer, despite all he'd done, I believed he was my future. Knowing what real unconditional love was, I—

I answered, "Spencer, please. Show some respect."

"Blake, I need to see you. If you can look me in my eyes and tell me that you don't love me, I'm out," he said, as though he was certain that I still had feelings for him.

This time I didn't say good-bye. I placed my cell on the coffee table, enjoyed my cocktail.

Never married was one thing, letting that woman lick between my legs was a first. My body shivered from the flashback. "Lil ole Blake Crystal. Country girl raised in North Carolina." Several of my siblings still lived in Charlotte. Work and vacationing with my fiancé left no time to visit Carol, Peter, or—

I dialed my sister, Ruby.

"Hey, honey," she answered. Immediately, I missed hearing her soothing voice.

"I love you," I told her.

"Love you too, Sis. What's up?"

I'd raised four gorgeous girls by myself. Who they developed into as women, they could credit themselves. My time had come.

"I called to tell you . . ." I paused, then said, "I'm engaged to one of the wealthiest men in America."

Why buy the cow was no longer my life.

"Shut up. Tell me more," she exclaimed.

Spencer stayed by my side, dabbed witch hazel on my black eye three times a day after (my at that time ex) Fortune had beaten me. Spencer and I used to soak in my Jacuzzi sharing our deepest secrets. He loved me the best way he knew. It wasn't enough. I had no regrets for moving on. Just memories I couldn't erase.

"I need a huge favor." Had to get it out. This was different from the secrets she'd kept.

"You know I got you."

"I'm going to set the stage for Bing, that's my fiancé, to call you and ask about the girls' fathers."

"Blake, you sure you want to do that?" she questioned. "You already lied to Alexis."

"She should thank me! Ruby, please. I have to. I can't tell my girls the truth about their fathers. I'll buy you a house, car, whatever you want."

THE ONE I'VE WAITED FOR

"Let me hear it first," she insisted.

I needed everyone to feel sorry for me. Not look down on me for my mistakes. There was one way I could assure my marriage would not falter at the altar.

"Since nobody in the family knows what happened to you, tell Bing those things happened to me as a little girl. Then when my daughters hear it from him, they'll accept Bing as their father figure and leave me the hell alone." I was tired of my children questioning me about putting "unknown" on their birth certificates and I didn't want them burdening Bing with their daddy issues.

I sensed her head shaking side to side as Ruby told me, "Blake. Why lie when I was the one who protected you?"

"I know, but I'm begging you."

"Okay. But if it backfires, I still want a new house, car, and hush money for this lie," my eldest sister said.

Taking another sip, I pinched myself to stay focused. Bing was real. I glanced around the living room. Should I sell or rent my property?

"You got it. I'ma call you back," I told her, feeling relieved based on my strategy.

"I love you."

I knew she did. "I love you, too. Bye."

I texted Brandon, **We need to do lunch asap**.

Bitch you back? I know you brought me a Parisian penis, Brandon replied.

Time to stop avoiding the inevitable. God knew my heart. I started with reading my boss's message.

Hi Blake. Hope you had a glorious time in Paris. Come to my office when you get back.

I could reply, *I resign*, or *how did you know where I was*, but my better judgment told me to type, **Will do**.

Scrolling on to the least dramatic daughter with real problems.

Sandara had texted, **Mother, I've never been more disappointed in you. I understand if you don't have time to go with me to court but not responding hurt my feelings. You didn't even respond when Max was sick.**

I sat up, my heart thumping, and typed, **How's Max?**

My Yorkie was sick? Deleting the message, I thought, *Okay, Blake. Calm down. How'd it appear if you were more concerned about your baby boy than your baby girl?*

Mercedes's message was direct. **Glad to see you haven't changed. A man shows up and you forget you're a mother. That's hideous! I won't cry for you when this one leaves.**

Cry? For me? Please. Mercedes didn't shed tears for anyone. Not her husband, her children, not even herself. If I hadn't birthed her, I'd swear that girl could've been cloned.

Devereaux was brief. **When I needed you the most, Mother**. Her emoji had a teardrop.

I closed my eyes to keep from feeling guilty. Defeated by my guilt, I cried through the cracks. Inhaling deeply, I blew cool air from my mouth. When could I stop being Mom first and become Mrs. Bing Sterling? That was how I desired to live.

Sighing heavily, I had to see what Alexis, the manipulator, had to say. **By the time you respond your grandchild will be in Heaven with my two siblings you aborted.**

Ruby promised she'd never tell a soul. What I'd just asked of her could destroy my bond with my girls, and end my engagement, if she'd break our promise. I knelt beside the chaise.

"Lord, give me strength. I don't want to lose this man. Dear God. I'm asking for forgiveness in advance." If I told the truth and lost Bing . . . I deserved to concentrate on me. Picking myself up, as I'd done all my life, I sat erect, welcomed the taste of liquor coating my throat. Maybe this was payback for my standing over my ex, Fortune. I could've called the paramedics while he was still breathing. Why should I have been the bigger person to a man who had beaten me until my eyes were practically swollen shut? I was glad Fortune was dead.

I was *not* going to—

Voices from outside interrupted my thoughts. There was a heavy knock at my door. Peeping through the hole, I saw Bing's handsome face. I needed more than a hug.

Exhaling several times, I opened the door. All four of my daughters walked in behind him. He stood in front of me. "Blake, we need to talk."

So he did have time. Suddenly, I was cornered in my living room. The only tail wagging happily at seeing me was my baby boy's.

As they chose their accommodations, I refilled my mimosa, then topped it off. The last time we gathered like this at my place was when Alexis's father, Conner, met her for the first time.

I took my appropriate place, next to my fiancé on the love seat.

"I'll do the talking and try to make this quick," Bing commanded. Scooting over, he'd left enough space to sit Max between us on the leather. Max crawled back onto my lap.

Not knowing what was about to be said, I was already pissed. Long as they didn't fuck up my engagement, they could say whatever. My stomach churned. Stroking Max with one hand, I began to calm down.

"So you knew our girls were having serious problems while you and I were in Paris?"

Was the question rhetorical? I waited for him to continue. They all remained silent.

"Yes and no," I answered. "I just read most of their text messages after you left a moment ago."

He countered with bass in his voice, "You knew when we were in Paris and you didn't tell me it was this serious. We should've been back here to assist our girls. I could've squashed Sandara's upcoming court hearings with one call. Did you know she'd stopped modeling?"

Who gives a fuck? Is that my fault? Hell, if he could've fixed it with a call, being here wasn't necessary. This is their selfish bullshit that is new to Bing. Not me.

Humiliation, heaped on top of anger, festered in my spirit. The girls remained quiet. I had no idea all of what they'd told my fiancé. Stroking Max, I opted not to say a word.

Bing addressed Devereaux, "Never lie with a man who cheats on you. A cheater is a liar. A liar is your enemy, not your friend. You're too good to give yourself to a Neanderthal. Never keep a man from his child. If Phoenix wants to see Nya, I'll arrange supervised visitation. I know Antonio personally. He used to work for me years ago. He's an upstanding guy. Give him a chance but never give a man your heart until after he gives you his."

Suddenly, Bing was Steve Harvey on steroids to my girls. My lips were tight, eyelids narrow. Drink in one hand, the other stroked my Yorkie's back.

Devereaux approached Bing. "Thanks, Mr. Sterling," she said, opening her arms for a hug.

"You can call me Papa Bing, if you'd like."

Tears streamed down her face. What the hell for? Bing hugged her longer than he'd held me before he'd left. Devereaux wept like I'd never seen nor heard.

My eyes scrolled toward the ceiling.

"It's okay. I'm keeping the promise I just made to each of y'all. You have a real father figure in your life now. Oh, and don't worry about finding your fathers."

That was the most exciting news I'd heard since they walked in.

"I'll put my investigator on that tonight. Shouldn't take him long. He's the best."

Really? At this point, I should intervene. I was not ready to deal with this. I'd die if Ruby divulged the lie I was determined to tell to put an end to the daddy madness. Didn't want to ruin their hopes or dictate the ending of this session. I sat quietly.

My girls gave him a group hug. Alexis nudged Devereaux and positioned herself directly in front of Papa Bing.

"I've had enough, girls. Have a seat," I insisted, wanting to offer them a group choke and strangle Alexis first.

"I love you girls too," Bing said, filling in the dent his ass had created next to me.

Love? Too? He barely knew my girls. I hated when men casually used the 'l' word.

My statement didn't stop him from saying, "Mercedes, you have to tone it down. You're trying so hard not to be your mom that you're actually sabotaging your marriage. You said, 'I do,' to prove a point. You had kids to show they had a father. You didn't do those things because that's what you truly wanted. You did it all to prove that you're better than your mother. From what your sisters said, you have a good man. Husbands are easier to come by than finding an honorable man. Emasculating Benjamin will push him away. Fall back. Chill. Be respectful. Be eager to listen. Slow to speak."

This would be a fantastic time for Mercedes to snap her fingers twice and exhale in Bing's face. All she said was, "Okay."

Time for the ringleader herself to get advice. I could not wait. Folding my legs like a chicken wing, I placed Max in the center of my thighs, lifted my drink to my lips, then sipped long and slow.

Bing said, "Alexis, baby girl."

I had to swallow to keep from spitting liquor on Max. *Baby what? Here we go!* I gave her a "Mama is mad as hell" piercing stare where I widened then narrowed my eyes to a slither. I knew she felt me. Her seemingly undivided attention was directed at my fiancé.

"You're not killing my grandson."

Humph. It's a boy. Well, lucky her.

"I'll be there for the delivery and I'll hire you a full-time nanny or two."

That was it! I uncrossed my legs, sat at the edge of the sofa with Max on my lap.

"Here we go again! A what?! Lil girl, you need to grow up." I told Bing, "She will take care of her own baby. I did it with four. She can do it with one!"

Calmly, he said, "Girls, give us a moment. I have each of your numbers. I'll be in touch. Oh, and Mercedes, think about coming to work for me. I have the perfect position for you."

I watched my daughters hug Bing before damn near skipping out of my house arm in arm. My entire face must've been shriveled like a prune that had been soaked in lemon juice.

"Blake, sweetheart," he said. "You're not the woman I thought you were. Next time a man asks you to marry him, don't send your representative." Opening my front door, he turned to me.

"Don't contact me. That's not a request."

Who in the hell did he think he was talking down to? I had options.

Soon as the door closed, I texted Spencer, **Come over**.

My hurt and my heart wouldn't let me press send. I no longer had feelings for Spencer. I was in love with Bing.

CHAPTER 25

Mercedes

Knock! Knock! Knock!

Feeling empowered, I left my mother's house and drove straight to Arizona's to get my husband. An extra hour with the sitter and our twins would be tucked in by their mommy and daddy tonight. I was sure of it.

Thanks to Dakota, I had Benjamin's mistress's cell, work, and home numbers. Addresses for her, her mother, father, her job, other relatives, and the last six men she'd dated were in my phone. Had a spreadsheet two years' long of places my husband had taken her, with the dollar amounts he'd spent of our money on his side. Now there was Toya, the new stripper trash on his lap and payroll.

If he wasn't leaving with me, he'd live to regret staying with her. I wasn't coming here twice.

The battle between Alexis and Blake was somewhere near the thousandth round. Alexis never tired of pulling hair and scratching eyeballs. She wasn't happy unless she could make someone else miserable. That was a fact. I couldn't stand by and witness our sister infiltrate our mother's relationship again. Had my own issues to tend to.

Bam! Bam! Bam! "Benjamin!" My car was parked next to his.

Bing was a brilliant man. I respected intelligence. Had faith that Bing would find my dad. Hearing advice from a fatherly figure, even if he didn't know us that well, ignited a different type of fight in me. My goal became reuniting with my biological family, meeting my father, and introducing him to his grandchildren.

Bam! Bam! Bam! "Benjamin!" I yelled, hanging on to the last syllable. He was going to come out eventually or I was going in. After Dakota had Devereaux slip her Phoenix's keychain and duplicated each one, bingo! One actually fit Ebony's door. I'd copied every key on Benjamin's ring. Surely, one would unlock this deadbolt.

None of my mother's exes had the resources or offered what Bing had. I should've asked for a nanny when he committed to giving Alexis two. That was one blessed chick. Landed on her feet once more. I was curious to hear details regarding the job opportunity Bing had for me.

The door cracked. I shoved it all the way open. "Benjamin, get out here."

Arizona closed her door to a crack. Calmly, she told me, "Don't show up at my house again, Mercedes. Your husband is here because he wants to be here."

I should've sucked his dick when he asked. Maybe I wouldn't be fighting for a man who was legally mine.

Remembering how Devereaux had Phoenix arrested, I got in my car, drove to the nearby Publix grocery store, parked in the lot, then texted Benjamin, **I need to see you right now!**

Me? he texted back.

I was no psychic but my guess would be that Benjamin, like most men, probably found it easier to smile in the face of a woman who wouldn't hold him accountable for his actions.

I replied, **Enjoy yourself. It's time I do the same.**

He asked, **Where are you?**

Giving him my next location, I texted, **Sweet Auburn Seafood**.

I wasn't there but I would be shortly. En route I listened to "Cry" by K. Michele. I had the upper hand. I dried my tears, then softly said, "Thanks, K." Replayed the song three more times, went inside.

What was taking him so long to get here? I texted, **I'm seated in the booth to your farthest right as you enter the restaurant.**

The band played on the opposite side of the room. Sweet

Auburn's was black-owned and they had some of the best food in
Atlanta. I kept my selection simple. A glass of cabernet was in front
of me. Reminding myself to be respectful to my husband when he
arrived, I questioned whether Bing meant for me to be submissive.
Being that woman meant I'd have to become someone other than
myself. Couldn't do that.

Deep in thought, I'd missed Benjamin's entrance. He kissed my
cheek, sat across the table. That was best.

Circling the base of my wineglass with both hands, I looked into
my husband's eyes. He placed his hand atop mine.

I told him, "I'm listening." Tears streamed down my cheeks. I
wanted to grip his hand as he cupped mine. I couldn't. I wondered
if his delay was contributed to his sexing Arizona. Had she performed fellatio on my man? Or had he licked her good good?

The evening sun descended upon us, casting a shadow of our
fingers against the painting on the wall.

"I love you, Mercedes. I'm proud of your accomplishments.
Your degree. How you operate your business. Care for our children. I don't need accolades for doing what's right. As protector of
my family, that is my primary responsibility." His grip tightened. "I
used to take my kids to school and pick them up every day when I
wasn't out of town. I cooked, cleaned. I told you I love you so
much I think you stopped hearing me."

All of those trips were not out of town and we both knew it.
Sometimes he was at Arizona's for three or four days. "Then why
are you sleeping with her?" I asked.

The waiter came near. Benjamin shook his head. "I'll let you
know when, man."

"No problem," the waiter said, moving to the next guests.

Benjamin's tone was low, yet strong. "Do you realize you always
have to be right? Always have to have the last word. Huh? Do you?"

No longer able to hear the conversations around me, felt as
though we were the only two diners. I dazed out the window at the
bumper-to-bumper traffic. Suppressing the strong black woman
yearning to defend myself, I could barely breathe.

What he'd said wasn't true. I shook my head. My lips parted.

"Yes. You do. If I tell the kids not to do something, you tell them it's okay. You do that all the time. In front of our families and friends. At home it's worse. I'm tired of your undermining me."

"Why are you sleeping with her?" I asked again.

My guess would've been my not wanting to have sex as often as he did.

Benjamin motioned for the waiter. Ordered a cognac.

When the waiter was at a distance, my husband said, "Maybe I'm tired of waiting for you to fall asleep so I can masturbate."

"How often were you doing that?"

Frustrated, he answered, "Three, four times a week and that's more often than we were making love. When was the last time you gave me fellatio or let me taste you? Your new pussy is meaningless 'cause you refuse to allow me to enjoy it. I always have to initiate sex. I'm a man, Mercedes. I have one heart and two heads. I also have a dick that stands up every morning before I do."

Okay. My husband's short-term memory was failing him. Wasn't my fault he couldn't penetrate me, but I didn't want to be the have-to-be-right wife right now. The lady at the table next to ours looked at my husband. Redirecting her attention to her guy, she had a blank stare. Her man raised his brows, then nodded at Benjamin.

Forget her, him, them. She'd better keep watch over her guy. I wondered, was I that bad?

"I'm not responsible for your dick," I hissed.

Benjamin stood. "As usual, you're right. Thanks for making my decision easier."

He was the one sleeping with his mistress! I refused to beg my husband to come back or follow him.

Taking his drink from the waiter's tray, Benjamin downed it in one swallow, tossed money at the glass, left the restaurant, and never looked back for me.

Maybe Bing didn't know every damn thing. My being submissive did not work.

CHAPTER 26

Sandara

"My boy. You know Dadday luv ya, right?"
Tyson nodded once.

Black spending time with Tyson was new. Brand-new. Day one new. This was all I'd wanted for me. My son. If I could get my other two children's fathers to drop their request for child support, we could come up with something that would work for all of us.

"Daddy, stop, that tickles," Tyson screamed, bent over with laughter. He wiggled his tiny fingers against his dad's rib cage.

The joy of hearing my man and my baby laugh together instead of Tyson being sad brought tears to my eyes. "I wish every day could be like this." Black was the only man I wanted to move in with us.

"Airplane, Daddy! Make me fly like Superman," Tyson pleaded.

I looked over at Tyrell sitting beside Ty watching television. Ty said, "It's okay, Tyrell. My daddy is coming to see me. Yours too. Tyson is the oldest so he gets to see his dad first."

Black had been here about two hours and I never wanted him to leave me again. I'd give him my world. Not my wallet.

"Come on, Ty and Tyrell. It's time for bed," I said to separate them from Black and Tyson. "Tell Mr. Black good night."

"Good night, Mr. Black," they said at the same time.

Black landed Tyson on the sofa. They laughed. "Black, the kids said good night."

"I heard 'em. I got mine," he said, plopping Tyson on his thigh.

"Come on, kids. You too, Tyson."

"Aw, Mom," Tyson protested.

Firmly, I told him, "Right this minute, boy."

"Yes, ma'am."

"Good night, son," Black said, then kissed Tyson on the forehead.

Taking all my kids into their bedroom, I said, "On your knees. Give the Lord his praise."

Ty knelt beside her bed. The boys did the same by theirs, placed their palms together, their elbows were on the mattress.

Ty prayed aloud, "God, where's my daddy? I want my daddy too. It's not fair for Tyson to have his and I can't have mine. Amen."

Tyson said, "That's not a prayer. God is gonna get you, girl."

Ty got in bed. Snatched the sheet and comforter over her head and started crying. I sat beside her. Held my little girl in my arms. Sympathizing with my daughter, I wanted to cry along with her.

"Sandara!" Black called from the living room. "What's taking you so long?"

Ignoring him, I comforted my child.

"Is Black my daddy, too?" Tyrell asked, crawling under the cover next to Tyson.

"Go to sleep, y'all," I said, then kissed all my kids before partially closing their door.

Black was on the sofa, in his boxer briefs. "Come pounce on this thang right quick before I go," he said, releasing his big dick through the opening of his underwear.

"I thought you were staying the night."

"Nah, you know betta. Do I eva?" He teased his thick shaft. Looked back and forth from his dick to me.

I sat on the opposite side of the couch. "Why didn't you say good night to my kids?"

"Your kids. Not mine. I ain't responsible for them. Now come ride this dick before I change my mind about giving you some," he said, stroking his shit long and slow.

"I'm not in the mood." I lied, then told him, "I have to decide if I'm going back to modeling."

His dick drooped to his lap when he let go. "Repeat that shit."

"You heard me. I quit modeling." Actually, I hadn't given it up. I needed a break until I figured things out. "You trying to take all my money. Got my other baby daddies trying to do the same. I'm not working to take care of y'all. I already do it all by myself. You need to support us," I told him.

Black was the quietest he'd been all night.

I couldn't say Tyson needed shoes, clothes, or a haircut anymore. Each of my children dressed well, ate at Red Lobster every weekend. Thanks to Alexis, we rolled everywhere in a Porsche. Soon I'd need a bigger car. Was thinking about that new Range Rover or a boss ride like a Hummer. I could buy a big house with a pool. The only reason I hadn't moved was this was my neighborhood. I didn't have any rich or well-off friends like my sisters.

Thinking about Bing, I added, "That's what real men do, Black. They provide for their family."

"You're not even worth choking out again," he said, getting dressed.

"Where you going? Tyson is so happy. I don't need money to be happy with you, Black. I just want us to be a family."

"I think your ass is lying 'cause you don't want to come up off the cash. We gon' see," he said, then pulled out two sheets of wrinkled-up paper. "Get back on the stroll. I'm sticking more than this good dick in your ass." He tossed the papers toward my face.

Batting them to the floor, I cried. "Why you gotta be like this?"

"You stupid bitch. We can rise up and you wanna hold us down. I'ma get mines. See you in court."

Black went into the kitchen. I followed him. He opened the freezer, dumped out all the ice, tossed the children's frozen treats in the trash. "Just in case you were planning on using my shit with some other nigga. Let him buy his own."

I wanted to say, *Like you did?* But I was scared he'd make good on choking me.

Quietly, he opened the door, then slammed it shut behind him. Ty screamed. I locked the door, then ran to my kids' room. "It's okay," I said, holding her.

I had to ask God, *What did I do to deserve him, Lord? Whatever it was, please forgive me. Please, God. If Black is not the one, show me a man worthy of my love.*

My tears flooded my daughter's headscarf.

"It's okay, Mommy," Ty said. "I love you."

"I love you, too," I said, tucking her in. The boys never woke up. Closing my bedroom door, I sat on my bed, called Remy.

She answered, "Hey, girl. I was just about to hit you. You wanna go to Taboo 2 this weekend?"

"Why not?" I said.

"What's wrong? What the fuck Black do this time? He'd betta not had laid hands again."

"Nothing like that," I told her, then started crying uncontrollably.

"You lyin', Sandara."

"I'ma be all right." Good or bad, nothing lasted forever.

"Fuck that. I'm on my way. Be there in ten minutes. Don't hang up 'til I got there."

I put the phone on the bed. Black was supposed to be here next to me. I got up, wrote a check for Remy so she could pay off her car. I had enough saved to comfortably do that for her.

Knock. Knock. "It's me," Remy said.

I let her in, and Remy gave me a hug and wouldn't let go. "Fuck that nigga," she said, closing the door.

"I love him though. What am I supposed to tell Tyson?" I hated disappointing any of my kids.

"That ain't love. You dickmatized. Go sit in the living room. I'ma open a bottle of wine. We gon' get smashed and come up with a plan to squash this shit. You getting back on that damn runway. That's where I've seen you your happiest," she said. "The only time Black makes you happy is when his dick is inside you."

Couldn't argue with her on that. I handed Remy the check. I couldn't put a price on our friendship. Maybe having my friend here to comfort me was God's way of answering my prayers.

Maybe this time I'd listen.

CHAPTER 27

Devereaux

Insisting on taking my mother to the airport was more for my benefit.

Phoenix acting, make that being, a fool was for his satisfaction. I was done with him. Taking him back would set me back.

"How long will you be in Charlotte?" I asked Mom, picking up her carry-on. After putting it in the trunk, I sat behind the wheel, fastened my seat belt.

"He ended our engagement," she said softly, buckling up.

Max was tucked under her arm. He was adorable. I wished I could adopt him. I was working extended hours between executive producing, writing, and spending a little time with Nya, so Max would become an on-set assistant to my assistant, Tiera.

Not sure how to respond, I took a while before saying, "Mama, no. I'm so sorry. Why?"

"I'm not sure," she said between tight lips, "how long I'll be gone."

Why was she upset with me? "Alexis initiated Bing's intervention."

Driving to Sandara's to drop off Max, I tried loosening up my mom. She'd be okay. We'd all be okay.

"I don't know how you raised all of us, got your degree, bought us cars, and put us through college. I can barely manage with Nya."

Mercedes and I had gotten our bachelors. Alexis was two years in. Sandara dropped out after her freshman year. There were a few professions where a high school diploma was sufficient. Talent accounted for a lot for my lil sis. Sandara should get back on her grind. I learned that staying preoccupied with my shows helped keep my mind off of a man. Phoenix and Antonio.

"That's nice," Mom said, staring out the passenger's window.

"Mama, maybe the timing was off for my telling Bing about my problems. If I had any idea he was going to end your engagement, I wouldn't have said a word."

She was quiet. I knew that kind of pain.

My heart ached knowing how losing my daughter's father initially hurt me. Bing moving on now was better than after the marital commitment. "Phoenix's first supervised visitation is later today." I didn't mention I was doing it because of Bing. I prayed their breakup didn't mean I couldn't call upon him for advice.

"That's nice, Devereaux."

What I needed to know from my mother, only she could answer. But she refused. Why?

Glancing at her, I said, "Bing's going to find my father," hoping she'd tell me something about my dad before I met him.

My mother nodded.

"Mama, please."

"Please what, Devereaux?" She snapped. "Help you solve the questions in your head? Help heal your broken heart? Be there for you? Is that what you want from me? I just lost the love of my life. My life! And all you give a damn about is who your father is."

Making my mother cry was not my intention. "I'm sorry, Mother," I said, parking in front of Sandara's place. My sister came to the car.

"Hey, you guys!" Sandara cheerfully said.

My mom kissed and hugged Max. "I want you to be a good boy. This is the last time I'll leave you, I promise."

Max's four legs wrapped tightly around my mom's arm as Sandara reached for him. He started whimpering. Mother's tears flowed again.

"I promise. This is the last time," she said. "Sandara, take excellent care of my baby boy. I'll be back next weekend."

Well, at least I knew she did have a return date.

"I will, Mama. I always do."

Sandara's daughter ran to the car. Max's tail wagged as she gently took him out of my sister's arms. "Hi, Grandma. Bye, Grandma."

I knew Mother was angry when she didn't respond to Ty.

Sandara said, "Bing is going to find my father! Thanks, Mom! I'll call you tonight. What time do you get in?"

"I'll call you later," I told Sandara. "We have to go before Mom misses her flight."

Explaining to Sandara what we'd done to the relationship with Bing might make Mom angry. Staring at our mom, my sister cried. Not sure if Sandara, like me, wanted Blake to be happy for us, I drove off.

Heading to Hartsfield, I had to let her know, "Mama, I didn't mean to mess things up with you and Bing. I sincerely apologize."

Our mother stared through the windshield. She didn't shift her eyes in my direction. The emotional tightening in my chest was suffocating.

"Mama, please. Say something," I begged.

Mom's eyes filled with tears that didn't fall.

I reached for my mother's hand, but she folded her arms.

This was the first time in my life I felt rejection so deep I wanted to die. Hurting my mother was killing me. Wished I could take it all back. Wished I'd kept my mouth shut instead of tagging on to Alexis's mess.

I parked curbside at Departure, and my mother opened her door, got her purse, picked up her carry-on from the trunk, closed the door, then walked away without looking back.

A police officer tapped on my window, motioned for me to move. Through tearful eyes, all the way to my studio, I tried to cry my pain away.

My mother didn't deserve to lose the best man she'd ever had. It wasn't all my fault but being the eldest, I'd definitely accept blame.

I parked, sat in my car, and called Bing to let him know no one knew our mom better than her sister Ruby.

Ending our call, I texted, **If you can meet with my aunt Ruby in Charlotte, she'll tell you more about our mom. Please don't give up on our mother. We all need you.**

CHAPTER 28

Blake

No one to handle my carry-on or unpack my bag, I dropped it inside the front door of my condo in Charlotte.

Uncorking a pinot noir, I drank straight from the bottle. Cried. Turned my liquid desensitizer upside down again. Gulped much as I could without stopping. Again. Again. Again. Refrained from throwing the empty bottle across the living room. Unleashing my anger wouldn't resolve my problems but bottle number two might get me there.

I sat alone. Lonely. Angry as hell!

A mother's responsibility was to protect her kids. At what point were my children obligated to, damn, at least be considerate of me?

Had I raised four selfish, insensitive girls? Not a one came to my defense. Max loved me more than the human beings I'd labored to give life to?

Mercedes and Alexis may never care that Bing left me. My youngest and oldest were concerned. I think. Hell, they may not be. Another failed relationship, Lord?

Give me a rest from it all.

Consuming as much pinot as I could, I was about to shut them out the way they'd done me. They hadn't seen anything yet. If I'd entertained Devereaux by answering her questions, and happily greeted Sandara, they'd be fine right now with continuing their relationship with my ex.

The tears flowed. I hadn't heard from the ringleader. Probably busy plotting on how to get in bed with my man. I meant ex-fiancé.

"God," I cried out. "Is it wrong of me to hate my child?"

He knew my heart. I knew my answer. She pranced her hot ass into my house like she owned everything and everyone in it.

Hostility. Sadness. Dejection. Overwhelmed me. Sitting in a chair, I swallowed alcohol until I couldn't breathe.

"I'm tired, Lord! Please don't take Bing away from me," I begged, then cried, "What did I do wrong this time?" There had to be a lesson.

I hated Alexis more than ever. What was she in competition with me for? She wasn't satisfied until she'd fucked Spencer. My breakup with Spencer may not have ever happened if it weren't for her spreading her legs and demanding to find her father.

Should've let Spencer come over after Bing left. Men didn't have loyalty to me. What difference did it make who I fucked?

I was satisfied that I'd changed my mind about inviting Spencer over while I was upset. One less regret. I didn't want any other man's dick inside of me yet. Spencer had cared for me like no other. When I barely cared for myself, he hadn't abandoned me. That meant something. If Spencer had only cheated on me with his ex-girlfriend Charlotte, I could've forgiven him.

Wash it down. Drown it all. Leave your sorrows in the bottle, I told myself.

Backtracking never worked in my favor. Not once. Bing's parting words for me not to contact him were unnecessarily harsh.

Told myself, "Blake, you're too old to chase any man." I'd done that long as I remembered. Including with Spencer. Gotta start somewhere not to keep lying to myself.

Taking off from work in the morning wasn't happening. I turned on more hot water than cold, prepared for a much-needed bath.

After opening a third bottle of red wine in the kitchen, I returned to the bathroom. My cell rang. The tone "Take Me to the King" played.

I couldn't deal with either of them right now. What had made all of them show up at my house at the same time? As I stepped into what felt like paradise, memories of being in this very tub with Bing brought more sorrow.

The tightness in my lungs squeezed until I gasped, then refilled my glass.

I'd lost the best man I'd ever met. My entire body hurt so badly. "Oh, my, God! Jesus! Why?!" I cried.

"What is the lesson? Is there a lesson? Show me, please Lord. You couldn't have given me this amazing man only to snatch him away."

Through my whimpering, I missed my Yorkie. I loved him so much. I needed him more than he needed me. I convinced myself not to call Sandara to check on Max knowing I wouldn't ask her how she was.

What could I have done differently?

CHAPTER 29

Blake

A ray of sunshine beamed through the window glowing on my naked flesh.

I glanced around the bathroom. Staring at the porcelain tub, I leaned forward, heaved. "Urgh!"

Purple vomit splashed all over my thighs, rolled down my . . . "Urgh!"

The morning after hangover was "Urgh!" nasty.

Calling in wasn't wise. Thankful I had the sense not to quit, I regretted finishing several noirs. Head going in circles, I turned on cold water, then hot, rinsed my body, then sat on the side of the tub. Had no idea what time it really was. Had to be in the office by eight.

I placed my feet on the tile. Stood. "Baby steps, Blake."

Shit! I was still hung over. A hot shower would help. I twisted the dial to the strongest pulsation. "Oh, hell!" I'd meant to put on my cap.

Blow-drying and styling my hair would take an additional thirty minutes. I checked the time on my cell. Staring in disbelief; it was seven-fifty. Not good. Brushed my teeth. Rinsed. Coating my hair with gel, I slicked it back with my hands, coiled my natural curls into a bun.

I sat on the bench at the foot of my bed. One foot. Two feet. I pulled my skirt up to my knees. I fell back onto my bed, and perspiration coated my face, neck, stomach, arms, and legs, soaking my comforter.

"No. Please don't." Pressing my lips together, I raced to the bathroom, bent over the toilet. "Urgh!" As the heat inside my body became hotter, I began sweating again.

A three-minute cold shower, brush, rinse, put on a fresh skirt. Eight-fifteen. Had to get it together. "God, was Eve's biting the apple that bad? You could've given men hot flashes."

I managed to fully dress—tan blouse, navy blazer, and matching skirt. Stepped into my tan one-inch heels.

Eight-forty. Driving the speed limit, I navigated the streets, instead of merging onto the freeway. I'd probably fail a Breathalyzer, if I was pulled over. Had never been and wasn't trying to go to jail. A car was parked in my reserved space. I took the spot one over, stood tall, concentrated on walking a straight line. My stomach hadn't recovered.

Bypassing my boss's office, I heard her say, "Blake."

Walking backward, I forced a smile the way I used to whenever Alexis asked how I was. I wasn't sure Alexis ever cared much for me. Seemed as though I disgusted her.

Should've gone with her to terminate her pregnancy when she'd requested. Maybe I'd be happily engaged. I'd bet she was fine. And I'd bet Bing was going to make good on his promise to her.

"Have a seat," she said. "You're an hour late. Did I miss your call? E-mail?"

I answered, "No."

"How was your vacation?" she inquired.

As I sat at the small conference table with a gorgeous woman young enough to have been one of my daughters, fond memories of Paris surfaced, settling the uneasiness in my stomach. "It was . . ." I paused, swallowed, then flatly said, "Quite an experience. Make that an adventure. My vacation was amazing."

I became a storyteller. Animating the carriage ride, to intimate walks in the park, I orally sculpted Bing's estate.

"Look what the wind blew in," my advisory said, entering. He smiled, mumbled, "A hot mess," at me, followed by, "Ou wee wee. Smells like someone is still on vacay."

My boss's exhale reminded me of Mercedes's. "What is it?" she asked him.

"Meeting in ten minutes. Should I? Or will you?" he asked.

I frowned, reluctant to speak. How could I reek of wine after I'd brushed my teeth and rinsed several times?

"I got it covered," she replied. "Don't start without me. Close the door on your way out."

"Ooookay. Sounds great. I was hoping it was fantastic. Blake, there's no easy way for me to let you go. If you don't mind clearing out your office, I'd be most appreciative."

Her words were sobering. I huffed. Not at her. To determine if I had an intoxicating stench. Her eyes widened. She leaned back.

"I don't understand. I worked hard for this promotion."

"We have a corporation to run. We're not in the business of doing damage control. It was brought to our attention that Sandara Crystal and Alexis Crystal tagged you on social media. Here are some of the posts." She slid the papers toward me.

I read how horrible of a mother I was—this was the ultimate slap in the face!

My mom aborted two of hers but won't go with me to terminate my pregnancy.

Caption: **Moms can be deadbeats too. My last run on the way. I quit!**

I never took social that serious. Hadn't been on these pages since my birthday.

"You can't be serious," I told her.

"You'll be fine," she said.

A tap on the door followed by "Three minutes, darling."

"He brought this to your attention, didn't he? He felt he should've had this job instead of me."

Shaking her head, she said, "It's irrelevant."

"Is there a severance package?" I questioned.

Laughing hard, she stared at my engagement ring. "Yes. But I doubt that you need it since one of the wealthiest clients deposited fifty million dollars into your account this morning. Our competition is going under massive investigation for internal fraud. We have to make sure our house is clean."

What?! Wow! That was news.

Leaving corporate wasn't a problem. I'd never been let go. "I may have been in Charlotte three months but I've been with this financial institution over twenty years. I demand and deserve to know the real reason for my termination and don't say it's social media. I don't control that."

She handed me a folder. "Read it on your way out."

I exited her office, closed the door in her face the way she'd done me. Okay, Lord. There were no more rugs for You to snatch from under me.

I surrender.

Getting in my car, I tossed the envelope on my passenger seat. My cell rang. Looking at the caller ID, I ignored Bing's call. He could have all his money back. If he'd found the girls' fathers, everyone should be pretty damn ecstatic!

Honk!!!!! The driver behind me leaned on his horn.

My presence in Charlotte was no longer required. Bypassing my condo building, I entered the freeway heading to Atlanta wishing I'd stayed in Paris, France.

Alexis may soon discover why I hated her. If she'd just left things alone. "Damn, that child!"

Conner Rogers was Spencer's father. He was not Alexis's dad. All that she owned legally belonged to her brother. She'd probably blame me for her having to give up her lifestyle but this one time, they all should've kept their mouths shut.

I had a foolproof plan to make all of my girls wealthy. They got what they wanted. I was done.

Alexis was most like me. Maybe I hated myself for telling one lie to cover another all my life. I should've thanked Conner before he died for accepting Alexis as his.

A call came in from Ruby.

"Hey, Sis. Where are you?"

"Leaving Charlotte. Heading back to Buckhead. For good," I said. "What's up?"

"Ah!" Ruby's scream startled me.

"Damn! You all right?" I questioned.

"I deserve an Oscar. I had a late dinner with Bing. He is so handsome. By the time I finished telling him what we'd agreed upon, he was sobbing like a baby. He hasn't called you?"

"So that explains the fifty mil he deposited into my account this morning."

Ruby screamed again. "I want my half soon as the check clears."

"If you tell anyone, I want all my money back."

"My word is bond," she said.

"Yep, just like you told Alexis about my two abortions."

Ruby was quiet.

Too late to reverse. My sister had protected all of her sisters from our father. Her reality had become my lie. I knew who my girls' fathers were but the day I gave birth they were all dead to me. Might as well be. Especially Alexis's sorry-ass dad.

It was time for my daughters to know: my father was their father.

CHAPTER 30

Alexis

"Okay, you're not going to believe this. I have spectacular news, chick."

I sat at the bar, needing my brother to stop servicing his customers and give me his undivided attention.

"If it's an apology for my taking off yesterday to take you to your appointment, keep it," he said all upset.

"You needed the time off. Wasn't like you called me," I retorted.

"I'm listening," he said, mixing drinks.

"Two seconds. Come here."

Spencer paused in front of me. "One."

"I've decided to keep the baby. Well, actually Bing . . ." I paused when Spencer stared at me.

"Sis, don't do him the way we got down. That shit ain't right for you to keep trickin' over your mom's piece." He placed a glass of water in front of me. "You thirstier than a dude, dude. Drink up."

He was sour over losing his puddy tat. A nigga was not built to outfuck or outsmart pussies when a pussy had nine lives. He'd fuck himself into an early grave.

"Cute." I knew how to get his attention with, "Bet you didn't know Bing ended their engagement."

Spencer's eyes lit up. I barely heard him when he said, "That's why she invited me over?"

"You over? Yeah, right." I laughed. "Blake isn't that desperate."

All of a sudden he cared more about my mother than I did. That was his conscience speaking for him. Wasn't my responsibility to show loyalty to either of them. I was about to drop this baby and run Bing's company. I'd heard him.

"Like I was saying. I'm keeping my son. Bing does not have any kids. I'm his baby girl and"—I touched my stomach—"this is going to be his baby boy. I'm thinking about naming him either Bing or Sterling."

My brother smirked. "So now you Charlie on *Willy Wonka* with the golden ticket and shit. That's cool. Do who you do best."

"Yasss," I said unapologetic. "I'm like thirty-two below freezing kinda straight ice, right. Bing is hiring me a full-time nanny and a nanny to the"—I sang—"na, na, na, nanny," then said, "He's going to be there for my delivery too. I don't have to do this all by myself, chick. Isn't that the best?"

I was no longer blowing smoke rings, and I thought Devereaux better hire me while she could afford to. I had madd options.

"You want something to drink? A slow screw is appropriate," he said.

I loved my brother. Had to laugh. "You mad, girl? Warning:"—I pointed then read—"Drinking alcoholic beverages during pregnancy can cause birth defects." Slapping a muzzle on his 'tude, I reassured him, "Your secret is safe with me."

That sent him to the opposite end of the bar with a quickness. With and on a dime he'd be begging me to visit him behind bars. I wouldn't have said that if his shade wasn't so dark. Getting ready for my role as Ebony, I had to practice on somebody.

"What are you so excited about, pretty lady?" West-Léon asked, hugging me from behind before sitting on the stool next to me.

"Spencer, give West-Léon whatever he wants. It's on you," I insisted.

Lots more heads turned in our direction when I announced the superstar was seated next to his future leading lady. Not that he didn't have a half-hour delay getting to me. I'd watched him grant Usies, Snaps, Instas. Whatever those females were doing, West-

Léon's girlfriend seat was filled until I no longer wanted to sit in it. That could happen at any moment.

My time to shine was coming before I popped out my kid.

"Are you always this flawless?" West-Léon asked, then ordered an Italian lemonade.

Grinning, I answered, "I'm slumming, man. Just wait until I'm settin' up next to you in front the camera."

"What's got you glowing? I mean besides my boy." He placed his hand on my stomach.

Spencer chimed in the convo. "A few days ago you were giving him up to a strange couple. Yesterday, you were the terminator. Now you're ruining your mother's relationship. And this guy has no idea." Spencer shook his head at me. "Dude, when are you going to give it up?" he asked, placing a glass of water in front of me and West-Léon's cocktail next to him. "The next dagger is in you." He nodded at West-Léon.

Spence reminded me. I texted Paul and Karen Ramsey, **I've de-cided to keep my baby**.

No need to thank them for what they hadn't done. Just didn't want them hitting me up for what they weren't going to get.

Paul replied, **Please reconsider. My wife started decorating our baby's room.**

Ignoring my brother and crazy Paul, I told West-Léon, "Sibling quarrel. So tell me all about yourself starting back far as you can recall."

Wow. He was adopted. He had two brothers who were also adopted.

Maybe Paul and his wife weren't crazy after all for asking for my child. They'd have to find someone else's kid to spoil.

I texted, **Bing, Hi Big Poppa! We're good. How are you?**

I'm well, baby girl. Thanks for asking. Ask your mom to call me.

Responding, **Sure!** I refused. Prayed he was not taking her lying, cheating butt back. I hadn't forgotten my mom had stepped side-ways when she was with my brother.

James texted, **How are you doing?**

Hit him with, **Your son and I are in capable hands. You're relieved of all obligations.**

"You wanna get outta here and go to my place?" West-Léon asked.

"Get out of my head," I said.

After I gave Spencer a wink, we left without tipping. That was how real celebs did it!

CHAPTER 31

Benjamin

Fighting back my tears, it killed me to abandon my beautiful super-mom wife at one of my favorite restaurants days ago. The ambiance, jazz, food was the best Atlanta offered. I was starved when I walked in. By the time I'd left, I'd lost my appetite, for my wife. If I had stayed, Mercedes would never understand I had a heart too.

"You okay?" Arizona asked, massaging my feet.

"No, baby. I'm not okay." There was no need to lie to her.

I was on the sofa, my mistress was on the floor, "Love Ballad" by L.T.D. started on my playlist. What I wouldn't give to rekindle that feeling of when I first fell in love with my wife. Something as simple as holding hands made me feel needed. I was still my wife's, my family's, protector.

"I'm so damn confused," I said, swallowing the lump in my throat. "My world would be perfect if my wife was you and you were her. Baby, you do all, and I mean all, the things I'd give a kidney for Mercedes to do."

Shit didn't make no damn sense! None! My father couldn't have been one-hundred-percent faithful his entire marriage. He shouldn't have taught me how to have it all.

The tone of Arizona's voice reflected her disappointment. "You agreed to stop comparing me to her."

Covering my face with my palms, I wiped away my frustration. She asked the question, now she didn't want to hear my truth. "You're right. I apologize."

I let the tears flow. I could never cry in front of Mercedes. She'd deem my quandary a weakness.

Arizona pressed deep into the arch of my foot, then she squeezed my big toe hard changing my melancholy mood to . . . "Damn, woman!" The nerve she touched must've been connected to my dick. Instantly, my shit stood at attention.

We laughed together when she did it again.

Freeing my erection from my pajama pants, I stroked myself wondering what the walls of my wife's new vagina felt like. I knew it was super tight. But was it dry or juicy? Plump on the inside?

Arizona's hand slid up my leg. I blocked her from making contact with my dick. It was cool for her to perform fellatio. That was my limit. Long as I wore my wedding band, my dick had not and would not risk taking any disease home to my wife.

"I've got him, baby. Keep massaging my foot. That feels amazing."

"Our second-year anniversary is coming up," she said proudly. "You promised me if we were still together, you'd divorce your wife and marry me. It's time for you to make good on your promise. Or I have to move on."

Damn, women hung on to every word? I forgot all about that. Did I say marry?

"When is it again?" I asked.

"Eight weeks exactly. In Georgia there are ways to make your divorce final in thirty days but you have to file soon."

Damn. I exhaled. The way she brought it up I thought it was coming up in a few days. "I'll honor that promise," I said, figuring by then I'd know for sure if I was done tolerating Mercedes's shenanigans or going back home to my wife and kids.

"You know what I'm looking forward to the most?" Arizona gave me a sexy, devious smile that only meant one thing.

Holding it in my hand, of course I knew. She wanted what a lot of ATL females desired, to ride my big, black, beautiful, irresistible dick.

"What? Tell me," I said, smiling, wanting to hear her say it.

Kneeling between my thighs, Arizona opened her mouth wide. Flicked her tongue on the tip of my head. She kissed. Licked. Licked. Sucked. Taking all of me into her mouth, she forced my head down her throat, then gagged.

I loved the, uhs, slurps, and seeing her saliva coat my shit.

What I wouldn't give to have my wife ease my dick past her pretty lips. Mercedes wouldn't let me put the head in and truthfully, I loved her so much, watching my wife suck me a little could make me explode a full load.

"We should do something special," I said, trying to take my mind off giving Arizona what she really wanted tonight.

The way she squirmed on the rug, I could tell she was hot and ready. Crossing her vaginal threshold tonight would fast-forward my promise to a permanent commitment.

Right this minute, I needed my mistress to . . . "Don't stop. Suck harder." Forcing down the nape of her neck each time she raised up, I asked, "You ready for dessert, baby?"

That was what she'd call my cum. I loved how she swallowed. Arizona's mouth stopped moving.

"Not now, baby. Keep going. I'm almost there."

She took my dick out of her mouth.

"Ah! Fuck! Shit!" I was pissed. "What the hell?!"

My parents reared me to respect women at all times, making me refrain from calling Arizona a bitch. "Please. Keep going," I begged, stroking my shaft. I had to bust this.

Straddling me on the sofa, she put my head at the opening of her pussy. "It's time, Benjamin."

The second I felt the warmth of her vagina I covered my head with my hand. When was the last time he was inside of a woman? I wanted to tell her to get up. My dick wasn't sure.

Arizona moved slowly, grinding both sets of her labia on my knuckles. Her shit was super wet. Fuck! I had mixed emotions. We were not supposed to have intercourse unless I was positive I was not going back to my wife and kids.

Placing my hand on Arizona's thigh, I teased her clit, trying to make her climax. She moaned. I had to have a way out. I'd resisted two years, not to cheat on my wife.

Arizona moved my hand, stared me in my eyes, then mouthed, *Benjamin, it's time.*

In the heat of the moment, I could make the worst decision ever if she became pregnant.

CHAPTER 32

Mercedes

"Kids, I said let's go! You're going to be late for school!" This single-mom life twenty-four hours a day while my husband, their father, laid up with his mistress was coming to an end. Empathy was what I was supposed to have from him.

I released the band from my hair, scratched my scalp, then tugged fistfuls of my natural curls. Benjamin should be pulling on this thick mane of mine. But I'd taught him not to touch my hair. Staring in the living room mirror, I picked up my purse.

"Now, Brandon! Now, Brandy!"

"Coming, Mom," Brandy said.

Brandon beat her down the stairs. His backpack hung on one shoulder. Brandy held hers by the strap. Brandon hugged my hips, his ear pressed against my stomach. I placed my hand on his head.

"I love you, Mommy," he said. "Don't be mad at us."

"Boy, stop kissing up. Let's go." Brandy walked out the door.

"Mommy is . . ." I paused. "I didn't mean to yell at you guys."

Brandy came inside, pried her brother away. "Momma's boy. You better not make me late."

I knew she missed her dad. I did too. It wasn't my daughter's job to parent her brother. She was taking her frustrations out on Brandon. Since I didn't have Benjamin to chastise, it was increasingly clear that my children had become my unintended target.

Dropping the kids off five minutes early, I didn't have the luxury not to pay for before and after care when I didn't feel like it. I was en route to a breakfast meeting with a client when my cell rang.

Answering the Bluetooth in my car, "What?" I became angry.

"Mercedes, I don't want to argue. I just called to apologize for walking out of the restaurant the other day and to say that I love you. I really want my family too, but my fear is that you'll keep hurting me," my husband said, then ended the call.

That was a coward move to dump his emotions on me and not give me the opportunity to respond. He was not the victim! The knife wasn't in my back deep enough? He wanted to hurt me for hurting him. My cell rang again. Immediately pressing the button on my steering wheel, I sent the call to voice mail, then realized it was my sister.

I returned her call. "Hey, Devereaux."

"You okay, Sis?"

Sniffling had replaced my two-finger snaps. I exhaled, then lied, "Yeah," knowing she could tell that I wasn't.

"You know, Bing's advice is the absolute best." She sounded genuinely excited. "I am so happy with taking my time dating Antonio. You remember him. He's the director I met at Haven @1411 when we were there." Everything she said seemed like one long run-on sentence. "I should thank you."

Should? Hmm.

"If it weren't for your meeting me that day, we would've never met. You'll be glad to hear that Antonio is the complete opposite of Phoenix. When I'm done filming this season, he's already booked an Alaskan cruise for, listen to this, Nya, his daughter, and me. A family vacation! Can you believe that?"

"Huh? What?" Hip. Hip. Hooray!

I didn't care if Antonio was taking Devereaux around the world. I was the first and only one married. All I wanted was my family back.

"You haven't heard a word I've said. Have you?" she asked.

I allowed my silence to speak for me.

"Where are you?" she asked.

"Heading into Another Broken Egg in Buckhead to meet a client." I parked in the lot. "This is a huge opportunity."

I'd canceled several meetings, one with her. Benjamin could work his IT technical job on his computer wherever he was at. Consulting required me to show up in person to make others comfortable about cutting me a check.

"When will you be done?" Devereaux said, a tad too cheery for me.

A text message registered. I wasn't sure if I should've been happy or disgusted. My client notified me, **Sorry for the last-minute cancellation, I have an emergency. Will reschedule next week.**

"Can you believe she can't make it? I'm going to go home and get back in bed. I'm tired."

That was the truth. I was exhausted from crying, trying. I was not a pessimist but my gut instinct told me it was too late to save my marriage. The enthusiasm for my vagina was buried in the bile of my stomach. I had to start preparing myself to transition.

"I need a break or I'm going to go insane. I have to consider giving Benjamin full custody. I'm not cut out to be a single mom like you guys." Mercedes Crystal was not cut from the seventy-percent-thread statistical cloth of African-American moms who didn't have a ring on their finger.

Chirpy, Devereaux said, "I just got a text from Bing. He flying in and wants us to meet at his house for dinner tonight. Without Mother."

The same message registered on my cell with his address. "I can't make it. I don't have a sitter," I said, not feeling like asking anyone new to keep my kids for a few hours. I needed days, weeks, by myself.

I had a nanny. I'd fired her. Actually, she'd quit. Same difference.

"I really like him. This could be that break. He did say he'd hire you. What if he's found our father? Even if he has, I'm still going to call him Papa Bing! You've got to come." Excitement grew in my sister's voice. "Sandara and Alexis just texted me. They got the same message. This is wonderful! I'll pick you up."

And do what with my children? It wouldn't matter. I wasn't going and that was final. Why did Alexis, aka baby girl, have to be there? She already found her deadbeat.

"I've got to go," I said, ending the call.

In transit to my house, I called my private investigator.

"Hey, Mercedes. You were on my list of people to call today. I have an unbelievable update to show you on Benjamin. He—"

Interrupting her, I said, "It doesn't matter."

"Oh, but it does," she countered.

"I no longer need your services. Thanks for everything. Send me a final bill," I demanded.

Ending the call, I detoured to Arizona's. My husband's car was parked behind hers. I blocked them in, left the engine running, knocked three times.

Benjamin opened the door wearing pajama pants, no shirt. His body glistened with oil.

"Mercedes—" he said, standing in the doorway.

I cut him off. "I need you to get your kids from school today. And keep them forever."

I wasn't trying to go in or see inside. Arizona must've been gone or else she'd be glued to my husband's ass.

"You love our kids as much as I do. I know you don't mean that. I'll pick them up for you and drop them off right after, but don't come here again," my husband said as though I were at his place of residence.

My heart wanted to say, *Come home, honey. Let's work things out. I miss you. I need you. I love you.* All of those things were true.

But I couldn't.

In this very moment, I hated him!

CHAPTER 33

Blake

I'd experienced, more times than I could count, a man hanging up on me, then my calling him back repeatedly to have a conversation with his voice mail. Showing up unannounced at my guy's residence, only to have the door slammed in my face. That was if he'd opened it. Thought I could drop by his place the way he'd randomly visit me. I was tired of choosing the wrong man.

Sitting in the back of a limo with Max in my lap, we were off to a fantastic day of shopping somewhere. I was destined to buy my son more outfits than he could wear in a month.

I answered his call. "Hi, Spencer," with zero enthusiasm.

Being that I was fifty, a man who told me not to contact him wouldn't have to say it twice.

"Hey, Fabulous, I heard about what happened with your engagement. You good?"

No need to question where he'd gotten the information. Nor did I care. "I am Fabulous. And you?" That was the best nickname any man had given me.

"I want to see you today. Listen, I admit I did the fool but I want things to go back to the way they were between us the first two weeks when we chilled." He could stop there.

Hadn't taken him long to stray. Seemed as though he still didn't know which bitch he wanted to piss on. I vividly recalled discovering Charlotte was somewhere underneath his sack the entire time and he still managed to make time to juggle Alexis and me between his balls.

"Took losing you for me to realize that you're the only woman for me," he said, sounding sincere. His plea was cuter than the name he'd given me.

Considering all I'd dealt with, I'd be not a fool but the biggest jackass if I'd give him an undeserved opportunity to make me squirt again. I was depressed and could use a friend but he didn't qualify. A shoulder to lay my head on, an ear to hear my sorrow, would be nice but I had no one since I hadn't communicated with my closest girlfriend in over a half year. Spencer was strong. Problem was our chemistry was too intense. I was certain, if we shared time alone, he'd expect at some point my clothes would fall off. Sex was what men desired, not love.

I wasn't interested in him. His dick. Conversation. Nothing. Period.

"Our flame has burned out," I told him. "Take care of yourself, Spencer."

He ended our conversation without saying good-bye. I wasn't surprised. Ex-men didn't want to see me doing well with the next man even if they didn't want me. Simply selfish. Spencer needed reassurance that he had access to my vagina whenever he wanted. Took time for me to figure out what men desired wasn't about me.

Thought my first and only fiancé was different. I was not returning his call no matter what Ruby said.

Maybe Bing and Alexis had done me a favor. I needed to get to know myself. Once I got over being angry with everybody, I realized my girls weren't horrible women.

"You can let us out here," I said.

The gentleman transporting us wasn't Uber or a taxi. I stood on the curb with Max cradled in my arm as my limo driver stacked Max's roller bag on the curb.

"I'll take it from here. Thanks."

Strolling to ticketing, I approached the agent. "What's the next flight I can get on?"

"Excuse me? Do you have a confirmation number?" she asked.

I shook my head. God, why me? I hugged my baby tight. He wiggled. My tears fell on his head. I handed the agent my credit card and driver's license.

"I wish I knew where I was going. I'll know in a, give me a minute."

"Miss, are you okay?" she asked loud enough for the person next to her behind the counter to hear. Now I had two attendants and no destination.

"Where would you like to go?" the second person questioned as though she had more authority than the first.

I stared at her. Spoke very slow with the same mellow tone. "Where's the first available flight I can purchase a ticket for departing to?"

She clicked keys for a moment, then advised, "Los Angeles. It leaves in two hours."

"Hm." I gave it minimal consideration. "You hear that, Max? You want to mark your territory in LA?"

He tilted his head, stared up at me as if whatever was good with me, was all right with him long as we were going together.

"Two first-class tickets, please," I told her.

I nodded at the agent. "He's never been to Hollywood. A one-way to LA is fine."

With so much time prior to boarding, I walked Max outdoors, let him empty his bladder a few times. Stopping at a restaurant, I ordered Max a grilled chicken breast for the trip. Thanks to Bing, I had preapproved security clearance. We made our way to Concourse A. Another thing Bing had taught me was how to be adventurous.

Entitled to a severance package from my job, I decided to accept it and move on. Shutting down all of my social pages, I didn't need any fans, followers, or friends I could not visit.

For the first time in my life, Blake Crystal did not have to answer to anyone. I could get used to this.

"Blake?"

Shaking my head, I recognized the voice. I ignored him. Wasn't sure how he'd found me but I was not surprised. Yes, I did know. Ruby.

Bing sat beside us at the gate. Max's tail wagged with excitement. My ass refused to acknowledge him.

"Blake, I am so sorry," he said. "Baby, can we get out of here? I had no idea."

Never again would I give a man a chance to belittle me the way he'd done in front of my children. Firmly, I told him, "No, Bing." I removed his ring, placed it in his palm. "Save all of it for the next woman."

Didn't ask for his money. Definitely was not offering to return it. But if he asked, he wouldn't have to mention it twice.

"Okay," he said. "Hear me out and if you never want to see me again, I'll accept that. I've arranged dinner with our girls tonight."

Our? Hm. I smiled. "Tell baby girl hello for me. Give her your best."

"With your permission, I want to talk with them."

Hmm. With my consent and the arrangements were already done. He didn't need my approval the first time or to set up whatever he'd planned this evening. All I said was, "If hearing me say, 'Sure,' makes you feel better. Sure, Bing."

"Dammit, Blake," he grunted.

Was that supposed to change my mind? Heal my heart? I doubted Bing or any of the men I'd dated felt the kind of pain they inflicted on me!

"Boarding all rows" was announced.

I stood with Max in my arm, placed him in his carrier. Bing had tears in his eyes. I did not. Patting his chest, I said, "Take care of yourself, Bing."

He followed us to the agent who was waiting to scan my ticket. Last call was made. There was such a thing as last chance. He'd gotten his and I no longer had to live a lie.

"Miss, if you're on this flight, you need to board now," she said, holding her hand open.

I gazed into her eyes.

"I'm closing the door in one minute," she instructed the other agent.

I handed her my cell, and she scanned the bar code for our first-class seats. I did not look back.

Soon as the attendant locked the door behind me, I heard my ex-fiancé shout, "I know what your father did to you. I'm so sorry," he cried. "Blake, I truly am sorry."

It was too late for me to turn around. Max started barking. My feet would not take another step. I fell to the floor, hugged Max's carrier, and cried like a baby.

Someone had to cry for Ruby.

I heard Bing demand, "Open the door. I need to take my wife home."

CHAPTER 34

Devereaux

"When is our mother getting here?"
Hadn't spoken with her since we were all at her house. I preferred to wait. She was back to her ways of not responding to texts or calls. I felt partially responsible. Should've been more considerate of her feelings.

Bing sat at the head of his table. "She's not coming. And before anyone speaks, we decided it was best."

Alexis had snagged the seat to his right. She should have given her cleavage the occasion off. "We decided? So y'all back together?" she questioned with disappointment.

"Baby girl. Never make me choose," Bing said.

Suspecting that Mercedes would take the other seat closest to Bing since Mother wasn't coming, I was shocked when Mercedes settled next to Alexis facing me. Mercedes relocated to the opposite side, then sat next to Alexis. I was prepared to protect my mother this go-around. Since she wasn't coming, I left the seat next to Bing for Sandara as she scooted close to the table. The other five places were unoccupied.

"Your advice did not work. Just thought I'd get that out before the deadbeats arrived," Mercedes said.

The real guests, our biological fathers, hadn't arrived and we were already divided.

"My advice? Or your approach?" Bing said, looking directly at Mercedes.

Sandara asked with wide eyes, "What time is my daddy getting here?"

"He's not. None of your fathers are coming," Bing said.

My heart skipped a beat, then thumped hard. "Is this some sort of joke?" I questioned. "I need to meet my daddy. You said you'd find him. My daughter needs to know her grandfather. Are you pretending, like our mother, to deliver the impossible?"

"That's on y'all. Glad I met mine," Alexis said sarcastically. "Since they're not joining us can me and my baby eat?"

"It's my baby and I," Mercedes corrected.

Alexis fired back, "That's why your husband has a mistress and you're the sitter."

"But I do have a husband," Mercedes countered.

Sandara picked up a bread roll, hurled it at Alexis. "Shut up! Why are you here anyway?"

"'Cause I'm the baby girl, that's why. Don't be jealous," Alexis retorted.

Mercedes stood. "I'm going to relieve my babysitter, aka husband, from watching my kids."

"Sit, Mercedes." The commanding tone in Bing's voice silenced all of us. "I was hoping to get to know you girls better but I'll get right to it."

"You can get to know me well as you'd like," Alexis said.

No more insults from me. We were justifiably dysfunctional siblings.

"I'll start with you, baby girl. There's no easy way to say this."

Alexis sprang to her feet. "You're my father!" Her eyes were wide. "That's why you call me your baby girl. I knew my daddy was rich!"

Sandara tossed bread roll number two. "You're lucky."

"Stop it, please," Bing insisted. "In anticipation of how one or each of you may respond, I have four professional therapists on standby. This is going to be the hardest thing you've ever had to deal with. No matter how heartbreaking this news I'm about to tell you may be, know that your mother has endured the worst."

Mercedes's lips parted, as she exhaled in Alexis's direction. "Here we go with justifying insanity," she said, then folded her arms.

"Dragon breath. Not today," Alexis complained, waving her hand in Mercedes's face.

Bing shook his head, took a deep breath, sighed, then continued, "Don't anyone interrupt me. I'm not asking. If you don't want to hear what I have to say, you are welcome to excuse yourself. That goes for each of you."

"I apologize for their rude behavior," I said, staring at Mercedes. Four rolling eyeballs scrolled in my direction.

"Alexis, I'll make sure you're okay, baby girl," Bing said.

Alexis's stare froze at Bing. Dropped from north to south as she smiled wide enough for all to darn near see her molars.

Bing exclaimed, "Conner Rogers was not your father. Everything he left you can be contested by Spencer and Spencer would win."

"Okay, this is creepy," I said. "You calling our mother a liar?"

"Hear me out. This is not about blaming your mother. Here's the real deal," Bing said. "Your mother is so embarrassed about having four children out of wedlock that she convinced Conner to cover for her."

Mercedes's lips pressed together, then parted. Shaking his head, Bing held up his hand to her. She sighed heavily. Relieved the distance between us was a good five feet, I watched Mercedes's lips tighten.

"I'm not done." He hesitated, then added, "Each of you has the same father."

Our eyes danced with one another. I did not remotely believe him. Outside of our thick, beautiful mane, there was no other common resemblance.

Questioning why Mr. Sterling was with my mother, I stared at him. Why had he quickly claimed us as his girls? He had this mansion that rivaled the Hollywood celebrities' mansions I'd seen on and off television. Bing had drivers, and a private jet. He didn't need Mother's money.

I asked, "Then why did our mother put 'unknown' on our birth certificates?"

Was Antonio planted? Did my family have an inheritance Bing and Antonio were plotting to acquire? Nothing made sense!

"All your mother needs right now is love, understanding, and you guys don't need to forgive her. She needs to forgive you."

Out of everything he'd stated, that was ludicrous. My mother was not incompetent.

Mercedes exhaled toward Bing's face. I waited for him to wave his hand in front of his nose. He didn't. Alexis didn't protest anything.

"Your father, Devereaux, Mercedes, Alexis, and Sandara, is dead. That's the truth. For now, let's leave it at that."

"Hell, nah. Don't put me in the lineup. I buried my father. I know who he is. We did a DNA test. And the money, house, Ferrari, Porsche, Benz, BMW, all that's mine! I'm not giving Spencer or anybody else shit!"

"I don't know where you came from, what your true intentions are, but if there's more to what you know," I said, "we demand to hear it right now."

Bing exhaled, "You're right. No need to prolong the inevitable. Your mother was raped by her father. Your father is your grandfather."

The silence in the room was deafening. Was incest how we were conceived?

"Can't y'all see she's lying?" Alexis angrily blurted. "One child, at the age twenty-two maybe. Two, suspect. Three, I'm not buying it. Four. Really? She was twenty-five when she had Sandara. The way I see it," Alexis replied, "that's not rape. Even if Granddaddy is our biological father, that was a relationship."

Mother wouldn't lie about something like that. I believed Bing. If my grandfather weren't dead, I'd kill the bastard.

If by chance, it turned out that Alexis was right, I'd hire her for a lead role on the spot.

CHAPTER 35

Mercedes

"Mr. Sterling, with all due respect, Blake Crystal is our mother." Bing requested we give *him* a day alone with *our* mother before my sisters and I went to see how *our* mother was doing. I made an executive decision; Bing had controlled enough.

"Mercedes, you're right. You're always right," he said sarcastically.

Reverse psychology was not going to work. "None of your advice has done me any good."

"I agree with Mercedes," Alexis said. "Not on the 'none' part. I need to find out what's going on with my mother."

Obviously, what Alexis really wanted was to find out if her inheritance was legit. Devereaux and Sandara were quiet until Devereaux said, "I'm going to see my mother now."

Sandara chimed in, "Me too. I'm not waiting either."

I wasn't sure if the real baby girl agreed due to being outnumbered or sincerity but the decision was unanimous. "Perfect." I needed something constructive to keep me from wondering what my husband was doing to his mistress tonight.

"Let's handle this your way, ladies." Bing stared at me, then added, "Just give me a few minutes to see your mom before you knock on the door."

A few meant three in my world. Did Bing have something to

hide? Had they concocted this molestation story together? He'd found out too fast for me. I'd hoped our mother needed us too and that she wouldn't let this or any man come ahead of what was important to us.

Bing escorted us to his front door. Alexis's Ferrari, the Porsche she'd given Sandara, and Devereaux's Benz SUV made the driveway appear as though an episode of *Lifestyles of the Rich and Famous* was being filmed. The only car that wouldn't fit in was my mommy SUV that I'd left at home, with the adjacent door handles on the passenger side.

I drove Devereaux's fancy foreign whip, following Bing closely. Alexis was behind me and Sandara trailed her. Mr. Sterling was going to have to make his spill with Mom quick.

I had to tell someone, "I have a new vagina."

Devereaux's head snapped in my direction. "Wait. Is it by default because you haven't used it in forever?"

"That too. There's this new procedure. Well, it's just catching on in the United States but women in other countries have been doing ThermiVa treatments for—"

"Thermi what?" she asked, smiling.

Explaining to my older sister how the procedure worked, I told her, "Since you're done with the lame and have a new guy, this is the perfect time for you to try it. I have to warn you, though, you might be too tight for him to fully penetrate you the first time."

Devereaux frowned. "Text me your doctor's info soon as we park. But I have something to share with you that you need to do."

What could she possibly know that I didn't? Definitely wanted to find out. "I'm listening."

"I haven't told anyone I had a VTox done at Sweet Spot Atlanta. It's a detox steam for your vagina."

I laughed. Were we keeping our vagina monologue a secret? "I'm listening."

"You sit on this chair that has a hole in the seat and underneath you is kinda like a Crock-Pot with nineteen herbs and you sit there naked for thirty minutes to an hour with a plastic drape covering you up and oh wee! The steam is hot and everything, all kinds of toxins, fall out of your coochie. Bad energy and anything that's not supposed to be inside, I'm telling you it falls out."

"Like colonics for your vagina?" I asked, trying to get a visual.

"Except nothing is inserted in you. And it tightened me up inside and out. The steam does all the work. I feel so ready to receive Antonio and any thought of Phoenix turns me and my vagina off."

"I guess we both have new pussies," I said.

"It's about time. You said the 'p' word," Devereaux commented. "I'll share the contact. Don't forget to give me yours."

I parked between Alexis and Sandara. Maintaining my position in the driver's seat, I motioned for my two sisters to get in the car with us. Devereaux gave Alexis the front, and sat with Sandara in the back. Mother welcomed Bing in, then closed her door.

I sat sideways to make sure I had everyone's undivided attention. "Since we have a moment, I'm going to go over the rules."

"You mean go over your rules," Alexis countered as though I was in her car. Facing me she arched her back, causing her baby bump to poke forward.

I envied her dark and flawless smooth skin. Wondered if my husband preferred Arizona's chocolate tone over my light complexion. I could tan in the sun for days and never get Arizona's color. The whites of Alexis's eyes were the brightest I'd seen. Had to admit to myself, being with child made Alexis more beautiful but only on the outside.

"Lil girl. Keep your voice down. This is not the time to have it your way," I replied.

Devereaux added, "Alexis, Mercedes is right. Don't go in there acting like you're more important than everybody else. For once, be considerate."

Deep inside I was jealous of Devereaux. If she had not asked me to join her at Haven @1411. If I had been early and she'd been late. If she hadn't taken Antonio's number. If I hadn't helped her see Phoenix for the loser he really was. Not trying to meet the amazing new man in her life, she'd stumbled upon a perfect gentleman who adored her and her daughter. It was my fault Devereaux was happier. She could possibly get married and I might be single.

I exhaled. Would I be that lucky if I divorced Benjamin? I did not want to find out.

"Stop that!" Alexis yelled at me.

I frowned.

"It's not about you, Alexis," Sandara commented. "Our father is a rapist. He raped our mother four times. That's why we're here. Mother did her best and thanks to Bing, I'll be back on the runway next week. Stop flirting with him, Alexis. And regardless of what anyone else is doing, I'm not putting my grandfather's name on my birth certificate as my father."

Bing was a man of his word. I believed he'd be there for Alexis's delivery. He was right about Antonio. With a call to his attorney, he'd resolved Sandara's custody issues. She had to show up at court but she didn't have to defend herself. Why didn't my attempt at reconciliation with my husband work? This was not the time to let tears fall. I was pissed.

"Everything is about me. Don't hate." Alexis wiggled her fingers at Sandara. "If you done with your insults, hand me the keys to my Porsche."

Alexis flipped her long, black hair. Whipped out her mirror, retouched her lipstick. She never took a day off from being the most gorgeous of us all. Styled in a minidress and heels, she'd said more men complimented her now than ever. Toya and her wife, who sat next to my husband and me at King + Duke, were sexy too. Where were they?

Sandara said, "It's not your car."

"She's right. You won't be popular after Spencer finds out all of your inheritance belongs to him," I added, with intent to bring Alexis's arrogance down a notch.

"Conner is my biological father. If what Bing said is true, Mother would still be with Spencer."

"Regardless of the fact that we now know Spencer is not your brother, you fucked our mother's man. So no, she wouldn't be with Spencer. You probably don't know who your baby daddy is," Sandara angrily said.

I'd put my money on Sandara being right, but she was not one to talk. What planet did Alexis come from? If she were in Mother's position, Alexis would not be with a man whom her daughter fucked. Slowly, I stared at Alexis with disgust. She was butt ugly on the inside.

Alexis's eyes locked with mine. "Even if Mother is telling the truth, which I don't believe her one bit, I have papers that prove otherwise. I'm not going backward for nobody and I mean nobody. None of you had better tell Spencer. It'll hurt him more than it will me anyway."

Reasoning with Alexis was a waste of all our time. "Mother didn't tell us, lil girl, Bing did. End of that discussion. Rule number one: let Mother do the talking first. Two: regardless of whether you agree or disagree with anything she says, do not interrupt her. She might shut down. And if that means you keep your mouth shut, Alexis, do that or I promise you I'll put my foot in it."

"Is that why your husband is still seeing his mistress?" Snapping her fingers twice, she exhaled, then added, "Now I'm done talking."

Determined not to let her win, again, calmly I continued. "Three: let's give Mother a group hug soon as we walk in the door."

"Forget all these rules. Let's let the situation unfold naturally," Devereaux said, leading the way up the stairs.

I rang the doorbell.

Mother's hair was uncombed. Her eyelids were puffy. Devereaux initiated wrapping her arms around Mother. I joined in. Sandara embraced all of us.

Alexis stepped sideways, squeezed through the opening between us and the door, went into the living room, and sat on the love seat next to Bing.

CHAPTER 36

Blake

I could almost count on one finger the number of times all my children held me.

The door was wide open. I leaned my head on Mercedes's shoulder.

The worst migraine I had came from the effect my secret (turned lie) had had on them. My intent was to take the embarrassment to my grave. In ten, twenty, thirty, forty years, they might've discovered the truth at my funeral. If they never knew what I'd done that would be best for everyone, including Bing.

Mercedes was not to fault for her controlling ways. Bing had shared she was the one who'd convinced the others to be here. I told Bing I wished he hadn't interfered.

"I'm sorry. Mama should've let all of you know"—I couldn't say the truth—"a lot sooner."

"I would've done the same, Mama," Sandara wept. "All you did was try to protect us."

"You're the strongest woman I know," Devereaux said, leading me to the sofa. She positioned herself to my right.

Mercedes comforted me from the other side. Sandara sat at my feet, placed her head against my thigh. Mucus streamed down my leg. I could tell her tears were for both of us.

Alexis was where I expected her, on the love seat next to my man. Knees flush together, ankles cutely crossed.

I heard Bing tell her, "Go sit with your mother, baby girl. She needs you."

"I just came for confirmation. I already know my—"

"This is not going to turn out well for you if you don't move." Bing had gotten a small, make that tiny, dose of what was coming from that one.

"But she was twenty-two when Devereaux was born? Y'all really believe her? Sounds more like affairs than incest. Just saying."

Let her stay next to him. Honestly, I didn't want Alexis near me. She came at his command. Plopped by Devereaux, reached in and held my hand. I pulled away.

"Mother, why didn't *you* let us know?" Mercedes questioned.

"Don't ask her that," Sandara said, clinging to my leg the way she used to when she was a toddler.

Bing stood, cleared his throat, then approached us. "I'm going to say this, then I'm going to let you guys have all the time you need."

Through heavy tears, I looked at the handsome man before me. Crying in his arms a few moments ago felt better than having my girls nurse me. I was tired of being alone. I needed a man, a husband, a companion I could cuddle and travel with. I needed a man to . . .

"I love your mother. I'm honored to be her fiancé. She knows my story. You guys do too. Sometimes we have to let go of things that hurt us. I'm here if any of you need me for anything," he said, gazing into my eyes.

Soon as all those tears and the ink dried on my marriage certificate, Mama was shutting down the charity factory.

Alexis placed her hand on her stomach, then said, "Thanks, Bing."

Seeing him shift his attention to her, I bit the inside of my mouth.

"Baby girl. I am your mother's fiancé. She is my woman. When you disrespect her, you disrespect me. When you hurt her, you hurt me. That goes for all of our girls. I'll give each of you the world. But not at the expense of losing my soon-to-be wife. I want you girls to help Blake plan our wedding. I love you, sweetheart. If you need me, I'm a call away. I have a meeting to go to."

Bing leaned over, gave me a kiss, then left.

The second the door closed, Alexis sarcastically told Mercedes, "You forgot your own rules."

This lil girl would steal the shine from a spotlight. "Please," I pleaded with Alexis. "Not now."

She lamented, "Conner is my dad. I don't care what you say. Who would go to the extreme of lying about something you have no control over? We did a paternity test."

We all stared at her. I knew the baby that she'd claimed she miscarried never existed. She lied and said it was for either James or Spencer. Alexis had to have everyone's attention revolving around her every second.

No denying she'd inherited my ability to weave a believable lie. I'd fabricated a story for Spencer. When he'd asked if I'd had sex with any other man since I'd met him, I said what I knew he wanted to hear right before he'd slid a relationship ring on my finger. What good would it have done for me to be honest?

The girls didn't need to know why I'd been terminated from my job. I'd never tell them that it was Alexis's and Sandara's fault. What mattered most was despite Alexis's attempts to toy with my man's affection and ruin my engagement, I'd earned Bing's love, trust, and respect.

Alexis stared at me. "When I find out your lie, I am going to tell Bing."

I snapped. "You need to pack your bags, move out of Spencer's house, leave the keys to his cars, give him his millions, and take your ungrateful ass and your unborn back to James. I'm sure Chanel won't mind letting you sleep in the guest room."

"I hate you!" Alexis yelled. "I should've aborted mine too!"

Mercedes shook her head. "I so see where I get it from."

Devereaux mumbled, "Lord, thank You for not letting me put her on payroll."

Alexis told Devereaux. "I don't need your money!"

Sandara stood. This confrontation should've never material-ized. Bing should've stayed out of my personal business. Ruby had better take everything to her grave this time. The new tracks I'd made were covered with premeditated deceit. I'd routed Bing to my eldest sister, Ruby, who'd agreed to settle for five million dol-lars, to tell him that her life story was mine.

Everybody had at least one secret.

"Say something else to me or Mama," *my* baby girl told Alexis.

Alexis rubbed her stomach. "Can't stand up to any of your ba-bies' daddy but you all up on me? What you gon' do? Nobody was talk—"

Smack! Sandara's backhand swept across Alexis's face. The toe of Alexis's shoe jabbed Sandara's pubic area. Sandara grabbed Alexis's foot, tried to snatch her off the sofa. Devereaux braced Alexis, then yelled at Sandara, "Let her go!"

"Stop it! You always have to ruin everything!" Mercedes shouted at Alexis. Each movement happened in split seconds. The action was over and I was trying to figure out how did we get here?

I watched Alexis scream, "I hope Bing leaves you!"

Softly, I told her, "You need to get your things out of your brother's house today. And don't call my fiancé to help you."

Conner was Alexis's father. Watching her squirm felt good. She was the ultimate user. If Alexis lost everything today, she'd find a way to get it back tomorrow.

No one deserved to go to hell for lying. I definitely did not want to run into my father if I made it past the pearly gates. If God didn't discipline me, my mother was going to beat my behind real good all over heaven.

Ruby's too.

CHAPTER 37

Alexis

No house. No cars. No cash. Why would Blake want to do this to me? I knew why. She was jealous of her own daughter. I was what she wasn't. An alpha female boss.

The thought of giving it all back made the sweetness of my inheritance sour in my mouth. I was not birthing a baby into poverty. Refused to trust Bing would take care of us. James and Chanel were not raising my child.

I had to do what I had to do. My mother left me no choice.

Backing up on his huge dick, I looked over my shoulder, then yelled, "Deeper!"

"Whoa, slow down," he said, then told me, "This is the best pussy I have ever had. I want to enjoy this shit."

If I had a dollar for every time I'd heard men and women tell me that I was their best in bed, hell I'd never gotten a W-2. I was here to handle my business.

To abort or not to abort was my constitutional right. Bet if these pussy-chasing, adulterous, escort-hiring, prostitute-paying, dick-sucking, porn-watching, male politicians were incarcerated for impregnating a woman before they put a ring on it they'd respect my vagina and my right to choose what I wanted to do with my body.

Dude was chilling; his fingers were wrapped around the monkey bars of my canapé. "Fuck me like it's your last time getting some pussy!" I couldn't grab his hands, placed them on my waist, and hold on to the headboard at the same damn time.

"You don't mean that," he said, rippling his abs. "I'm trying not to hurt you. My dick has a reputation for being hazardous." He nodded, then winked.

"Do your thang. This pussy is built for big dicks, dude."

I had references. My fiancé, James Wilcox. My mom's ex, Spencer Domino. And a host of other whores.

Pretty boys were the worst. Gave him a chance because ballers were known for head bangin'. He was recently recruited to our football team but this chick did not qualify to be in my rotation.

I was six months, but I wasn't ready to become a single mother. Refused to struggle the way our mother had done with us after not one, not two, or three, but four men impregnated, then abandoned her.

Clueless about motherhood, I came to the realization that I didn't know how to change a baby's diaper nor did I want to figure the shit out.

After leaving my mom's house, I refused to schedule another appointment. I didn't need them. An Uber driver could've gotten me home from a clinic but I wasn't brave enough to go alone to have my pregnancy terminated. Since no one cared about me, I had to find another way before my stomach resembled a basketball.

Wait. That was it. My mother wanted Spencer to have my financial flow so he could be with her if things didn't work out with Bing. She always believed she was entitled to my inheritance.

Backing up on his salami, I looked over my shoulder again, then yelled again, "Deeper!"

Nya was practically a fourth child to Sandara. What was Devereaux going to do when Sandara stepped back onto the runway?

Not my problem.

My entire life my mom was preoccupied with working, sleeping, or dating ruthless men that never stuck around. With the exception of the man-sticking-around part, Devereaux was missing out on Nya's childhood.

How in the fuck did Mom have four kids and not one of our fathers thought highly enough of her to put their last name on our birth certificate? I should legally flip from Crystal to Rogers.

All men were good for was fucking or trying to get fucked. Literally. I hated all of them, including my deadbeat dead-ass father. Didn't care if he did will me this mansion, all of his luxury cars, and $2.5 million. He'd probably only done it because he hadn't invested anything worthwhile in any woman, including me. Now my mother had created the most hideous lie.

"Faster, man!" I yelled, praying for a miscarriage.

The siblings I had. The women I knew. They were all too damn emotional. Didn't know their fucking value.

"Chill out," he replied, grinding.

"Deeper and faster. Can you do both at the same damn time, nigga!" If I wasn't on a mission, I'd throw this lame out of my house on his balls. Surely, I'd chosen to bring home the wrong dick tonight.

"Girl, I am trying to make love to you," he said, dragging out the "l" word with the heaviest Georgian accent I'd heard.

I swear I wanted to pull out my nightstand drawer, get my gun, and hit him upside both of his heads. My wallet was wetter than my ass. I didn't have to pretend I wanted to breastfeed an infant.

Long as Alexis Crystal was, as my peeps claimed, using everybody—I say positively influencing my man, girlfriend, and family to give me whatever I wanted—people didn't recognize that I had feelings.

"Chick, you'd better beat this pussy like somebody stole your brand-new Hummer that's in my driveway." Dude stopped midstroke.

Money did not make his dumb ass smart. I mumbled, "You must've had too many brain injuries on and off the field."

"What?" he said, yanking my hair.

"Bitch, let go! You can't do shit right! Not even hike a ball. That's why your ass is fucking third string."

"Fuck you," he grunted. "You not my daddy."

"Actually, I am your motherfucking daddy." He'd call me that if he knew what I was capable of doing to his asshole. "Okay, maybe from all the contact, you're hard of hearing."

This dude should've never been in my bed but I'd given up on going to the clinic. One way or another, this chick and this baby had to go.

"Okay, bitch! You want this dick?" he asked.

"What dick? I can't feel anything."

Bam! Bam! Bam! Bam! Bam! He fucked me fast and hard. I was speechless.

Bam! Bam! Bam! Bam! Bam! My head hit the wooden part of my headboard. Tried to reposition myself in front of the cushion.

Bam! Bam! Bam! Bam! Bam! Tried to holler, *Bitch, stop! That's enough!* Nothing came out.

Bam! Bam! Bam! Bam! Bam! "I can't hear you. You trying to say something?"

Bam! Bam! Bam! Bam! Bam! "I'm cumming," he hollered, releasing semen deep inside my vagina.

If he was messing up my night, I was returning the favor. When he pulled out, I screamed, "Nigga, you crazy!" digging, then dragging my pointed nails deep into his thighs.

"Ow! Bitch! You crazy!" he said, collapsing sideways onto my Egyptian sheets. "I gave you what your ass begged for. All you females talking about how we don't care, but you don't give a brotha the opportunity to satisfy you. Damn. You messed up my legs."

"Your legs," I hissed, "were jacked up before you got here." Cupping my ears, I stared in his face. "You need to leave." My head was throbbing.

Placing his hands behind his head, he bent his knees, planted his feet on the mattress. "You'll be all right. You got a nice ass, cool spot, rolling on wheels fit for a boss lady, all that but you 'bout the craziest chick I've met in my life. If I hadn't cum in you, I'd swear you had a dick. I like that, though."

Hmm. I could strap-on for this dude the way I'd done for Spencer's friend LB and he'd be in paradise like James. A sharp pain darted up my neck. "Ow."

He laughed as his body shivered. "You weren't talking a buncha shit at the bar an hour ago. You invited me over 'cause you like me. I'm feeling yo' ass too. I'ma have two tickets waiting for you at the box office for Monday night's game. Come here. Let Daddy massage that crick."

I didn't have minutes to waste on watching him stroll the sideline like the cheerleader he was. Lying about how good he ate pussy and telling the truth about how big his shit was got him here. I stood, stumbled, composed myself best as I could.

Had to let dude know. "You suck at suckin'. Those three sorry licks on my clit with your dry-ass tongue didn't get me wet. Raise up." I snatched his hands from underneath his head. "Get out my house." I plowed a king-size bamboo pillow against his chest.

Grabbing the pillow, he threw it to the floor. "The old me would show you just how street I really am," he said, sitting on the side of my bed. "All you bitches are fucked up," he said, shoving me. I stumbled backward.

Why was I wasting my time with this arrogant asshole? Opening my drawer, I took out my gun and pointed it at him, then twisted my wrist sideways. "Ten, nine . . ." I didn't get to five before he was dressed with his shoes in hand.

Following him down twenty steps, I kept counting. I didn't wait for his second foot to clear the threshold. I slammed my front door.

"Get help. Professional help. You easy, bitch," he said, then kicked my door.

Let's see how much pussy he gets when he's cut from the team. I could cry rape but too many niggas and bitches would probably rise from my past and the grave in his defense.

I watched him climb into his SUV. He gunned his engine, and his tires spun creating a cloud of smoke before he sped off my property making a screeching sound.

I'd never shot anyone. Dude came close to being my first. If Alexis Crystal was getting her mug shot taken, someone was going to be ICU- or cemetery-bound.

Returning to my bedroom, I slipped on a pink satin, spaghetti-strap teddy, then checked my cell. No texts or missed calls. Staring at my bed, I touched my vagina.

My fingers were covered in blood.

"Ow!" Pressing against my temple, I cried, dialing the person who was always there for me. I placed the call on speaker, and red fingerprints coated my smartphone.

"Hey, Alexis," James answered.

Crying louder, I heaved repeatedly, then pleaded, "Please come take me to the hospital. I think I'm losing our baby."

"Hang up and call an ambulance. I'll meet you at the hospital."

"I'm not sure what's happening. Something doesn't feel right." That was true. "Please, James. I need you to come now!" I went to the bathroom, plopped down on the toilet.

"Babe, we have to go or we're going to miss the opening," a woman's voice resonated in his background.

James told me, "I'll be on standby, Alexis. Call me when you're sure of what's happening."

Bracing my hand on the vanity, I stood. "Don't bring that bitch with you."

Sarcastically, he replied, "That bitch is my fiancée."

What the hell? For real? "So you're marrying my ex-girlfriend and y'all doing this shit while I'm pregnant with your child?"

"Babe?" Chanel whined.

"James. Ow! Please!" My voice faded. "You need to tell her this is serious."

Calmly, he replied, "Sure, Alexis. Whatever you'd like. You've got your money, house, cars. You don't need us. All you do is manipulate the people who love you."

"Babe. Motown," Chanel said. That bitch was always whining.

"Tell that ho, ow! To go slide down a different pole!" I shouted, hoping she'd hear me. "I think the baby is . . . !" In part, the pain made me holler.

Keeping it one hundred, James had been nothing short of fantastic to me. Chanel too. I hated that they were happy and I wasn't.

"I'm here for my child, Alexis. Keep me posted. Oh, and thanks for introducing us."

Why the fuck he had to say that shit? "Don't do this to our child. I think the baby is . . . Ow!"

"We love you too, Alexis. I gotta go. Bye."

I cried aloud. "Why? Why me? I can't do having a baby by myself. I can't live like this. I won't live like this." If James didn't care about my being in pain, how would he respond to me feeling like I was in labor?

Life was about choices. Holding on to my phone, I had to get myself to the hospital. I walked to the top of the staircase, looked down. *Oh, my, God!*

My inner thighs were red. The stream down my legs to my feet was slimy. Touching my vagina, my fingers were covered in blood. My body swayed back and forth. I gripped the left handrail tight as I could.

"Lord, please. I'm scared."

I took one step. Made it halfway. Stopped.

Leaning forward, I swayed backward staring down at the remaining stairs. I had to make it on my own. My cell rang. I answered. Faintly, I said, "Help me."

Not sure of what was happening to me, my fear escalated.

"Hey, dude! What's up?"

Everything in front of me was blurry as though clouds floated over my pupils. I tried to move my feet. Told myself if I could sit, I could slide down the steps on my butt. Squatting, the sharp pain in my stomach felt like someone had stabbed me.

Maybe God was punishing me for what I'd done.

"Hey, dude. You answered by mistake?" he asked.

It was my brother. I tried to scream, "Help!" I couldn't hear myself.

"Dude. I'ma hit you up later."

No. God. No. God. I'm sorry.

Mustering everything inside of me I yelled, "Spencer! Help me!"

Oh God. Another pain stabbed my belly button. The phone slipped from my right hand, tumbled to the floor below. A throbbing pain in my belly felt like my uterus was trying to escape my body.

God, forgive me. Please don't let me . . .

I reached for the rail to catch my fall.

As I tumbled in slow motion, every wooden step felt like concrete. Hitting the bottom, I couldn't move my arms, my legs, or my head.

"Dude! Dude! Dude! I'm on my way!"

I prayed, *God, please. If one of us has to die, let it be me.*

CHAPTER 38

Benjamin

Inspired to do the right thing, I was ready to step it up. I stopped at the jeweler on Peachtree Street, picked up the $8,000 amethyst infinity ring with a princess-cut solitaire. "Man, this is beautiful," I said, imagining how it would look on her finger.

"She's a lucky woman," the jeweler said.

Truthfully, I said, "I'm the one that's lucky."

In and out the liquor store, a bottle of chilled champagne was on my front seat. Next, I dashed into Lenox Square mall, went to Macy's, where Gena Lavigne had my package waiting. I purchased a pre-wrapped bottle of perfume that came with a cute tote bag, then headed to the last location on my list of errands.

"Here you go, Mr. Bannister, two dozen long-stem roses in a crystal vase. I only put a little water so you don't get your car all wet," my florist said, then explained what I already knew about how to cut each stem on a slant. "You normally get red but pink is a good switch. Women like nice surprises. Pink signifies love, gratitude, and what all women want, and that's appreciation. Your wife will enjoy these."

No need to pray for her to love me more. I hoped she didn't kill me when I told her I'd made up my mind.

Parking in the driveway, I managed to cradle the vase in my

right arm. The other items were in the complimentary tote on my shoulder.

I knocked on the door. "Special delivery."

If my lady's mouth could stretch to her beautiful firm breasts, I was certain the gap would be wide enough for the doorknob to fit. "Happy early anniversary," I said, kissing her sweet lips.

Jumping, she cried the same as she'd done each time I'd brought her a bouquet. "These are absolutely gorgeous, baby. Thank you. Thank you, thank you. I love you so much for always thinking about me, baby," Arizona said, scooping the arrangement out of my arm.

Following her to the kitchen, I removed the bottle of champagne, left the ring inside the bag. "We have to celebrate."

There was a price a smart man paid for his mistress's consideration. I was giving respect where it was reciprocal.

"Our anniversary isn't for another few days. So you've made your decision already?"

Nodding, I told her, "Yes, I have."

"So you told her?" she asked.

I smiled, staring at Arizona. Her deep brown eyes glowed with joy. Her lips were painted a seductive flaming red. She only wore that color at home and for one reason. The second I saw her smile, I knew I was getting my dick sucked real good. The sleeveless mid-thigh dress was tapered to her breasts, waist, and hips. My manhood started rising at the thought of softly licking her body all over.

The decision I'd made was harder than my dick. There were three more people I had to tell. Soon.

Your woman, your wife, your family, and your mother come first. Heard that from my father and grandfathers all of my life. They'd told me stories that their father and grandfathers shared with them about the sacredness of fidelity.

I'd dedicated my marriage to pleasing my wife in and out of bed and she refused to suck my dick even after I begged myself into embarrassment. What about my happiness? Mercedes had been officially relieved of her wifely duties.

All of them.

Removing the perfume from the tote, I gave it to Arizona. "It's not nearly as sweet as you."

She cried unraveling the paper, sprayed a little behind each ear. "This is why I love you."

I took the gift, placed it on the counter. The tote rested on my shoulder. "You deserve more. This is a new beginning for us." I braced my hands on her butt, pressed my lips to hers, then I closed my eyes.

I never wanted to forget this moment.

"I have to leave for a moment but when I get back I'm going to take a nice steamy bubble bath. I want you to oil every part of your sexiness. Put on some jazz and the hottest lingerie you have. I'll be back shortly."

"You don't have to go home to her right this minute, do you?" she asked, unbuttoning my shirt.

Leading her to the bedroom, I placed the tote on the dresser. The parting amethyst gift for my wife could wait. I wanted to go but . . . Mercedes wasn't going anywhere.

My wife could wait. I let Arizona undress me. Why didn't my wife pamper me this way? Wasn't as though she had to do this all the time, but having a wife meant I shouldn't have to go elsewhere to release myself.

After I followed Arizona's command to "Lie down," she removed my shoes. Let them fall to the floor. She disrobed me, my socks and pants preceding my underwear.

I covered my dick right before her open mouth reached my head. "I've been running all day, baby. I can't let you do this. I'ma shower first," I said, torn between sticking to my original plan or letting things unfold naturally. I wanted to penetrate Arizona the second after I'd officially ended my marriage.

Arizona leaned over, picked up a bottle off her nightstand. Pouring oil into her palms, she massaged from my ankles up to my knees. Her fingers gripped my thighs.

"Relax. I want to reward you by showing how thankful I am," she said, climbing on top of me.

Watching her sexy painted lips, I started salivating at the thought of devouring her plump pussy. Holding her perky breasts, I squeezed her already-hard nipples. She slid her hot, wet pussy juices up and down my shaft.

"Can we go all the way?" she moaned. "The walls of my vagina feel like they are going to combust, baby."

I told myself I deserved this moment. Hell, I was thirty living like an old man with a wife and twins. Would Arizona become like Mercedes if we had a baby together? Women had a way of changing after they got a ring.

The touch of her nails along my stomach made me close my eyes.

"Aw, man. That feels amazing. Do it again," I said, moaning.

"You think we're going to be a good married couple?" she asked.

I stared up at her. The passion between us had grown more intense over the two years we'd been together. My father would be greatly disappointed if he'd overheard that question. Sex with Arizona was undeniably better than being with my wife simply 'cause she'd never denied me.

"I love you," escaped my mouth. The first time I'd spoken those three words to my mistress, words that were once reserved exclusively for my wife, I knew I was in trouble.

"Love you more," she said. "But you didn't answer my questions."

My dick wanted action that I wasn't ready for. Rolling her off of me, I answered, "I'm not sure."

"I know. You're legally married and I'm . . ." She paused. Exhaled. Continued, "I don't know what I am."

What if I changed my mind about divorcing my wife and impregnated Arizona? Cumming inside of her wasn't worth the risk.

Sliding her tongue from my nipple to my dick, she sucked the head, then glanced up at me. Sucked a few more times, then asked, "Am I your pre-fiancée?"

My dick felt amazing. I held the nape of her neck. Watching her mouth lower over my shaft, I applied enough pressure to redirect her attention. Right or wrong, cheating or not, Arizona's head game felt like I'd seen the bright white light people who'd died and came back described. I concentrated on the overwhelming sensation.

I still had to go handle my unfinished business. The question now was, when would I make it to my other home? Enjoying the moment, I didn't want to cum too fast.

"Slurp. Slurp. Slurp," was all I wanted to hear.

My legs started trembling. She sucked harder. Faster. Slowed her pace. Sped up. Tapered off.

Bracing my palms on opposite sides of her head, I yelled, "Ahh-hhhh! Shit!"

I swear I couldn't hold out any longer. It felt ridiculously amazing. I wanted to pull out but didn't have the willpower to ask if she was ready for me to unload. My nuts fired three fast squirts, then two more rounds of cum down her throat.

"Ahhh!" Arizona screamed.

My wife picked up the tote from the dresser. "What do we have in here?" she said, opening the ring box. Mercedes slid the infinity band on her right ring finger. Her wedding ring was appropriately placed. I liked her loose and wild curls. The blue halter was more Alexis.

"When you're done playing house, Benjamin, you have a wife and two children at home. Oh, and don't ever buy me pink roses."

Mercedes took short, quiet steps out of the bedroom. We heard the front door close.

"Why didn't you say something to her?" Arizona asked. "That's my ring!" she said, getting out of bed, then yelled, "Why did you give her a key to my house? Are you crazy?!"

I pulled her back in. "We must've left the door unlocked."

"I never leave my door unlocked," she complained. "I want her arrested."

"No one is going to jail. I'll get you another ring." I wasn't spending another eight grand. Mercedes would return the jewelry to its rightful owner. Me.

"Get me a locksmith first!" *Slam!* The bathroom door closed. I heard Arizona crying.

The decision I'd made was no longer harder than my dick.

Putting on my clothes, I stood on the opposite side of her bathroom door. "I'm going to talk to Mercedes. I'll be back."

"And bring back my ring!" she shouted.

"No problem" were my last words.

CHAPTER 39

Sandara

A man who'd kept his promise meant the world to me.
"Sandara, I have an emergency meeting. I won't be at the courthouse this morning," Bing said, making my heart drop.

I stood. Paced in front of a wooden bench in the hallway staring at my phone. First my dad disappointed me all my life. Now the man who had impressed me, said he'd be there for me, couldn't make it. I wanted to hang up and go home. Maybe his being a no-show was a sign not to trust any man.

"I switched you to a young, capable attorney. Delvin Brown has done his homework on Blackstone. Call me soon as the judge dismisses the case."

It was eight thirty. "Okay" was all I'd said.

A friendly face approached me extending his hand. "Hi, Sandara. I'm Delvin Brown. Looking forward to representing you." The deep tone was accompanied by a firm shake as he focused on my eyes.

"I hear he's arrived. Gotta go," Bing said, ending our call.

Suit. Tan. Shirt. Tan. Shoes. Brown. Skin. Tanned. No tie. Ice blue irises. No mustache, no beard. Full brows. Thick lashes. Black hair long in the front, parted on the left, swooped to the right, shaved in the back.

"Nice meeting you. And thank you for representing me." I noticed two piercings, one in each ear but no jewelry.

Admiring Delvin's professional attire and demeanor made me feel important. Not because he appeared Italian and black. He was a runway delight.

Black arrived dressed the best I'd seen him since we'd met on the lawn at a concert at Wolf Creek Amphitheater. I was twenty-one. He was thirty-six. We turnt up—danced, sang, got drunk off of my raspberry vodka. Should've enrolled for my sophomore year at Baylor instead of having my first child. Black had said education was a waste of time and money.

Maybe that was true for some. Not having a degree didn't keep me from becoming a successful model.

Blue jeans, hard-sole shoes, and a short-sleeved, button-down, blue striped shirt. The hairline to his spiked afro was clean as usual. His sideburns connected to a thin line that trailed to his goatee. Black stroked his chin. Stared me up and down. Gave Delvin a, "Hmph," then told me, "Get ready to break me off that Porsche," in front of the attorney.

"Excuse me, Mr. Blackstone. You need to respect my client," Delvin said with authority.

Delvin's posture was erect, shoulders back. He stood about six-two, two inches shorter than Black but Delvin's demeanor made him appear taller.

"You'll find out in a minute, bruh. Don't let the Sunday school swag fool ya." Black flipped my bow in my face. "Sandara is *my* bitch, bitch."

Delvin stared at Black without blinking, then said to me, "A forty-year-old wannabe pimp with no job or employment history trying to eat at your expense. This hearing won't take long. Let's go inside."

"Fuck you, you fake-ass lawyer," Black lamented.

"Did I mention limited vocabulary and illegal activities?" Delvin said. Holding the swing door for me, Delvin allowed me to enter the courtroom first.

"Thanks," I said. Glancing at the other people, I felt we were overdressed.

I didn't see nor did I expect to see Tyrell's or Ty's father. They'd threatened to file for child support but once they learned I had legal representation, they went back to being silent dads. Guess they thought the judge might find out they were selling weed.

Mercedes had told me to wear off-white and nothing revealing. My puffed sleeves tapered above my biceps with a wide band. My buttoned-up blouse had a big pussy bow that drooped. The pencil skirt stopped right above my knees. I wanted to wear my red pumps but put on the beige ones and carried a matching designer clutch purse. I'd smoothed my hair back into a bun. The black-framed glasses were for effect.

If Black hadn't filed these papers I would've freely shared with him. He could've driven the Porsche or the Bentley I was about to upgrade to. I sat in the front row.

Black squatted next to me. He whispered, "You sho' you wanna do this?"

He was the criminal. Not me. Should've asked himself that question.

Scooting over, I didn't answer him. He moved closer. Delvin glanced at me. I pleaded for help with my eyes, then lowered my head as Black kept calling me a bitch and a whore.

Remy warned me he'd act an ass. Actually, I thought he'd raise his voice or choke me like he'd done at my apartment.

"You need to move," the bailiff told Black.

My eyes shined as I connected with Delvin. The closed-lip curve of my mouth was a sign of relief.

"Man, fuck you. You don't own this courtroom. I'm free to sit wherever I'd like. If she's feeling some type of way, make her fake ass move," Black said.

The bailiff placed his hand on his cuffs. "Let's go."

Black stared at Delvin. "I got you, bruh. They might put me out but I'll be right outside waiting for what's mine."

"Don't make me do my job," the bailiff said, standing at the end of the bench.

When Blackstone versus Crystal was announced, Delvin motioned for me to sit on the defendant side next to him. I stood, checked over my shoulder. Black wasn't back.

The bailiff approached the judge and whispered something I couldn't hear.

"Blackstone versus Crystal is dismissed," the judge said, handing a folder to a clerk.

"Thank you, Your Honor," Delvin said, then told me, "Let's go."

Exiting the courtroom, Delvin asked, "You have time to grab a cup of coffee?"

Concerned about where Black was and what he might do to me, I replied, "I'd love to but I have to get my kids. I have three young babies. Two, three, and four," I mentioned in case he didn't have all the facts.

Delvin smiled. "Well, here's my card. I'd love to take you to dinner and if you accept, I'll take care of the cost for your sitter."

Usually, guys came over and chilled. Didn't care if my kids were asleep or awake long as they could hit it or get head before they left like they'd come, empty-handed.

Placing his card in my purse, I walked away crying.

No man had offered to do such a generous thing for me.

CHAPTER 40

Alexis

When I opened my eyes, my mother was the first and only person I saw. I scanned the room, lifted the cover.

"Who put me in this?" I questioned.

"Take it easy, baby," my mom said. "You're lucky to be alive. You have Spencer to thank. He found you unconscious."

Where was he? Did he know about the money? Was he at my daddy's house moving me out? "My head hurts," I said, touching a bandage. "Please tell me they didn't shave my hair off."

"You still have your hair," Mom said.

Felt as though someone had stolen my personality and my energy. I touched my stomach. "I'm still pregnant?"

Silence divided us.

"Mother?"

"Relax. I'll be right back," she said.

What was I thinking, God? I never wanted to see that ignoramus football player again. Asshole.

A doctor entered, before my mother, then asked me, "Which one should we save?"

"What kind of stupid question is that?" I lamented. He couldn't be serious. A baby can't care for . . . I froze. "Oh, hell no! Tell me I'm not having him now. I'm not ready. He's not ready. He's still growing. He's just six months."

"Do you recall what caused you to fall down the stairs?"

Mother's mouth hung open. I waited, expecting her to answer.

Talking to the doctor, I demanded, "I need pain medication."

Sandara, Mercedes, and Devereaux entered along with a nurse as the doctor repeated, "If we can only save one of you?"

Sandara was beautiful. The most conservative I'd seen her dressed, in off-white. Mercedes had on . . . I frowned. A blue alluring halter. Her hair was spastic in a sexy way. Devereaux was in a black pantsuit.

"If we can only save one—"

"I heard you the first time. That's not a chicken or fish meal choice. Mother, what's happening?"

"Everything is going to be all right, Alexis. Doctor, we can't lose either of them," my mother said, standing by my bedside.

Sandara cried, "It was an accident. Don't let them die. It's all—"

Slap! Mercedes's hand landed on Sandara's cheek, then she rubbed off the fake mole. "I apologize, Sis. Thought it was a bug."

"Is there more we should know?" the nurse inquired. "This is a life-or-death situation."

"Yes, there is," Mercedes said, approaching the short woman in light blue scrubs. "You should know how to do your job. We are family. And—"

Calmly, my mom interrupted. "Yes, it was an accident," then told me, "I warned you about wearing those high heels, didn't I?" firmly squeezing my hand.

Mother could let go. Sandara almost pulling me off the couch had nothing to do with why I was here.

I had my mother and everyone else convinced this was my second pregnancy but my mother's lie was bigger. When I told my brother I had a miscarriage, I knew he'd tell my mom. Wasn't sure why mother had kept that secret when she publicized all my other business. We all knew Devereaux had falsified information to the police about Phoenix in order to protect Mercedes.

Lies were a necessary part of life.

It was my turn to be my sister's keeper and if this was how it would end for Alexis Crystal, I'd let them bury me with all the secrets I knew.

The doctor looked at me. "I'll be right back."

After he left, I stared at Sandara. Her face was red, eyes bloodshot. With each sniff she wiped her tears, mucus, then dried her hand on her skirt. I didn't know how that child made it on anybody's runway with that nasal drip.

She mouthed, *I'm so sorry. Please forgive me,* then cried.

I nodded, then winked at her. I questioned the nurse, "How much longer before you guys decide if I can go home? My head and back aren't hurting as much."

I watched her chest rise, then fall. Her eyes shifted to everyone in the room, then back to me. "You have a few minutes to think about what I asked. Seriously."

"My doctor's question is relevant. You're not," I said.

She had a job to do. I had a decision to make.

As I swallowed the heartbeat thumping in my throat, my eyes swelled with tears. I might really die. I had to ask, "Wait. If I ask that you save me, will you abort the baby?"

Devereaux, Mercedes, Sandara, my mother, and the nurse were quiet. Wasn't as though I hadn't contemplated that alternative.

The nurse stated, "If that's what you want, I'll prepare the paperwork."

I nodded.

Devereaux blurted, "I have the perfect part for you, Alexis, after you have the baby. You're my leading lady. You can have your nanny on set. You're going to be a great mother." She forced a smile, then started crying.

What was I supposed to do? If I didn't stay with my decision, I could be the one with a toe tag.

Mercedes commented to the nurse, "Tell the doctor to do his absolute best and save them both. There is no other option here. Got that?"

Just as I mouthed back to Sandara, *I forgive you,* James raced into the room. Chanel was one step behind him.

He stood beside my mother, who'd not relinquished her position of being closest to me on the right. James frantically asked, "Baby, are you all right?"

Chanel echoed, "Baby, are you all right?"

I tried to say, *Fuck both of you.* Truth was I was scared and no words came out. I'd never been afraid of anything. Dying at twenty-six hadn't entered my mind.

Spencer busted through the door, raced to the side of my bed opposite James and Mother. He created space closest to me, nudging Sandara over a few steps. "Sis, you okay?"

Nine people were in my birthing room, including the nurse who hadn't asked anyone to leave. Surely, there wouldn't be an audience if this might be my finale.

I was glad everyone was asking about me, but it saddened me that no one asked about my unborn son. Looking at James, Chanel, and Spencer, I realized they hadn't heard my decision. And they wouldn't.

The guilt of my requesting to take my son's life made me cry. One tear chasing another couldn't wash away my confusion. Why was God making me choose?

"Before we take you into the operating room, we need you to sign these papers," the nurse said, handing me an electronic pad.

The only person who promised to be here for me wasn't. Bing was really excited about being a grandfather. I knew if my son survived, he wouldn't want for anything. I took the pad, placed it on my lap.

James would take great care of him. "What's that?" he asked.

No one answered him.

Mercedes told the nurse, "She's not signing that. I don't understand how a simple fall can create a life-threatening situation. I demand details before you start cutting."

"Have you ever fallen on hardwood?" Spencer asked.

Memories of the random men I'd slept with, the vigorous workouts, the things I'd done after my missed abortion appointment, chased one another. All to rid myself of being like my mother only to discover I wasn't as strong as her.

My mother said, "You're a fighter. You and my grandson will get through this."

Out of all her children, I was the one who gave her the hardest time. I blamed her for . . . "If you can only save one of us," I cried uncontrollably, looking at James, then said, "save our son."

The nurse tapped the screen, handed the pad back to me. This time I signed off on everything.

James's coming had nothing to do with my decision. I knew either way—God or his earthly father—our son would be in great hands. Spencer was my brother no matter what and I'd take his secret to my grave.

I looked at my brother. "If I don't make it, chick, everything I own is for you and my son," then said to everyone, "Name my son Domino Blake Wilcox." Domino was Spencer's last name. There was no need to hyphenate by adding Crystal or Rogers. Didn't want my grandfather's name associated with my son or me. If I survived, the first thing I was doing was tracing my roots to Africa and changing my last name to something African.

The doctor entered the room, then ordered, "Prepare Ms. Crystal for a C-section."

"It's time," the nurse said. "All of you can go to the waiting room."

"Doctor," my mother said. "Please give her a tummy tuck after the delivery. She's a little vain."

"No! Mama, don't go! I need you, Mother! I need my mother!" I screamed, clinging to her forearm.

"I'm not going anywhere. Neither are you. Alexis, you are the strongest person I know. No matter how long it takes, Mama will be right here for you and my grandbaby."

"I love you, Mama!" I yelled as she gently pulled away.

A voice stood out above mine. "Baby girl. Everything is going to be okay, baby girl. I promise," Bing shouted as they rolled me down the hall.

I cried for my mama all the way to the operating room. The anesthesiologist leaned me forward, told me not to move, then gave me a shot in my lower spine to numb me. A tent was placed at my waist. I couldn't see or feel what the doctor was doing. An oxygen mask covered my nose and mouth, the same as they'd done my father when he was in the hospital.

Everything around me was cold. I looked at the nurse.

She asked, "What's your favorite color?"

Softly, I said, "Purple."

"Mine too," she said. "Where's the last place you vacationed?"

I had to think about that. James and I used to travel two to three weekends every month. "Miami."

"Sweetie, you're doing fine. We're taking your son to ICU. How are you feeling?"

He was here. That was quick. Now, I could relax and let go.

"Sweetie, I need you to answer me. How are you doing?"

I heard her. In my mind, I answered each time but she kept repeating the same question. "She's losing consciousness!"

"No, I'm not! I can hear you!" I yelled, then repeated, "I can hear you!"

The light became the brightest I'd seen. I pretended I was on stage performing a one-woman show.

"Get her to emergency immediately. I think she's having an amniotic embolism," the nurse said.

I, Alexis Crystal, would forever be everyone's shining star.

CHAPTER 41

Devereaux

Alexis's unexpected situation made me visit Phoenix's mother, Etta.

The BMW I'd bought my ex wasn't in the driveway. Nervous that I hadn't called first, I told Nya, "Stand behind Mommy." Before I pressed the bell, Etta opened the door.

"Grandma!" Nya danced in front of me, then stretched her arms. Her eyes beamed. Her smile was wide. "I miss you, Grandma."

"I miss you too, my little angel. Come on in," Etta said. "I was just about to bake chocolate cupcakes to take to Bible study tonight. I sure could use a helping hand."

Nya wiggled her little fingers in the air as she skipped to the kitchen. "Me, Grandma! I'm your helper. Follow me and raise your hands, Mommy. You can help too."

"How about I watch?" I sat on a counter-height stool, told Etta, "It would be good for her to visit you more often."

Nya climbed on a stool, then leaned her elbows on the granite like she was accustomed to doing at Sandara's and at home when she was with me.

Time with my daughter was more frequent since I'd started dating Antonio. We were becoming a blended family. Etta used to keep Nya during the week. Not wanting Phoenix to have access to our daughter, I'd cut Etta off.

I expected Etta to scold Nya, but instead she placed two twelve-cup muffin pans on the island, then held a stack of paper cups. "What colors should we use this time?"

"All white," Nya said.

"Hmm," Etta said. "Don't you think the pink cups would be jealous, Teacake?"

Nya smiled.

Teacake? Cute. I hadn't heard that word since my grandmother passed. Not many people made the old-fashioned pastries. Nowadays the closest I'd come was a scone.

"You're right, Grandma. I'll use some blue ones, too," Nya agreed. "Let me count them."

"Have you seen him lately?" I asked, avoiding saying Phoenix's name.

Etta told Nya, "Go wash your hands, Teacake."

"Thanks." I shouldn't have asked about him in front of Nya, but I hoped he was okay.

Nya hopped off the stool. "Okay, Grandma."

Etta waited until Nya was out of the room, then told me, "Honey, I owe you an apology. If I had raised him, he would've turned out like my other two. His sister is married. No kids yet but she has a wonderful husband. She's a makeup artist. My other son owns a restaurant down in Fort Lauderdale. Took me a good while to get over him having a husband but his partner is a nice, successful man. I keep my two good ones away from"—she deepened her voice—"the bad seed."

"What's a bad seed, Grandma?" Nya asked, reentering the kitchen.

Etta lifted Nya onto the stool. Carefully filling the first cup with chocolate batter, Nya touched the spoon then licked her finger.

"You know what you have to do," Etta said.

"I know. Wash my hands again." She left the kitchen without protest.

"Devereaux, I love Nya so much she could live with me but I can't give Phoenix a reason to show up at my house whenever he feels like it. He's not welcome here. You're an amazing mother.

You are exactly the type of wife I'd want my son to have. I can't tell you how he's doing."

"I—"

Etta interrupted, "I wasn't finished. He's not good enough for you. Phoenix will destroy everything you've worked for, then he'll blame it all on you. You shouldn't have bailed him out of jail. His picture is all over the news. Got folks at church questioning me. Don't ever take him back. Ever. Now, I'm done."

I spoke fast trying to get what I had to say out before the extra set of ears returned. "I was going to say, I don't want to take you for granted. My sister was fine yesterday. Today, she's under the doctor's supervision. I'd feel horrible if anything happened to you or us and we let something bad come between what is wonderful. You don't have to answer now, just think about sharing time with Nya the way you used to."

"Here I am," Nya sang, skipping into the kitchen. She held her hands in front of Etta waiting for her grandmother's approval.

"Great job, Teacake," Etta praised.

Seeing Etta teach Nya how to bake, I'd thought my daughter was too young. I was more interested in having Nya learn ballet and gymnastics than teaching her how to be a homemaker.

Nya mixed frosting colors. She covered some with solid frosting, others she topped off with as many sprinkles that stuck. Decorating the last cupcake, she said, "Time to do yours, Grandma."

"Well, we'd love to stay and help your grandma but we have to get going. I have to get back to the studio."

Nya shook her head. "Mama, I don't want to sit still and be quiet. What about Grandma's cupcakes? I have to help her."

I looked at Etta.

She nodded. "I'll bring Teacake to you after Bible study. If that's okay?"

"Please, Mommy," Nya pleaded. "My friends be at Bible study."

"Thank you," I said, offering Etta a hug.

Embracing her, I wondered why she'd given Phoenix to her mother. Maybe her father had done to her what our grandfather had done to my mom. Whatever the reason, it didn't matter.

Women had to constantly make tough decisions that men would never understand.

Etta dropped off Nya to us at Big Pie in the Sky Pizzeria.

"Mommy. Sarah!" Nya yelled, running toward our table.

My daughter bumped into Sarah. Antonio caught them before they fell to the floor.

"Not so rough, Nya," I said.

The girls laughed. Nya said, "This is my grandma," then squealed with joy.

"They're okay, sweetheart. They're just playing." Antonio stood beside me.

Etta smiled, handed Nya a cupcake. "I have to go, Teacake. Be good."

"I made this one for you," Nya said, giving it to Sarah. "It has the most sprinkles."

Nya was a naturally happy little girl. She loved being with Mercedes's and Sandara's kids, too. Anyplace except the studio was fun for Nya. I prayed one day I'd say the same for my nephew, Domino. He weighed fourteen ounces at birth. The doctor said that was good considering Alexis delivered three months early.

The joyous expressions on Etta's face meant I had to find a way to convince Etta to keep my daughter during the week the way she used to before Phoenix messed everything up. "Ms. Et—" Before I could introduce Etta to Antonio, she was heading toward the exit.

"Bye, Teacake. I love you."

"Bye, Grandma!" Nya yelled, waving frantically. "Love you too!"

Sarah looked up at Antonio. "Indoor voice, Daddy?" she asked as though she wanted to scream too.

"That's right, darling," he responded, then asked me, "Is Etta okay? I was just about to say hello."

"Don't take it personal, she always has some place to be," I told him, feeling slightly embarrassed.

"How's Alexis?" Antonio asked.

I prayed endlessly for my sister. Mother texted us group updates. Said there was no reason for all of us to sit and wait.

"She's the same," I replied, swallowing my sorrow. I'd make good on my promise to give her a part.

"You want to place the order like the last time?" Antonio asked, then told Sarah, "Save your muffin for dessert, darling."

Sarah sat her cupcake near me. "Don't let my daddy eat it."

I winked at her. It was best to request separate toppings considering none of us had the same favorites. I ordered, "Meat lovers for Antonio. Vegetarian for me. Cheese for Nya. Pepperoni for Sarah. And a pitcher of unsweetened iced tea."

"My daddy always eat my food," Nya said.

"Always" was an exaggeration, though Phoenix did occasionally consume what Nya left on her plate. I made it a practice not to consume unnecessary calories.

Sarah questioned Nya, "Where he at?"

Nya hunched her shoulders. "You want me to teach you how to bake muffins?"

Sarah smiled, shaking her head.

I was glad Nya didn't mention Phoenix often. Primarily all he'd done was transport my baby from one place to another or leave her alone in Ebony's guest room while he fucked Ebony in a different room. She'd declined our million-dollar offer. Refused to give a reason.

I wondered where Phoenix was. Didn't care enough to find him.

"I have a surprise for everyone," Antonio announced.

I had a love-hate relationship with the unknown. If I never had another surprise in my lifetime, that would be okay. The girls stared at the envelope in Antonio's hand.

"Please, end the suspense," I said, wanting to snatch the mystery that he waved in front of us.

"We are all going on an Alaskan cruise," he said, then handed me the envelope. "All you have to do, sweetheart, is select the dates."

CHAPTER 42

Blake

A mother was not supposed to outlive her kids.

"Train up a child in the way he should go: and when he is old; he will not depart from it." Proverbs twenty-second chapter, sixth verse. I knew that Scripture well.

Holding Alexis's hand, I wondered, had I instilled my characteristics in her? "Don't give up, Alexis. I'm right here, honey, and I'm not going anywhere until you open your eyes and speak to me. You won't believe how beautiful Domino is." I smiled. Squeezed her fingers. Yes, she would. "He looks just like James."

In parts, I'd read the book of Psalms, John, Proverbs, and Ecclesiastes to Alexis. Alternated massaging her extremities—arms, hands, legs, feet—every hour to circulate the blood. The only time I'd left her side was to visit ICU to see my grandson, use the restroom, or to freshen up.

"Ms. Crystal, here's a little something for you to eat. Please. If you don't, we're going to have to admit you to the hospital," the nurse said.

Guess she never had a child this close to death. With every breath my baby was fighting for her life. I would never mistreat or disrespect her again.

"Okay," I said, taking a few bites of the bland chicken salad before setting the container on Alexis's bedside table. Until the Lord made His decision to bring my child home or give her back to me, this hospital was my new residence.

Bing texted, **Give baby girl a kiss for me. I'll be there tomorrow morning**.

Whenever anyone requested I hug, kiss, or say hello to Alexis, I did.

The door opened. A familiar face entered.

Spencer gave me a much-needed endearing embrace. I didn't want Spencer to let go. Sobbing, I released my fear. His comfort was temporary yet welcome. I didn't want him as my man. His compassion wasn't sexual. I had a fiancé whom I could not wait to marry.

The negative things that I thought were worth my time and energy? Watching someone who may not recover taught me to release my animosity. I was striving to forgive and appreciate others. Give and receive love, not hate. Determined to value family instead of devaluing people, I knew it was time for me to focus on being my best. That meant I had to start with my truth.

"I can take the night shift. You should go home and get some rest," Spencer said, sitting next to me. "I'll take care of dude."

She called him chick. He referred to her as a dude. They were definitely related. Before Alexis was born, Conner told me not to contact him. I hated him, yet I'd honored that. Being here with my daughter, I was glad she'd met her father. Conner was the third in the lineup of four men to abandon me. If I counted my dad, that would up my count.

Men justified being irresponsible and inconsiderate.

I'd changed my mind. Telling the truth wasn't happening. I didn't owe my exes, my daughters, or society a confession.

"I don't need a break," I told him. "I believe she's going to come out of this coma. I know you hear me, lil girl. Stop pretending. You know what? I talked with the nurses today. Domino is getting stronger by the hour. He's gained two ounces. He's a fighter. I need you to do the same. For Domino. For me."

"Me too, Sis," Spencer added. "I got you."

Spencer's last words made me chuckle. I thought when he'd told me, "I got you" or "I love you," I was special. Hearing him say it to another woman let me know that was how he expressed himself with everyone.

"I'm really sorry about your uncle raping you. And for what it's worth, I deeply regret not keeping your secret," I told Spencer.

His chest rose, then deflated. "Wasn't your fault."

That I'd told or that it had happened? Focusing on my daughter, I knew this would not be the time for Alexis to let go. Crystal women were born warriors.

Spencer held my hand.

"For what it's worth, I will always love you, Blake. We were just two damaged people looking for someone else to repair our broken hearts. Isn't it funny how we want it all yet we don't believe we're deserving," he said. "I mean, I expect the best in my head but my heart is all fucked up. I wonder if my real ride-or-die unconditional woman is out there looking for me."

My eyes shifted toward Alexis.

"Dude knows how I feel about you, Fabulous."

Not putting a thing past Alexis, she could probably slip into the bright white light, come back, ruin my life, then return to heaven. God would give her a pass to get in. I did not know a single person who had stayed mad with Alexis. Chanel and James had justifiable cause and they'd both forgiven Alexis.

"I used to feel the way you do until I met Bing." Breaking his grip, I had to emphasize, "He shows me what real men do. Vacations without expectations of any form of indebtedness. He never asked me what my girls needed. He asked them and he handled it. Nothing he does is to impress me. Everything he's done has blessed me. I never believed in my heart that you were genuine. And I was right. But"—I placed my hand over his—"it's time for the man inside of you to stop being afraid to grow up. You're a good person, Spencer. And, your ride-or-die is out there. And when you meet her . . ." I paused.

"What?" he asked softly.

"Don't stab her in the heart. Men are good at doing that."

A tear fell from his left eye, then his right. I looked at Alexis. "Oh, my, gosh," I whispered, then pointed at her face. She was crying through closed eyelids.

I told Spencer, "Hurry. Go get the nurse."

He yelled from the doorway, "Nurse! Nurse!"

I shook my head. He had a ways to go down that grown-up trail but I knew he'd get there. I saw her eyeballs shifting. What was it that made her cry? I didn't care.

"Baby, I know you can hear Mama. Alexis, I want you to open your eyes. You can do it. Domino needs you. Your family needs you. Your mother needs you."

Spencer said, "I need you. You can't leave me. Dude, you already knowing James gon' dress Dom with all that plaid stuff. I'm telling you. You better wake up."

Her eyelids fluttered. I whispered to Spencer, "Keep talking to her."

I recorded a video of my baby opening her eyes. Spencer started telling funny stories, then said, "Dude, you're the only person I know that knows how to keep a secret. Thank you."

Alexis stared at him. I scanned back and forth between the two.

Was he referring to the secret I spoiled or was this something new?

CHAPTER 43

Mercedes

"Have a good day, kids."

I gave Brandy a kiss. Brandon turned sideways, gave me a one-arm hug. Straightening his tie, I told him, "Tuck in your shirt."

"Mom," he protested. "You're embarrassing me."

"Son, give your mother a kiss," Benjamin said. Picking up Brandy, he asked, "Who's Daddy's girl?"

"Me. I am. I'm Daddy's girl. Love you, Daddy. Love you, Mommy," she said. She interlocked arms with her girlfriend, and they walked toward the gymnasium where the students assembled before class.

Brandon scanned the playground. Stared up at me with wide, fearful eyes.

Not wanting to go against what Benjamin told Brandon to do or make my son uncomfortable, I told Brandon, "Save my kiss. I'll get it later. Go."

This was the first time Benjamin and I had been in the same vehicle since I'd let myself into his mistress's house, thanks to Dakota. Long before I'd fired her, she told me to have a locksmith copy all the keys on Benjamin's chain. Only one didn't fit any of the locks in our home.

There were limited places a man could keep a key, if a woman gave him one. Car. Under the mat in his car. Glove box. Armrest. Change or sunglass compartment. Key chain. Tiny spaces in his car, backpack, or wallet. Inside his cell phone case. With the proper tools provided by my investigator, I could expeditiously pick a lock. And if there was a keypad, I knew all the combinations Benjamin used.

Bet that bitch Arizona started setting her home alarm.

I tried doing what Bing advised. It was not in my nature to cater to my husband or kids. I was where I was accustomed to being, in the driver's seat of his car. His life.

Starting the engine, I said to my husband, "Explain the ring, the flowers, the champagne, the perfume that you bought your mistress," knowing he hadn't given me a gift outside of my birthday, our anniversary, and holidays in two years.

I heard him exhale through his nostrils. His lips were so tight saliva couldn't ooze out. "Mercedes, I told you last night and the night before, I bought everything as parting gifts. I was ending it with her. The ring was for you. Not her."

The bullshit men came up with. Was I supposed to believe any of that?

"Her sucking your dick was a parting gift too, Benjamin? I didn't see you fighting her off as your cum spilled out of her mouth."

My fingers gripped the steering wheel. I plunged the accelerator.

"Honey, pull over. Let me drive."

"No. You like living on the edge. Fucking her. I shouldn't have let you stick the tip of your head inside of me. No telling what you gave me." Rattling my head, I merged onto the freeway. "You might want to answer me, Benjamin."

Calmly, he replied, "Honey, please. Pull over. I'll drive."

I accelerated to ninety. Weaved between cars. Heading south on Interstate 75, I had no physical destination.

"Nothing I seem to do pleases you. You don't want to suck my dick. You get mad when another woman enjoys it. You don't appreciate my dropping off and picking up the kids, cooking, cleaning, nothing. Why are you so angry?"

I switched pedals. Stumped the brakes, then sped up. "Didn't you forget something?"

"No!" he yelled, bracing his hands on the dash.

"Yes, you did!" I yelled. "What do you do for me?"

"Everything!" Heaving, he continued, "I do is for you and our kids."

"You take that bitch out three to four times a week to make me happy. Is that it?" I drove faster. "Oh, you humiliate me, then call me angry, then lick her pussy to apologize for the fucked-up shit you've done to me!" I increased my speed. "Is that it? When was the last time we went on a date?"

Plunging the accelerator, I screamed, "You can answer at any time!"

"When was the last time you put on lingerie?" he lamented.

Really? "So that's it. I'm no longer the mother of your children. I'm a piece of ass that don't put out. Is that my worth to you?"

"You said it. Not me."

I slowed my pace—in the fast lane—to fifty miles per hour, then told my husband, "Get out."

"You can't be serious."

"Okay, if you won't get out, I will."

Parking in the emergency lane, I opened my door, stood near the rail, started crying. I wasn't going to jump in front of traffic. Killing myself was never a consideration. I was just having a moment. The worst part was my husband was clueless.

Benjamin lowered my window. "Honey, please. Get in the car. If you want me to prove to you it's over with Arizona, we can go to her house now. I'll tell her in front of you."

I got in the car. Drove the legal speed limit en route to our house. His offering to tell her he was done while I was there gave me the satisfaction I needed. I reached into my purse and gave Benjamin the ring.

"Take it back to the jeweler, get my money back, then take your ass back to Arizona."

CHAPTER 44

Sandara

OMG! Containing my emotions was not happening.

Delvin parked his Bentley in front of my two-bedroom apartment in Little Five Points. Remy's car was in front of his. She'd agreed to watch the kids at my place.

Standing in the doorway beside me, Remy squealed, then mumbled, "Damn, girl. You have my permission to stay out all night and until the sun comes up."

The best thing Black had done for me was take me to court for child support.

Delvin exposed Black's insecurities. Black wasn't tough dealing with an intelligent, well-dressed, articulate man who didn't view him as a threat.

There was no easy way to tell Remy I was moving soon as I found a place I liked in Buckhead. I wanted to be closer to Alexis and Domino, my mother, and my other two sisters. Maybe I could buy a house big enough for all of us and convince Remy to move in with us.

"Hi, Delvin," I said, smiling inside out.

The black-and-white checkered fedora had a tiny red-and-white feather on the side. I loved the black, buttoned up shirt with fine white pinstripes. Black skinny slacks revealed his well-endowed manhood. His spotless white shoes added character to his outfit.

Kissing my cheek first, he answered, "Hey, beautiful."

Remy cleared her throat.

"Oh, come in. This is my girlfriend, Remy. She's watching the kids."

"Hey, handsome. You'd better take good care of my girl," Remy said.

It was a first date, not a departure to a foreign country, I thought.

"Word is bond. She's in great hands." Delvin spoke with confidence.

Holding his hand, I escorted him to the living room. Before I could introduce Delvin, Ty sprang to her feet. "Daddy!"

Delvin's brows formed a unibrow, then raised toward the brim of his hat. He picked her up. "Hey, princess. I'm not your dad but I see where you get your gorgeous features."

Ty's face shined. "Thank you."

Delvin nodded at me as if to suggest "job well done."

Tyrell said, "He's my daddy," hugging Delvin's leg.

"This is Ty, Tyrell, and that's my eldest, Tyson. Say hi and bye to Mr. Delvin Brown," I told them.

Tyson stared at the television. I didn't make him respond. Doing so would've been more for me than him. He was sad that I'd told him Black wasn't coming by. Truth was, I told Black what Delvin advised me. Black could see his son when he got a custody order from the court.

If Black could file for child support that he didn't deserve, then he could legally request to spend time with his son. When he showed up at my place that night after court thinking he was going to fuck me, I called the police. Hadn't seen or heard from him since.

Delvin handed Remy an envelope. "I'll have her back at a decent hour."

Remy and I frowned. She opened the envelope. "Take your time. Tomorrow is fine."

Delvin laughed. "You ready, beautiful?" he asked, lowering Ty to the floor.

"Girl, I got these kids." Remy's two were on the sofa reading a book aloud to each other.

I was really going to miss being able to walk to my best friend's house. "Thanks," I said, then followed Delvin. He opened the door. Waited until I was in, then closed it.

Buckling up, I thought, I had to stop being afraid to embrace my success. "Where are we going?"

"I made a reservation at Chops. That's cool?"

Nodding, I asked, "How old are you and what made you want to become a lawyer?"

"Twenty-nine. Guess you could say I went to law school by default. My dad, brother, and sister are attorneys. My father is good friends with Bing Sterling."

"I like him," I answered.

"He's a stellar kind of guy. Straight shooter. Hard to find these days."

"What about you?" I asked.

Delvin smiled. His teeth were perfect. "Never believe a man who toots his own horn. I'll let you be the judge of my character," he responded, parking at valet.

Attendants opened our doors. Delvin escorted me to the elevator, up one level, to our destination. The host seated us at a booth in the corner.

"You mind if I order for us?" he asked.

Wow, I could get used to this. "I don't mind at all."

The next three hours, we shared a bottle of Charles Krug cabernet, a jumbo crab cake, and calamari. He ordered the seafood trio for me, a six-ounce Kobe steak for himself, and for dessert we shared crème brûlée.

We retraced our steps to valet. His car was parked up front. Delvin insisted on opening my door. Securing my seat belt, I said, "I had an amazing time."

He said what no man had told me. "You're amazing. And I'd love to take you out again."

"You don't mind my having three children? You know my situation."

Delvin parked in front of my apartment. "Sandara, lots of men take advantage of gorgeous women. I represent those women on a daily. The more beautiful a woman is, the more she's probably been used and abused. Men who lie and cheat make women heartless. I already told you I have a large family. I'd like to get to know you better. Let's enjoy getting to know each other. But first I need to know if you're interested in date number two."

Staring into his eyes, I said, "Yes. I'd like that," then paused. "No. Actually, I'd love that."

Opening my door, he held my hand until I was on my feet, then escorted me to my door. Delvin placed his hand at the back of my neck, leaned in, and gave me a passionate kiss. His tongue wasn't all down my throat. His dick wasn't grinding against my pelvic area trying to impress me.

I cried.

There went my heart again saying yes to a man before he'd asked me to have sex.

CHAPTER 45

Devereaux

Antonio placed his hand on my knee. The warmth from his fingertips increased my temperature. My body was on fiyah!

I knew the moment would come when neither of the girls was with us. We didn't have to pick them up or drop them off. Just the two of us for the remainder of the night until other obligations would demand our attention at sunrise.

This time we were enjoying a candlelit dinner for two in front of the waterfall at my place without our children. Nya and Sarah were in the overnight care of a reliable person, Etta.

My cell was on do not disturb with no exception for my favorites. Antonio's phone was powered off. I'd prepared a simple meal. I'd oven-broiled three whole lobsters, diced them into bite-size chunks. Didn't want either of us to bother with the shells. Garlic smashed potatoes and spinach were the perfect sides. Dessert, if we indulged, was Bananas Foster.

I was a decent cook, just hadn't had a reason to spoil a real man. Wouldn't stand over a hot stove ever again for a man who didn't uplift and respect.

"You know how hard it is to meet a woman of your caliber?" Antonio asked, dipping a piece of his tail in drawn butter.

No, I didn't. Thought it was easy for a man to meet any type of woman he wanted.

"What I do know is it's harder for a woman to meet a man who's not hesitant to make a commitment and respect his woman when she's not with him. How about trying to meet just one guy who's open and honest? Even the decent ones are liars and cheaters."

I paused, the agitation creeping in my spirit from having been a fool for Phoenix for four consecutive years, from twenty-five to twenty-eight. The ages made me think about what Alexis had said about our mother.

I didn't want to believe our mother would lie to us about something as important as paternity but her reason wasn't plausible. Phoenix wasn't perfect; lately he was horrible. Despite the road he'd chosen, he'd always be Nya's father and Nya would have a relationship with him. Antonio could not take Phoenix's place.

"You're okay with my being fifteen years older than you?" he asked.

"Age is just a number." I know that was cliché. It was also true, for me. Time for me to let a man love me more. If he happened to be a decade and a half my senior, I was good with that.

I dipped my lobster, fed it to him. He dunked his, put it in my mouth. We shared a buttery kiss.

Antonio whispered, "Let me make love to you, Devereaux," then he pressed his lips to my ear.

The gentleness of his touch against my wildly full afro made my body reheat.

"Your hair is beautiful," he professed, stroking my cheek with his thumb.

Was it too early in our relationship to give myself to him? I hadn't been with another man since Phoenix. I needed a man's touch.

Praying he wasn't one of those men who would change after I shared my body with him, I held his hand, led him from my dining room table to the sofa. The room was filled with silence.

"I can turn on some music," I said, giving myself a reason to pause this intimate moment that created the urge for me to prematurely climax.

"The music is already playing," he said, pressing his lips to mine. "Can't you feel it?" His hand moved slowly from my knee, under my dress, to mid-thigh.

"I'll get us something to drink."

His hand moved closer to my rejuvenated, detoxed vagina. "Please don't be the type of man who says and does what's necessary to get laid."

Closing my eyes, I prayed he'd stop there. Give me time to dispel the sexual tension taking over my body. He grazed the edge of my outer lips. I gasped, opened my eyes, squeezed my thighs, trapped his fingers inside my labia.

"I want you now, Devereaux." He paused, then asked, "What would make you comfortable?"

Naturally, I replied, "A ring."

"Tomorrow isn't promised to me or you. We work hard. Let's make love the same." He lightly kissed me. "I hear you. If a ring is important to you, you deserve it."

Lawd, I was on fire . . . ready to explode! Jesus, it had been too long. Men were different. They could easily be into the orgasm and not the woman.

"I reassure you. I'm not interested in any other woman. I won't toy with your emotions. When love comes first, yes, I said love, intimacy is created. I'm not a character. Don't write me into a script. Hold me," he said, leaning his body into mine. "I need to feel you embrace me."

Relieved that his hand was no longer between my thighs, I held him. "You're right. I do feel the music."

Melodic energy lightly strummed my vulva, encouraging me to add my own chorus line, "Make love to me."

The beat of his heart thumped rapidly when he placed one hand behind my back, the other under my knees, then carried me upstairs to my bedroom.

"Let me do what you've asked of me," he said, lowering my feet to the carpet.

Neatly, he peeled the comforter to the foot of the bed, held my hand, then led me to the bathroom.

Warm water splashed against our naked bodies. He coated my skin with body wash, cleansed my genitals front to rear, rinsed me well, toweled me off, escorted me back to my king-size bed, then tucked me in.

What the hell?

"Don't move. I'll be right back."

With each passing moment, the heaviness of my tired eyes battled my will to stay awake.

Completely uncovering my body, he held my foot. Gliding his tongue between my toes made me laugh out loud.

"You'll get used to it. Relax."

This was no pedicure at the spa. The sucking made me cringe, in a good way until I became comfortable. "Oh, my, gosh." The sensation was unbearably orgasmic. I was dying to kick. Didn't want him to lose a tooth.

As he trailed light kisses from my ankles to my knees, this time I did kick a little when the ticklish feeling crept throughout my body. Antonio quickly moved his tongue up to my clit, then licked softly. If he licked one more time I was going to cum.

I was determined that our first explosion was coming at the same time. I tugged under his armpits, suggesting he stop licking, climb between my sizzling thighs and penetrate this freshness.

Reaching under the comforter, he retrieved a black cock ring, slid it over his corona, to the base of his shaft, then over his balls. Phoenix had never used one with me.

The patience Antonio exhibited did not exceed the control he had over releasing himself. Each time I was on the verge of exploding, he'd stop thrusting and tease my nipples.

The music in my soul was more intense than any song created for my show.

He slid his head all the way in until he couldn't go deeper. The walls of my vagina pulsated with the throb of his shaft. Felt as though we'd never stop climaxing. This moment was heavenly.

We were quiet. Pounds at a time, his weight grew heavier by the minute. Never wanting this experience to end, I pressed my lips to his shoulder, rolled him onto his side, wrapped my arm and leg atop him, then I closed my eyes.

CHAPTER 46

Alexis

Mothers were like wives. They did what was expected out of obligation.

"He looks just like you, dude."

Touching Domino's tiny fingers, I didn't know a single mother who had given up on her kid. Trifling fathers who never showed up? I could start with my dad.

"I have a little person depending on me, chick."

I'd never had what I'd considered a best friend. My mom didn't have to be by my side the entire time. She could've left, let the nurses do their job, and come back to check on me like everyone else or left and never returned. Mother wasn't my bestie but she was the greatest. I'd try my hardest to never take Blake Crystal for granted again.

"Whatever you do, you cannot call my son 'chick.' Deal." I wasn't asking. After my recovery, I refused to leave Domino's side.

"Done," he said, sitting beside me. "I kinda feel like I'm that boy's pappy."

We laughed hard.

I told my brother, "Don't start no buzzing, man. You're Uncle Spence." Didn't need my mom questioning me. "To silence the shit talkers, I'm insisting James do a paternity test."

"So you're not sure?" my brother asked in front of my son.

I wasn't sure what my baby understood. I heard the nurses and my mother when they were speaking to me. Rolling my eyes, I chose not to dignify with a direct response.

Exhaling, I confessed, "I feel hopeless." My baby could fit in the palm of my hand. His diaper wasn't much bigger than a bandage.

After washing my hands, I uncovered my breast. "You've seen it before, chick."

I suctioned the nozzle to my areola, and the machine did all the pumping. I watched my baby's milk collect into a sterilized bottle.

"Dude, that looks like it hurts," Spencer said. "And your boobs are humongous."

"It's not painful . . . anymore. At first I was about to quit. But the nurse said it's best for Domino."

Life wasn't about sacrifices. Not for Alexis Crystal. Everything I'd do for my son, he'd deserve. The moment he understood right from wrong, there'd be accountability with no entitlements. He had to earn what he got. If my mother had taught me responsibility, I realized, I wouldn't have hurt the people I love.

Not spoiling Domino to the hilt sounded great. Hoped I could look into his eyes and tell him "no." When I manipulated family, friends, and lovers, they couldn't deny me. Already I was doing the unimaginable. Staying by Domino's bedside.

"You have a visitor," the nurse said with a wide smile. "It's Mr. West-Léon. Again."

Slowly, my smile grew the widest I could spread my lips. He'd come every evening after set.

West-Léon sat beside me in the intensive care nursery. Scrubs were hot on him.

"You get more beautiful every day. I swear. How's our lil man doing?" he said. "You need help with pumping? I can relieve that machine."

Not requiring assistance, I answered, "Yes."

The way he placed his hand underneath my breast made my pussy twerk. I was advised to wait six weeks before having intercourse. Ready to dig into my treasure chest filled with toys, I whispered, "You have no idea what I'm going to do to you."

Spencer told us, "I'ma get outta y'allz way. I'll be back tomorrow to check on y'all."

My brother and new closest friend was never in my way.

"Why don't you let me take you to dinner when you're done. I promise I'll bring you right back," West-Léon said.

"I'd love to but I can't. You should've asked before Spencer left. I'd feel horrible if anything happened to Domino while I was out enjoying myself."

"How long before he can go home?" West-Léon asked, closing the flap on my bra.

"Three, maybe four months. Depends on how fast he gains weight and how well he does breathing on his own."

Domino had what they'd called a hole in his heart. And if the fluid continued to accumulate in his brain, he might need surgery. I hadn't shared that information with anyone. Knowing my son might not survive, I realized how my mother felt about me.

My baby's condition was my fault. Was thrilled to see they cut that head-banging fool from the football team. I had to stay with Domino. This might be our only time together.

"You can't stay here that long, Alexis. Dev has an opening for my love interest," he said, placing my hand over his heart. "I have a vacancy on and off set that only one beautiful, amazingly talented woman can fill." He raised his brows. Smiled. Kissed me.

"For clarification. What do you want from me?" I asked. He didn't know what my pussy tasted, looked, smelled, or felt like. Maybe he wanted to use me to secure his role.

"I want to see where we can go," he said.

Men had a tendency to spark interest in a woman for a relationship, do a "no-show," then pretend they were never the costar. I had a baby who needed me. All of me. I refused to be dickstracted.

"There's always another episode. If it's meant to be. If we're meant to be." I stared at him.

James entered the room, handed me an overnight bag. "Spencer told me to give this to you. He forgot. What's up, West-Léon?"

If James knew the truth about our son's health, he'd be here day and night too.

"It's all good for me, man. And you?"

Softly, I said, "Hey, James," then told West-Léon, "Give us a moment alone. James needs to see his son."

"Sure thing. I'll grab you something to eat," he said.

"Thanks, babe," I answered to make James jealous, then added, "Wherever you go do not go to Spondivits Seafood."

"I feel you. I hate the way they treat their black customers too. I'll get you something from Pappadeaux or Six Feet Under."

"Cool." I loved both.

James sat beside me. Chanel had stopped coming at my request.

The pre-mommy Alexis would enjoy watching two men compete for my attention. I was still a diva but clearly over being petty.

Didn't like the way the loose skin of my belly made me cover up my sexiness. Mercedes's demanding a tummy tuck was ideal. I almost went from delivery to plastic surgery. Dr. Paul McCluskey reassured me he'd sculpt me a new stomach with a six-pack that would make me look like a workout fanatic. The new me could wait. Plus, I didn't want to have or look like I had a body harder than a man's.

"I want us to become a family. Don't answer me now. Think about it," James said, looking at Domino. The love in James's eyes brought tears to mine.

I shook my head. "Chanel is better for you," I said, knowing James would never become my best friend or my sweetest lover. That position was currently reserved for West-Léon.

That was if West-Léon didn't mess things up.

I'd grown tired of strapping on to make James cum his hardest. Chanel was pretty good at penetrating but she'd never perfect my techniques. James would never give up anal and eating pussy was my vice. Earlier, I thought the three of us would make the perfect family. Now that I was a mother, I'd never subject my son to growing up in a confusing environment.

"It's over with her, Alexis. I'm not asking you to decide this minute. Keep my engagement ring, wherever it is. If you ever give it back, I'll accept that as your final no."

I held James's hand.

"I will always love you . . . Always."

"I feel the same," he said, admiring our baby.

"James."

"Yes."

"There are some things you should know about our son's heath condition. There's a serious possibility Domino might not make it."

In a split second, James's love turned to blame. "Alexis, what did you do?"

CHAPTER 47

Benjamin

I dug myself into a bond with my mistress that was so strong only Jesus could save my marriage.

Again, our children were at school. We'd dropped them off this morning. In a few hours, we'd have to pick them up. Together. Life was good for my wife and kids but I missed the hell out of my Arizona. Not just the way she cooked, cleaned, and performed fellatio. She was cool. Chill. Made me feel like a man. The man. I needed that. Needed her. Needed my wife but all she made me feel was pain.

"You paid eight thousand dollars for a ring for me to signify you've ended the relationship with Arizona? Really? One of us is full of shit and it's definitely not me, Benjamin Alexander Bannister."

The woman in front of me had changed. Or had she? Cursing. Badgering.

Every damn day, I swear, I had to answer the same motherfucking questions. I was done with her relentless bitching. I exited my home office, went downstairs to the living room, turned on Steve Harvey, praying he was doing an intervention for somebody that might help me relate to my situation.

Mercedes sat beside me. "Steve can't save you, Benjamin Alexander Bannister. I am your wife and I demand an answer."

Exhaling, I asked, "What was the last question?" wondering why my father believed I should value a piece of paper over my sanity or what was in my heart. I sincerely loved Arizona. Missed hearing her sexy voice, her listening to me, her drawing me a hot bath. Her touch. All that and more.

A repeat with Toya and her wife sucking my dick couldn't eradicate my frustrations. Fuck! I wish my wife would shut the fuck up. I couldn't hear myself think.

"Forget it! Just recommit to making your family a priority and an exclusive and we'll be back on the right track."

"My family has always been my priority."

My wife created my second-class ranking. I flipped through channels. Selected HGTV. Arizona and I dreamt of buying a fixer-upper in Conyers, customizing every detail. Exploring the world together starting with Bora Bora. If Will and Jada could redesign homes, maybe I could repair my household.

Exhaling the loudest, "Ha!" Mercedes couldn't stop laughing.

I'd have to tear my wife down first. Not sure it or she was worth my trouble, I picked up my keys, "I'll be back."

My decision to stay married could have been easier if she would have stopped bitchin'. My God!

Mercedes clawed at my shirt, scratched my back. Crying, she begged, "Don't leave me for her! We need you!"

She sure as hell didn't act as though she loved, appreciated, or needed my ass. The kids did.

"Get off of me," I yelled, shoving her. She stumbled to the floor.

"I hate you!" she screamed up at me, then started crying.

Dropping to my knees, I held her. "Honey, I'm sorry but you have got to stop. Attacking me is making our situation worse. First you degrade me verbally. I'm not going to become a battered husband."

I helped her up. "Say what you mean," I said, sitting beside her on the sofa. "I'll listen. Then you need to shut up and let me get it all out without judgment."

Sniffling, my wife regurgitated the same concerns. This time I heard her. She was hurting. She was embarrassed. My wife was scared.

"I have something I want to show you," Mercedes said.

She stood, raised her dress, lowered her panties, and put her pussy in my face. I'd seen it before. What was different?

Hold up Wait. Show? Or give? She was going to let me go all in? Picking up my cell, I texted Toya, **Pick up my kids, please . . . and keep them for a few hours. I'll pick them up from your house later.**

Toya texted back, **U Sure?**

Positive.

CHAPTER 48

Mercedes

When had I stopped acknowledging that my husband loved me? I'd rationed my vagina to Benjamin as though it was a treat reserved for special occasions—birthdays, holidays, good behavior. The way Arizona sucked my husband's dick, I saw how much she enjoyed pleasing him. I hated seeing her do what I wouldn't even do upon request. Arizona would do the same in her next affair. She was a whore. I was sure of it.

"Let me take a quick shower," I said, bracing my hand against Benjamin's forehead.

He held my wrist, buried his face in my new vulva, then inhaled. "Ah. I missed your natural scent." His next inhale was longer.

"This is your pussy," I whispered, feeling uncomfortable. Sounded vulgar to my ears. If dirty talk was what men wanted to hear, I might as well practice on my husband.

"That's what I'm talking about, bitch. Let me fuck my pussy."

I froze. Stepped back. "Where'd you learn to speak such language?"

He moved closer to my vagina. I was no man's bitch.

We were a young couple. I was twenty-seven. He was thirty. I made time for the twins, for my clients. Sex should be on my list of things to do once a week. Honestly, I didn't want it as much as he did. I'd never cheated on my husband. Revenge was not what I wanted. Sexing another man would degrade me, not him. I needed a man of my house more than I had to have a man in my house. If he was done straying, I'd meet him halfway on the mattress. Benjamin was the only one for me.

"Lie down," he dictated.

My eyes widened. "On the couch or the floor?"

"The couch," he said, sitting me down.

I stood. "But the kids and our guests sit there."

"Woman, would you relax for a moment and stop overthinking everything."

"Okay, let me get a sheet." I hurried upstairs.

Grabbed a sheet. Decided to check my cell. Responded to a few e-mails from clients. Texted Alexis, **How's Domino? I'm going to see you guys today. Do you need anything?**

Devereaux had texted me a photo. Her face shined brighter than I'd ever seen. **It's a relationship ring. Isn't it gorgeous? I love this man!**

The diamonds were absolutely blinding. Was that what Benjamin had bought Arizona? A relationship ring? Never heard of it. But I was sure he hadn't gotten a ring a half size too big for me.

I replied, **Congratulations.**

My enthusiasm for my husband faded. I showered, dressed. It was almost time for us to go pick up my kids. Entering the living room, I didn't see my husband.

I called out, "Benjamin. Where are you, honey?"

The garage door closed. My stomach cramped. I rushed to see what I feared. I stood in the driveway.

"Where are you going?" I asked. "I just need a little more time. Please don't go."

Watching me drive him away again was hard. What was wrong with me? Alexis was suddenly supermom. Devereaux was in love. Sandara's modeling career was back to business thanks to Bing. Her babies' daddies stopped harassing her for child support. The new guy Delvin was a good fit for baby sis. Then there was my mother. She was planning her first wedding. I was so jealous of Mother, I'd stopped returning her calls and responding to her texts about colors, cakes, dresses, flowers, and so on.

No time for pity, I told myself.

Grabbing my purse, I got in my car and went where I knew I'd find Benjamin. This time I wouldn't be considerate of him or his mistress.

I was putting an end to my husband's conveniently running to his mistress every time I didn't do what he wanted, when he wanted.

One way or another, this was the end.

CHAPTER 49

Blake

"Twenty dozen long-stemmed roses for the altar."

"Scratch that. Make it fifty dozen," Brandon said. "All white. I'm ordering magnolias and lilies, too."

Brandon appeared more excited than I, which was impossible. In ninety days, I'd be Mrs. Blake Sterling. The sound of my new last name thrilled me. I'd practiced enunciating it over and over.

"That's overkill," I told him.

"Yes, darling, if you were marrying me. Stop acting like you're not getting hitched to a man who can not only give you the world but can buy your replacement too if you fuck up. I wish he was a little gay. Straight women are too conservative for rich men."

Leave it to Brandon, he had everybody's relationship figured out except his own.

Magazines, books, planners, and color swatches were scattered atop my dining table. I could no longer see the oak wood.

Sitting next to Brandon, I reminded him, "I got my eight-hour-long mile-high wings."

"Gurl, you just went along with the program. So jump on board for this whirlwind wedding," he said, twirling with his arms spread east and west. Settling into his seat, he noted, "We need four cakes. Five hundred, long-stemmed, white chocolate roses for our guests."

"What? Have you lost your mind?"

I understood why Alexis hadn't offered to assist. Sandara, Devereaux, and Mercedes, regardless of what they were dealing with, they had no excuse.

"The leaf on the stem will be eighteen-carat gold. The boxes will be black. You can never go wrong with black, honey, which reminds me, I need to send the tailor to Bing for his measurements and I'll be here for your appointment. I have the perfect design for you. First things first. These thank-you gifts to your guests will be presented by black ballerinas toward the end of the reception." Brandon raised his left brow. "You know I have to include a few guys."

My winning this battle was not happening but he was drastically reducing the number of attendees and that was non-negotiable. The official wedding planner quit shortly after my partnering her with Brandon. I was not telling Bing, nor was I hiring a third.

"Cut the white chocolate roses order by a third. You can leave the gold leaf. I like that. Make it small."

"With all those folks in your family? Four hundred. Final number. I refuse to be embarrassed."

I sighed, then countered, "Three fifty."

"Cool," he said, smacking his lips. "I'm parched from all this planning. Let's quench my thirst at the Ritz-Carlton. Lunch is on Mr. Bing's Luxury Black Card. And don't forget who ignited the union for you two." He pressed a few keys on his cell. "Reservation confirmed. Shall we?"

Thank goodness there was a spending limit assigned to the card Bing told me to give Brandon. Cruising in my Ferrari, our drive was less than ten minutes.

Brandon ordered filet mignon. I had grilled salmon. We shared a bottle of champagne.

"What would I do without you?" I told my friend. Exhausted from talking about my arrangements, I asked, "Are you enjoying being president of the bank?"

I was proud of Brandon and of myself for having taught him how to do my job. He was my loyal VP deserving of his promotion.

Brandon never left me. Claimed some things were more important than his money.

"Honey, you know me. I love telling people what to do," he said, placing his tie over his shoulder. "And I learned from the best on how to value my employees. They will do anything for me. I mean kill and hide the body, darling." His voice lowered when he said, "So tell Bing he'd better treat you right. I'm so happy for you, Blake."

Brandon rubbed his eyes. The teal-colored suit complemented his pink button-down shirt.

"You may be the only one," I commented, extending a hug.

"You gets no pity, bitch. You're getting married. That's all that matters. What I want to know is why you haven't mentioned they terminated your ass in Charlotte." His voice returned to normal range.

Should've known he'd know. "I haven't told anyone."

"Child, if you think that man doesn't know, you ain't fooling nobody but yourself. Word is, he was the one who'd made it happen. But you didn't hear that from me."

Normally, I'd be upset. "After sitting by Alexis's bedside praying not to lose her or my grandson, I have a different perspective on my life. Bing loves me. And if he wants me by his side instead of working nine-to-five for someone else, I can live with that."

I hadn't mentioned the sizable deposit. Didn't want anyone treating me differently. Not that Brandon would but if he loved me for sure not knowing, he might not feel the same if I told him. I was okay with marrying Bing, not his money.

"Speaking of Ms. Alexis, I have to be Domino's honorary godfather and fashion consultant slash baby room decorator slash personal shopper."

I laughed. "She'll love all of that."

"I've been thinking about opening my own clothing store but I have to trim my budget first. Which brings me to, what are you going to do with that fabulous house of yours?"

"If you want it, I'll gift it to you after the ceremony."

"Bitch, stop it!" Brandon's mouth hung open. He leaned close, giving me a tight hug. "Now I know I've gone to heaven and God let me come back to move in when?" We laughed as he said, "Thank you. Thank, you."

"There's one catch," I said.

"Bitch, I should've known it was too good. What?"

Tears swelled in my eyes. Brandon held my hand. There was no one else I could ask.

"Will you give me away?"

"Like no woman has been given away before, bitch."

"Thanks."

CHAPTER 50

Devereaux

Letting go was easier when you had someone to break your fall. "Just dropped the girls off at Etta's and I'll pick them up after I'm done. Meetings all day for me but I promise to call you in between. Text me an hour before you finish filming. We can take the girls out for ice cream or something and all spend the night at my place," Antonio said, getting out of the shower.

"Thanks, babe." I kissed him, adjusted my cap, then closed the door.

Visions of making love with Antonio scrolled through my mind as hot water splashed against my body. Spooning when we were too tired to make love. Early morning quickies. Waking up to his head between my thighs. I'd never tire of this man or take him for granted.

Slipping on a summer dress and sandals, I powdered my brows, then coated my lips with a cotton candy–pink gloss. Dabbing perfume behind each ear, I exited into my garage. There was a handwritten note on my windshield.

Miss you already. Have an amazing day. — *Antonio*

The little thoughtful things Antonio did made me realize there was always time for couples to bond. He'd pick up the girls, cook or order takeout for dinner for the four of us. I'd comb hair and lay out the girls' clothes for the next day, eat with them, then I'd go to my writing room for a few hours while Antonio responded to e-mails.

Phoenix was consumed with trying to become successful at my expense. He'd sexed me but that wasn't the same as making love to me. I wasn't sure Phoenix knew how to give all of himself to a woman in a way that would leave her feeling like his queen. I was blessed to have met Antonio.

En route to the studio, I commanded the Bluetooth in my car, "Call Antonio."

"Good morning, beautiful."

"I wanted to hear your voice before starting my day. Thanks for the note."

"I'm glad you called. Let me know if you're available for a quick cocktail before I get the girls?" The enthusiasm filled my heart with love and lust.

"Is seven okay?" I asked.

I thought about my sister Mercedes. She had many challenges to overcome. She was learning a valuable lesson. I liked the new her. Benjamin's zero tolerance for her rudeness forced her to respect me.

"Seven is perfect. I'll text you the location, babe. And . . ." He paused, then said, "I have a film deal opportunity. For us."

"Ah! Are you serious?" I screamed with excitement followed by, "Ahh!" filled with fear. I ended the call, got out of my car.

"Are you okay? Say something, please!" I cried. "What have I done?"

The body was stretched in front of my tires. "Are you okay?" I yelled.

Reaching in my cup holder, I got my phone. A call registered from Antonio. I ended it.

Calling 9-1-1 was more important. "Yes, I hit someone. They're under my car. God! Please! Send an ambulance. Quick," I cried, giving them the address to my studio.

"Is the person breathing?" the operator questioned.

"I don't know. Let me see."

I hated how pedestrians in Atlanta walked in front or behind moving vehicles. This was all my fault. I should've been paying attention.

They were facedown. A hood covered the back of their head. Kneeling beside the person, the combination of the stench and the nervousness in the pit of my stomach made me puke on them.

"I'm so sorry," I cried, then asked, "Are you okay?"

Antonio parked off to the side. Hurried to me. "Babe, what happened?" He placed his arm around me. "Don't touch 'em. Get up and stand back. Let the paramedics do their job."

They rushed to the person on the ground, turned them over, and proceeded to check the person's vitals.

"He's breathing," one paramedic said. "Goddamn!" he said, then rattled his head.

"What is it?" Antonio questioned.

"That's what I want to know. He alive but he smells like he's dead." The paramedic walked a short distance. Inhaled several times.

Both paramedics placed masks over their nose and mouth. Rolling the man onto the gurney, I threw up again. I was speechless.

Antonio asked, "Babe, you okay? Do we need to get you checked out?"

Staring at the man lying before us, I said, "Antonio, Phoenix. Phoenix, Antonio."

The paramedics strapped Phoenix's legs, waist, and chest.

"I love you, Dev. I will always love you," Phoenix said.

"You know this person?" one of the paramedics questioned.

Staring at the man who fathered our child. The man who'd asked me to marry him. The man whom I still had love for but was no longer in love with. I shook my head.

Phoenix sat up. "You gon' know me when we get to court." He reclined on the stretcher, folded his arms over his chest, said to the paramedics, "Let's roll."

I parked my car. Watched the ambulance drive off with my ex, with my daughter's father. With a liar, user, and cheater who I knew would settle out of court for a few dollars.

I had no regrets leaving Phoenix. Should've left him behind bars.

I texted Mercedes, **Thanks, Sis. I love you.**

CHAPTER 51

Sandara

"Please. Stop. You're gonna make me cry," I said, holding my friend.

"I'm happy for you," Remy sobbed. "If anybody deserves a good life and a great guy, it's you."

I wiped the water from her cheeks. Remy had never met her dad. Her kids didn't know their father. Were we to blame for our bad choices? Or did black men only want to stick their dick in us, then fuck the next chick? Dating a man with a black mother and Italian father showed me that men of other nationalities loved, adored, and respected black women.

"You can move with us. I bought a house large enough for the seven of us. We'll work it out," I told her, not wanting to leave her in Little Five Points. "And, I can ask Delvin to hook you up with one of his boys."

Shaking her head she forced a smile. "Welfare, Section 8, being the best mom I know how, partying and making a few dollars on the side, that's what I know. What my kids are familiar with, you know. I'd move to Bankhead before I do Buckhead. Your mom works for a bank. My mother doesn't even have a savings or checking account. You were on Section 8 by choice. I'm not a fashion model like you. Look at me," she said.

I did. And I saw a beautiful plus-size chocolate woman with full lips, fierce hips, and a luxurious twenty-four-inch weave that could make her favorite artist, Remy Ma, jealous. Having her babies left stretch marks on her stomach but Remy rocked shirts that rose above her belly button.

"I can't leave you here. I won't. Please, move with us," I cried. "We'll figure it out."

Remy shook her head. "I'll be watching you on social," she said, sniffling snot as she stood.

"I have a house with a pool. Promise me you'll bring the kids over to swim."

"A pool? Wow! That's cool, Sandara." She hugged me. "I gotta go."

"You and the kids coming to my mom's wedding?" I asked, trying to keep her in my presence long as I could.

"Of course," Remy said, letting me go.

Not wanting to watch her walk away, I closed the door. I strolled through my two-bedroom apartment for the last time. Everything here except for my pictures on the walls would be donated. What I was doing was best for my children and me.

A text registered from Delvin, **We're still on for movie night at your new place with the kids?**

What did I do to deserve him? Was there a Delvin or a Devon out there for Remy? I replied, **Yes.**

Great! I'll bring the popcorn.

Locking the door, I got in my Porsche, drove by Remy. She waved. I cried.

Success shouldn't make me lose my best friend. That wasn't fair.

CHAPTER 52

Alexis

"If you don't stop eating like you're having another baby, dude, you're going to get fat."

I fucked up the mashed potatoes and meat loaf my brother brought me from the Cheesecake Factory. That seven-layer chocolate cake was next. I was no stranger to hitting the gym harder than most guys. These calories would burn off before they settled anywhere on my body. If that didn't work, plastic surgery was always an option and Dr. Paul McCluskey was the only surgeon snatching me to perfection.

"You're the one that keeps bringing me appetizers, entrees, and dessert."

Three months in the hospital, Domino was at his should've-been birth weight. Spencer was the only one who visited us every day. That was okay. People had their own lives to tend to. My sisters had more important things to do. Couldn't wait to case Sandara's new spot. My mom was the only person other than Spencer who I'd told we were going home in a few days.

Didn't need all the fuss to determine whether James should pick us up. West-Léon spat all that rhetoric about my filling the vacancy on *Sophisticated Side Chicks ATL* until Devereaux convinced Ebony Waterhouse to come back, then his popularity soared the highest ever. Just as I'd expected, he'd barely texted and never called. I refused to respond to him.

Life for Alexis and Domino was blessed. I had my brother and best friend by my side. From now on, family was my priority.

"He's still light to me," Spencer said, cradling Domino in his arms. "You think Venus is a cool name for a boy?" He placed the blanket over his shoulder, propped my son on his chest.

I stared at my brother. "You're having a—"

He laughed. "Hell, no. I'ma do my shit right. Stroll down the aisle like Blake and give my woman my last name. But when I do get hitched, I want my mother's name to live on."

Venus Domino? "Hm, that could work, chick, but you'd better pray he's finer than Denzel and John David Washington rolled into one."

My baby had fallen asleep on Spencer's chest. My brother was already a second dad to my son. I'd keep it that way.

"The first thing I have to do is decorate Domino's room," I said, admiring the six pounds my son had gained. I wanted to keep breastfeeding him but my ducts had stopped producing milk when I'd switched from the machine to his mouth.

"I can't believe he's a normal size now. Didn't take long at all. I can tell you this. That chick, I mean my nephew, is greedy as hell. He damn near eats more than me. You'd betta make sure he doesn't overdose on formula. You know how that happens to some premies."

"I love my son no matter how much he gains," I said, glad we'd made it.

Spencer stared at Domino, then said, "Unc will bring you cheesecake every day, Nephew."

"No, you will not," I protested.

"Dude, you just scared you gon' eat it." He laughed.

"Seriously, I want to know what you think. Mom said her friend Brandon wants to decorate Domino's room before I take my baby home. She said he has the perfect theme but just because he's planning her wedding doesn't make him great with decorating for my baby."

I'd heard more about Brandon over the last few months. Couldn't wait to get to know him for myself.

"That's her gay friend from work, right? Well, where she used to work."

"Don't be jealous, chick. This isn't about you or anything that happened to you when you were little."

Silence filled the room. I didn't mean to sound insensitive. Spencer gently rocked Domino.

Spencer's childhood molestation was tragic. My son wasn't going to be negatively influenced by anyone regarding anything. Being gay did not mean a man would rape or molest a child. It was the undercover self-proclaimed heteros I'd keep my baby away from. A pastor molested my brother so preachers were on my mommy protection radar too.

I told Spencer, "My mom and stepdad-to-be delayed their ceremony so my son would be there and so I could be a bridesmaid."

All of my sisters had agreed. Auntie Ruby was the matron of honor. Mom's other siblings would each be there. Bing's side of the family included no one. Well, he didn't need them. He had us as his family now.

If my momma died, I'd lose my mind. I know I was her thorn but I felt sad for Bing. The one person who loved him was gone.

Not everybody had family but anyone could create family. I looked at my brother. I'd take his secret to my grave. That was how much I loved him.

"Straight," he nodded. "Who's paying for it?"

"Bing is covering everything."

"Humph. Cool, that. Spend all that nigga's money."

Toning down for my brother's noise, I was super excited!

Brandon had been there for my mom when I was being a spoiled brat. The one thing Brandon and I shared was extraordinary taste.

I wasn't requesting chick's permission. I texted my mother, **Brandon can stage Domino's room. If I don't like it, I'll redo it myself.**

"Who you seeing now?" I asked him.

"Random. No time for the crazy head-bangers," he flatly expressed.

"There's my number one gurl," West-Léon said, entering the room.

The nurses must've been tending to patients. I'd have to inquire how he got past them. Placing a bouquet of flowers on the stand, he kissed me. "You taking up residence in this joint or what? I might have to kidnap you and my son, to take y'all home." West-Léon tossed a baby blanket over his shoulder, then scooped Domino from Spencer.

Scanning the fitted, cropped-sleeve, pewter shirt exposing West-Léon biceps, the relaxed-fit jeans covering his big dick, and the black, square-toed shoes instantly made my pussy wet. Didn't want to be one of those females who go back for a checkup and find out they're pregnant. I'd never gone this long without sex. All that shit about celibacy was obsolete.

He gestured for another kiss. I stood to the opposite side of my son. Our mouths suctioned together.

"I'm out," Spencer said. "Tell your mom hi for me. Hopefully, she'll send me an invite."

Nodding, I refused to break the passion with West-Léon. His energy spread through every part of my body.

West-Léon sat in the seat Spencer had abandoned. "I apologize for not coming sooner. I've done a lot of thinking. I know Domino has a father. I'm not going to interfere with that. We both know the show is going well with Ebony. But I think Devereaux fitting you in would take us over the top."

Firmly, I replied, "My son is my priority."

"Our son," he said, then added, "I want you to be my lady for life."

"For life?"

"I don't believe in marriage but I do feel that relationships should be based on love. Love should last forever. In the event it doesn't, I don't want a piece of paper to be the reason I stay in a situation. You feel me?" *You stay?* "Too many women are the trapped ones but I know how to leave."

Finally, a man who thought the way I did. "Uh, that forever temporary commitment thing does come with a ring? Right?"

West-Léon reached into his pocket. "You thought it didn't?"

Damn! I held up my right ring finger. The show was trumping out like that? Maybe I should reconsider. The diamond solitaire was at least ten carats.

"Domino, say hello to our new daddy."

CHAPTER 53

Mercedes

"Mercedes?" she answered as though she hadn't recognized my voice.

"Put my husband on his phone," I demanded.

The call ended. I redialed.

"What, Mercedes?" Benjamin answered this time. "Please stop calling Arizona's phone."

The one thing I wasn't was insane. I knew what number I'd dialed. "I need you to come home. Now. We need to discuss—"

The call ended again. I was accepting of our not being together. What I wasn't going to do was wait for him to make up his mind how and when he felt like being a daddy. I grabbed my purse, got in my car, and drove to her house for the last time.

Bam! Bam! Bam! "Benjamin Alexander Bannister, get your ass out here!"

Arizona opened the door. "You're trespassing. Leave my property. I'm not asking."

"Really?" What was she going to do? "You have my husband in your place and I'm the trespasser?" I exhaled in her face.

She closed the door.

Bam! Bam! Bam! Pacing, I waited for him to come to the door.

Bam! Bam! Bam! My not sexing him could not be so serious that he'd gone back to her. For good this time. She was clearly the one he wanted.

Bam! Bam! Bam! "Benjamin, I'm not leaving until you get out here!"

We were close to working things out. He was about to choose his family. I loved my husband. He didn't love me, us. I was done! But he was going to deal with our kids.

Bam! Bam! Bam! "Bitch! Stop sucking his dick! He legally has a wife and kids," I yelled.

Benjamin opened the door. "You can't keep coming to our house like this."

"Our house? Is in Buckhead."

Looking down at me, my husband said, "Show some respect. Please. I'll pick up the twins from school and drop them off to you."

"So now you're a transporter. I'll take your kids away from you."

"You don't mean that. If anyone is unfit, it's you. Any judge would grant me custodial rights."

"Good! When you pick them up, keep them! Forever! I'm tired of your shit!"

I might be a lot of things but unfit? Never. He was their father as much as I was the twins' mother and he could have full custody. Who said a mother had to bear all or the majority of the responsibility?

Folding my arms to keep from slapping the shit out of my husband, I said, "Don't drop them off. Seriously, keep 'em. You love Arizona so much. Let's see how much she loves your kids."

Softly, he said, "Anything else? We were in the middle of something."

"Like her sucking your dick in the middle of something?" Fighting a battle already lost, I was exhausted. Knew I should leave. I couldn't. I wanted him to hurt.

"Not yet," he calmly answered. "You should go. Now."

I shoved the door, stepped inside. "Make me go! You want a threesome? Is that what you want?"

"Listen. I don't know any other way to put it, Mercedes. I'm tired of you."

"You're tired? Of me?"

He nodded. "Of you. Yes."

Placing my hands over my face, I broke down crying, longing for my husband to hold me in his arms. Sniffling, I gazed into the eyes of a man who once only had love for me. How did he come to hate me?

Benjamin raised his palms, stepped back.

"You made it easy for me to love another woman. Arizona doesn't bitch at me. She cooks, draws my bath, gives me massages, and well . . . you know the rest," he said.

Wedging my hand between his, *Smack!* I slapped his face hard as I could.

My husband grabbed my wrist, held it tight. I recalled the day he'd shoved me to the floor. I didn't mean to scratch his back or slap his face.

"I'm sorry."

"For once, you've got it right. I'll take the hit. But don't do it again," he warned.

Sirens grew near the front door, then stopped. Arizona escorted the police inside. "Please get her out of my house," she said.

I stared at Benjamin. He was silent.

"Ms., you have to go. Now," the officer said.

His tone reminded me of the officer who had arrested Phoenix. My situation was different. I had just cause.

"Mrs.," I replied.

"Ma'am, Mrs., Ms., Miss, it doesn't matter. The owner wants you out of her house. Sir, do you know this woman?" the officer questioned my husband.

Benjamin's stare penetrated my soul when he responded, "I used to. Not anymore."

This was not the damn time for him to be sarcastic.

"Arrest her," Arizona demanded.

The officer opened his handcuffs, put my hands behind my back. "You have the right . . ."

"So you're going to stand there and let her do this?" Tears streamed down my cheeks. "Let them do this?" My eyes pleaded with and for my husband to rescue me.

He exhaled. "After I pick up our kids, I'll be down to bail you out."

I gargled saliva in my throat, then I spat in Arizona's face.

CHAPTER 54

Benjamin

The more I struggled with doing what my parents, what society, and what I thought was right, the more I couldn't deny the fact that I was in love with my mistress. If I had lived my life my way, I never would've married Mercedes.

"Your wife left me no choice," Arizona said, slamming the door. "This is the third time she's shown up at my front door. Second time she entered without permission. It was only going to get worse if I hadn't done something to stop her. My question is why didn't you handle her?"

I couldn't throw my wife on the floor again, stab her in the back, or leave her for dead. We had two kids. My one regret was not having been a better father. If Arizona didn't watch her tone, she'd be searching for another man. I did not deal with her for two years to start taking her shit. I could go home and get talked crazy to.

Not supporting either of their positions, I told Arizona, "I've got to pick up my children, then post bail for my wife. I'll text you later. Okay." I paused, thought about kissing her forehead.

"Don't bring them here. That'll give her another reason to go back to jail."

Shaking my head, I left Arizona's house wondering if she were a wolf in sheep's clothing.

The twins were excited to see me. Brandon asked, "Where's

Mom? I have a big surprise for her and I was going to give her a big kiss right here."

"You're not the only one with a present," Brandy said. "Mine is bigger and better than yours."

"No, it's not," Brandon said, looking to me for support.

I wanted my son to learn how to verbally defend himself. If he could prevail over his sister, he'd be okay. Maybe being an only child with no one to argue with made me passive-aggressive.

"Yes, it is, and you know it." Brandy was inches from Brandon's face.

I interjected, "Why don't we let Mom decide when she gets home."

"Where is she?" Brandon asked.

"With a client, silly," Brandy said.

I wished that were true. Instead, my children's mother was going to have an arrest record and her mug shot would be online for all of her clients to view. Mercedes could lose her business license.

Why didn't she leave when I told her? She was so damn onerous.

All that had happened hadn't altered my feelings for Arizona. A text from my mistress registered, **Is Mercedes okay? I'm going to drop the charges**.

Guess she had time to reflect on her role in the altercation. Arizona's consideration for others, including me and now Mercedes, was what made me fall for her. Most women would cheer, call their girlfriends, and boast about having my wife arrested.

I texted back, **Not sure. Trying to figure out where to take my kids.**

I didn't want to answer a lot of questions from Mercedes's family. **Bring them here.**

My options were limited. Had to do what I had to. They wouldn't be at Arizona's long.

Thanks babe, I replied, then told the twins, "Daddy has important business to tend to. You guys have to stay with my friend for a few hours."

"Who?" Brandy asked.

"Why?" Brandon inquired.

They alternated questions that I never answered.

"What do you have to do?"

"Why can't we go too?"

"Where's Mom?"

"How long will we be there?"

Eventually, Brandy said to her brother, "I told you. She's with a client. Right, Daddy?"

Parking in Arizona's driveway, I thought, they were my kids, too. I was doing what was best to bond their mom out before she was processed in. Couldn't leave her locked up all night in inmate attire. The twins weren't old enough to be home alone. They had to meet my mistress one day.

Mercedes owed Arizona an apology and a thank-you.

Praying they hadn't processed her in, I headed directly to the precinct. "I'm here to bail out Mercedes Crystal."

The clerk researched her computer. "I don't have a Mercedes Crystal. Could she be under a different name?"

My heart raced. "Try Mercedes Bannister," I said, spelling each name.

The clerk shook her head.

"My wife was arrested two hours ago for trespassing. If she's not here, where is she?"

The clerk stopped typing. "Hopefully she's not there, but try Fulton County."

CHAPTER 55

Devereaux

"I have some news for you, Devereaux."

Etta sounded matter-of-fact as usual. Hadn't seen nor heard from Phoenix since he'd stretched out in front of my car. Antonio told me we didn't need a protective order; he had a license to carry a weapon. If Phoenix came near either of us, next time he wouldn't be lucky. Antonio also refused to allow Nya or Sarah to visit with Etta after Phoenix's stunt.

Being submissive to a man who protected my child and me, I didn't want to deny Etta seeing her grandchild but Antonio was right. We were not putting our children in danger.

We needed Etta in our lives. Timing was bad. The one thing Phoenix was great at was fucking up other people's lives.

"I'm finishing up set. Can I call you back in say, thirty minutes?"

I had to go over details for tomorrow's shoot, pick up Nya from Sandara's and drop her off at Mercedes's, then get ready for a dinner date with Antonio.

"Hold on a moment, Mrs. Etta, I have an important call coming in."

"No need to hold, dear, I wanted to let you know before you saw it on the news. I shot Phoenix in his ass. He's at Grady."

My mouth was wide open when she ended the call. Was she joking? If that was true, this was not funny at all.

I answered, "Hey, Mercedes. Glad you called. I'm running a lil—"

She interrupted, "Unless you want to bring my niece to visit me behind bars, I—"

My turn to stop her. "Where are you?" Was the moon full? No one would prank or double prank me.

"Long story. I don't have Bing's number memorized. Can you call and tell him I'm in Fulton County? Hurry," she said, snapping her finger twice. "He needs to get here before I'm processed in."

I grabbed my purse. "Fantastic job, everyone. Ebony, it's like you never missed an episode."

West-Léon gave me a quick hug. "Going to see my lady."

Whatever Alexis had was worth cloning. "Give Domino a toe tap for me." That was if he could get past those nannies Bing had hired.

Motioning for my director, I instructed him, "I need you to wrap up for me. Let's meet a half hour early in the morning."

"You okay?" he asked.

"I'm good," I lied, heading out of the building.

Getting in my car, I told Mercedes, "I'll call Bing and I'm on my way."

"Wait!" she yelled, making me slam on my brakes.

"What?!" I didn't mean to yell. I took several deep breaths recalling the day I could've rolled over Phoenix and killed him. If suicide was his goal, it would be the one he'd come closest to accomplishing. Maybe he had some sort of death wish.

"Devereaux!"

Nervously, I screamed, "What?" nearly rear-ending the car in front of me.

"Go to my house, and get my kids from Benjamin!"

"Okay. Okay. I'm on it."

"I have to go. Hurry," Mercedes said.

In transit to my sister's house, I called Bing, realizing I'd left Etta on hold. I'd call her back when things settled.

Bing answered, "Hey, Devereaux. How's it going?"

Exhaling, I told him, "Mercedes is in jail. She's at—"

"My attorney is already on the case. When he's done it'll be like it never happened. She'll be out within the hour."

"But what happened?" I couldn't imagine how scared Mercedes must've been. Her emotional trauma could never be expunged.

"Benjamin called Blake. Mercedes will be out shortly. And Benjamin. If he's wise, he'll never allow such a thing to happen to the mother of his children again."

"Speaking of the twins, where—"

"They're okay. They're with us. You can come to your mother's house. We need to have a family intervention for Mercedes."

"I'm on my way," I said, ending the call, then commanded my Bluetooth, "Call Antonio."

"Hi, babe. We're still on for seven?"

"I need to cancel. I have a family emergency."

"Anything I can assist with?" he asked, calming my spirit.

"Can you pick up Nya from Sandara? I'll come straight to your house after I leave my mom."

"Babe, if no one is dead or in the hospital, we will get through this. Breathe. Take your time. I'm on my way to get our girl. Okay?"

A text registered from Sandara, **Nya can stay here with Delvin and my kids. Bing just messaged me. I'm on my way to Mom's.**

Wow. "Yes. Okay." I ended the call.

Talked a text to Sandara, **Thanks but Antonio will get Nya.**

Antonio restored my faith in men. If I hadn't met Mercedes at Haven @1411 that day . . . I had to help my sister. "Family intervention," Bing had said. That meant whatever Mercedes had done was worse than I'd imagined. I thought Mercedes was always the strongest of us all.

Maybe I was wrong.

CHAPTER 56

Blake

Family gatherings with Bing and me were becoming increasingly popular.

The circumstances could've been better. Before today, none of my girls had been arrested. I opened then closed my refrigerator. Decided catering was best.

I called BRIO on Peachtree. "Yes, I'd like to order for six adults."

"That comes with our homemade chips," she said, then asked, "Is that okay?"

"Ready when you are," she said.

"Two of your roasted garlic and spinach artichoke dip, three spicy shrimp and eggplant, three lobster bisque, and four Caesar salads. That completes my order. What's your delivery time?"

She told me an hour. That was perfect. I went upstairs, removed my navy dress, freshened up, changed into a basic pink cotton jumpsuit.

"Sweetheart, we're here!" Bing called out from downstairs.

"Coming, babe!" Smearing on clear lip gloss, didn't want my lips cracking. When I saw Mercedes, her eyes were devoid of any emotion. I held my child in my arms.

"Let it out," I told her.

"I'm okay, Mother, really. I brought it on myself," Mercedes said, breaking my hug.

Pouring three goblets of her favorite cabernet, I handed a glass to Mercedes, then one to Bing. I sat beside my daughter, sipped my wine twice, then placed the glass on the table.

"I'll give you guys a few minutes alone. When the others arrive, I'll come back," Bing said, then retreated upstairs.

The pain on her face showed Mercedes was doing what she'd done since she was a child. She was suppressing her feelings. First Alexis and the baby. I prayed there wasn't a fourth family tragedy. Definitely not the revelation of my secret to Ruby. My wedding was a few weeks away.

"I've been where you are, honey," I told her.

"Bing already gave me that speech, Mother. And no, you have not. You were never married with children. You never had a husband who left you for another woman." Exhaling in my face, she added, "I'm good, though."

I insisted, "You've got to let him go."

No one was there to protect me from the men I'd dated. Family and friends told me to leave. That wasn't the same. Maybe if just one had held my hand the way I interlocked my fingers with Mercedes's, I wouldn't have stayed until I was used up by every black man I'd dated prior to Bing. One good man, unbeknownst to him, helped eradicate my anger.

I took her glass, set it on the table next to mine. "Come here." I wasn't asking.

Embracing my child, I confessed, "I've done a lot of things that I was ashamed of. I had no shoulder to lean on when I had my two abortions. I was barely out of high school supporting my boyfriend and his mother. I worked long hours to give you girls what I thought was my best. Cars. Clothes. College degrees. This is the first time in my life that I know what real love feels like. Benjamin wants to love you, baby, but like a lot of men . . ." I paused. Thought about Spencer. Continued, "They don't know how. And for the ones who do, sometimes love is not enough because they need more than they have to give. You and Alexis are my alpha females. Devereaux and Sandara are beta. You need a strong man who's not in competition with or intimidated by your dominant personality."

Mercedes cried like I'd never heard. Between the sniffles, snorting, she asked, "Am I a bad person? No one likes me. I have no real friends. My sisters tolerate me. He watched them cuff me, Mama, like I was some sort of wild animal. He went back inside as though I were a stranger." My baby gasped like her life depended on him.

"Get it all out. When you're done shedding tears, Benjamin is going to regret, not leaving you, but how he left you," I told her.

"He hates me—"

Sandara and Devereaux arrived on the tail end of Mercedes's comment.

"Are you okay?" Sandara asked, sitting next to Mercedes.

Sandara hugged her sister, then started crying.

I stood, let Devereaux sit in my place.

Devereaux said, "I'm so sorry that happened to you. I love you so much. Next to Mother, you are the strongest woman I know. You helped me to see that Phoenix was no good. I'm here to return the favor with Benjamin."

Sometimes there weren't enough words in the dictionary that one could speak to show another person love. This was a time when no words were needed.

Alexis entered the living room empty-handed. Her nanny carried the baby that was hidden under a blanket. The second helper had a diaper bag and the portable diaper changing station Bing had bought her. She should thank Mercedes for paying for that after-delivery tummy tuck that Alexis was getting tomorrow. Motherhood agreed with this one more than the others.

"What's all the tears for?" Alexis asked, sitting on the love seat.

"She was arrested," Sandara retorted.

Alexis squinted an evil stare at Sandara, then retorted, "Exactly. Arrested. Not kidnapped. Not locked in a hotel room with some asshole selling her pussy to scumbags. Now you're officially a bad-ass bitch, Mercedes. This is the best time to make Benjamin your bitch. I'll help you."

"Is that my baby girl making all that commotion?" Bing asked, coming down the stairs.

"Grandpoppa! You want to see your grandson?"

"Of course I do," he said.

The nanny peeled back the blanket. Yes, indeed. That boy had

Brandon's plaid, blue, yellow, and white designer short set with monogrammed blue socks.

Domino looked at Bing. A quivering lip proceeded a cry.

"Don't worry, Grandpoppa. He doesn't get out much."

I motioned to pick Domino up. Alexis blocked my hands. "Mother. Give him a few more months," she said, then directed the nanny, "Cover him up, then rock him. Don't take him out of his carrier without my permission."

Shaking my head, I told the nannies, "Follow me. Make yourselves comfortable in the family area. If you need anything please let me know."

"No peeping, Mother!" Alexis yelled from the living room.

Change was difficult for some, impossible for others. The strongest of my girls was now the most vulnerable. In time, Mercedes's heart would mend and I prayed she'd find true love like her sister Devereaux. Sandara had discovered the woman inside of her was most powerful now that she'd uncovered her passion for Delvin. No one was going to love Domino more than his mother, including James, Bing, Spencer, and me, combined.

Admiring all of my children, I was in a good space.

CHAPTER 57

Mercedes

Love was a decision.

Sometimes a woman made a man a better man for the next woman.

Awakening in the middle of my bed, I was not lonely. Wishing Benjamin and Arizona well relieved my heartache. I loved my husband the best way I knew. Finally accepted that deep inside I didn't want him back.

Arizona wasn't better than me. She was better for him. Devereaux and Antonio kept the twins while Benjamin moved all of his clothes from our house to hers. I didn't survey what he'd taken. All material things were replaceable and some people were expendable.

I had what was most important.

"Good morning, Mommy," Brandon said, kissing me on the cheek. "I made you some orange juice." He placed the crystal glass on the nightstand beside my bed.

Sitting up, I gave him a hug. "Look at you," I said, straightening his tie.

"You did not make it," Brandy exclaimed.

"Did too!" my son lamented.

"You can't make juice that comes out of a carton," she explained.

"So what am I supposed to say? Mommy, I poured you some orange juice."

She exhaled, put her hand on her hip. "Yes, silly. Why do you have to claim you did something you did not do? Mom, tell him I'm right."

My forever-correcting-others, nothing-was-ever-my-fault daughter's condescending tone reminded me of when I was her age.

I was unconsciously raising my son to bow down to girls. "Your brother is right. He made the effort to make me this juice." I swallowed a sip, then told Brandon, "Thank you, son."

"Ugh!" Brandy shook her arms toward the ceiling. "We'll settle this at school with the teacher."

Watching her turn away, sternly I told her, "Come back here, lil lady."

Toot! Toot! Benjamin's horn indicated he was here to pick up the twins for school.

Her eyes bulged in protest. "Daddy is here!"

"If you take one more step, girl, you will be . . ." I paused, picked up my daughter, sat her on my lap. "Boys are as smart as girls. Sometimes you have to find a way to compliment your brother. There's nothing wrong with encouraging him and others," I said, wishing someone had told me that when I was in kindergarten.

"You mean the way you compliment Daddy?" she asked.

I refused to debate with a five-year-old. "I love you, sweetheart. Be nice to your brother and your father. Go. I'll see you after school."

She hopped off my lap, raced out the door.

Brandon waited for me to put on my robe. I wanted to avoid seeing Benjamin's face. Had to confront him later. We'd agreed to meet with our attorneys in hopes of amicably dissolving our marriage.

"Brandon."

"Yes, Mom."

"If your sister bosses you today, stand up for yourself." I kissed my son.

"Brandon! Let's go!" Brandy yelled up the stairs.

"I like it," he said. Quickly hugging me, he whispered as though he didn't want Brandy to hear, "I love you, Mom. Hope you feel better. Bye."

Picking up my cell, I had five new text messages from my sisters, Mom, and Bing sending inspiring notes.

Mom texted, **I'll pick you up in an hour**.

Bing let me know, **My lawyer will speak for you. Anything you have to say, whisper in his ear. Shield your mouth before you speak. You'll be fine. See you and the kids for dinner tonight.**

Bet he hadn't imagined dealing with our family problems.

I showered, put on a white, form-fitting, sleeveless dress that stopped right above my knees. Smeared on a mocha matte lipstick, pulled my hair back. Staring in the mirror, a very conservative married woman reflected.

Snatching the band from the neat afro bun, I bent over, fluffed my hair, stood, fluffed my hair over my shoulders, then put on my black-framed designer sunglasses. I removed my wedding rings, placed them inside the box. Dropped the box in my purse. Stepping into my four-inch mocha pumps, I switched my personal items (including the ring) to a new white Dior purse I'd bought two years ago.

Mother was in her red Ferrari. "You look gorgeous," she said as I fastened my seat belt.

"I need to get me one of these," I told her, then laughed.

"Bing is way ahead of you. How are you feeling?" she asked.

"I'm good" were my last words until we arrived at the courthouse.

Seated across the table, with my mother and attorney, Benjamin, his lawyer, and Arizona, faced us. My mother's hand was under the table on my knee. I sat directly in front of my husband, and between my mom and Bing's lawyer.

"Let's start, shall we," Benjamin's representative led. "Since Mrs. Crystal has an arrest record, we've concluded it's in the best interest for my client to be awarded sole legal and physical custody of the twins with supervised visitation for Mrs. Crystal until after the ruling."

My mother patted my thigh. I sat quietly. No expression. I was truly done with exerting emotions for a man who had stuck a knife in my back that severed my heart.

Directing his attention toward me, he continued, "And, he'd like the residence sold and the proceeds shared seventy-five percent for him since he'll have the children and a more than generous twenty-five percent for Mrs. Crystal. Hopefully, you'll spare yourself the embarrassment of going before a judge by not objecting."

Arizona sat beside my husband as though she was his wife and I was the mistress.

Placing my hand over my mouth, I whispered in my lawyer's ear. He looked at me. "You're sure?"

I nodded.

My lawyer responded to Benjamin's attorney. "First, I recommend you do a better job of fact checking before misrepresenting your client. Mrs. Crystal does not have an arrest record."

"You're right," Arizona interjected. "I dropped the charges against her for trespassing into my home so she could raise her children."

Addressing Arizona, my attorney said, "This is not the time or place for you to speak. Mrs. Crystal can sue you."

I could? Definitely had to gain insight on the basis.

He asked me, "Would you like to have her removed from the room?"

I shook my head. If Benjamin was dumb enough to bring her for support, I'd let her stay. At least she had sense not to follow through on her charge.

Continuing, my lawyer said, "Mrs. Crystal has one counter."

Benjamin did a quick raise of both brows, gave me a corner smile on one side of his mouth. Kind of how he'd done trying to impress Toya and her wife when we were at King + Duke.

I remained motionless.

"Effective immediately, Mrs. Crystal grants Mr. Bannister's request for full legal and physical custody. Her visitation shall be according to her availability without supervision, unless you can present evidence as to how she's an unfit mother."

I watched my soon-to-be ex-husband swallow his Adam's apple a few times. He looked at Arizona.

"Perfect," Benjamin's attorney said.

My mom patted my thigh again. Benjamin wouldn't last thirty consecutive days being a single dad but I'd let him try.

"One more thing," my lawyer mentioned. "Mrs. Crystal will vacate the house *and* deed her rights to the property to Mr. Bannister, in seven days. If you have no further concerns, my client has to move into her new home."

My mother dug into her purse, handed me a set of keys.

I laughed. Shook my head at Benjamin.

"Thank you, Mother." As I hugged my mom, the expression on Arizona's face was priceless.

"It's fully furnished, sweetheart. The movers are packing your belongings right now," Mom said. "Oh, I almost forgot the keys to your"—she dug into her purse, placed the keyless remote in my hand—"Bing knew you'd look awesome in a brand-new all-white Ferrari. It's his divorce gift to you."

Those two, make that three, were amazing.

I stood, embraced my attorney. "Thank you."

"No, thank you. You made one of the smartest counters I've ever presented."

Exhaling softly, I felt better already. I wasn't worried about my children. Didn't need to see them all the time. Long as I knew they were fine, I'd be okay.

Arizona told Benjamin, "I told you I didn't want to raise *her* kids full-time. I refuse to do that. I want our own."

I hadn't noticed the ring he was supposed to return to the jeweler was on her finger until she removed it, placed it on the table.

"I'll accept it and you back, when she takes care of her own kids," Arizona said.

I'd almost forgotten. Handing her the ring box, I said, "These belong to you. You've earned them. Let's see how long it lasts when you find out he's fucked a stripper and her wife. Yes, while he was with us."

Arizona refused to take the rings. I placed the box in front of Benjamin.

My mother held up her hand, gave me a high-five. "I'm so proud of you, sweetheart."

Bing had warned me that men who'd done wrong by their

women would never be satisfied. He said Benjamin would do all he could to make me miserable. Following Bing's advice to give Benjamin everything he wanted and more gave me the freedom to love someone new.

Benjamin wasn't smirking. He stared at me. "You look nice."

I winked at him, slid on my sunglasses, then said, "Take excellent care of my kids."

CHAPTER 58

Blake

"**B**itch, you're going to make me marry you."

I stood in front of the full-length mirror, dressed in all white, not caring what color the world thought I was or wasn't worthy of wearing. I was done caring about anyone's opinion of me.

Brandon's original design weighed forty pounds, not including an extra ten for the fifty-foot train that I'd practiced to perfection dragging gracefully. I felt like a cross between a mascaraed diva with my diamond-crusted, hand-held eye-mask, a madam cinched into a white leather, back-laced bustier, and the queen at the highest regal ball.

"You nervous?" he asked, smoothing back my hair.

"When I turned fifty and no man had proposed to me, I'd lost faith in becoming a bride. Having a man hold to his commitment to me was a challenge."

"God saved the best man for last," Brandon said, giving me cheek-to-cheek air kisses. "Never lose faith. It's the key to all things possible, darling."

A light tap at the door. Someone announced, "Mr. Sterling is ready for his bride."

"It's your time," Brandon said, lowering the veil.

As I held on to his arm, sweat coated my forehead. My girls suspected I wasn't telling the truth about their father. There were only two people who were certain I'd lied.

Brandon lifted my veil, fanned my face. I stared into his eyes.

"You're no virgin and he's no LeBron, honey. Whatever is on your mind, save it until after he says I—" Brandon motioned for the guy in the doorway. "Quick, lower the temperature to sixty-five," he ordered, then told me, "You will not ruin my creation with sweat."

"How could you see me perspiring?"

"Honey, see it? You can't hide the onset of a hot flash. You're moist all over."

Get it together, Blake. Think Paris. No, not Paris. Your girls. No, not them. That'll lead to the lie and the liar in me.

Spencer wasn't invited. This was the only church he'd sworn never to step foot in again. It was my church and the new pastor performing my ceremony was not the minister who'd molested Spencer. I was not supposed to let thoughts of an ex enter my mind. Not today.

Get it together, Blake.

A tear fell right before the double doors opened to a paradise that would make all of Paris's gardens envious. I cried on the first note of "Here Comes the Bride."

These tears were for the little girl inside, who survived. The woman who reared four beautiful daughters. The executive who went out on top. The soon-to-be wife who would help her husband make a difference in other people's lives.

I was ready for new beginnings.

Scanning faces, I saw that every man was suited in a tuxedo. Every woman wore a gown. That Brandon. I paused midway down the aisle to take photos with my mind as Brandon escorted me to the altar.

Looking ahead, I noticed my four girls. Their gowns were off-white, each one tailored to their beautiful personality. Alexis's top was haltered. Her skirt was the longest I'd seen her in. Ever.

"You have outdone every event planner in the world," I told Brandon as I smiled at family and guests.

"You, my dear, are the belle of everything," he replied. "Wait until your reception."

Following the trail of rose petals, I stopped. Softly asked, "Where's Bing?"

Brandon reassured me, "Keep walking. He's watching."

The music changed from the bride's theme to saxophonist Antoine Knight. Then I looked up and saw white shoes on a wooden plank. White pants. As my eyes scanned up, the most handsome man in the universe descended from a white cloud blanketing the ceiling.

Bing stood tall. I smiled at Brandon when I saw the diamond crown on Bing's head. His manicured hands gripped thick, white ropes.

Light tugging at my hips and I felt my train release. When I arrived at the altar, the swing lowered to the platform. Bing stepped off. I handed my mask to Alexis. Brandon bowed, then took two steps backward to the first seat on the front pew.

Ruby looked as though she'd inherited a million dollars. She winked. I winked back, then gave her a single slow nod.

Bing extended his hands to me. We face each other. My fairytale wedding was really happening.

The pastor stood before us as we exchanged our vows to love, protect, and honor each other.

The pastor firmly said, "I now pronounce you husband and wife."

Husband and wife. Not man and wife. Bing had insisted as he never wanted to be the man his father was.

This was the first day of the rest of my life as Mrs. Blake Sterling, no hyphen required.

In life, there were secrets.
Some to share.
Others you take to your grave.

THE ONE I'VE WAITED FOR

Mary B. Morrison

ABOUT THIS GUIDE

The suggested questions that follow are included to
enhance your group's reading of this book.

Discussion Questions

1. Blake, was she a good mother? Would you put your grown children's happiness and needs before yours?

2. If someone willed you $2 million, then told you it was in error, would you give all the money back? If you could keep it, how would the money change you?

3. In Blake's engagement to Bing, do you think Bing was controlling or Blake wasn't used to dealing with a real man? Give examples.

4. Was Benjamin a man of great character? How much influence do you believe his parents had in his decisions with Mercedes and Arizona?

5. What was Alexis's biggest fear? What's yours?

6. Are you an alpha or beta personality type? Why?

7. Do you think Sandara will adjust well to having money, success, and a man who cares for her and her children or will she eventually return to Little Five Points?

8. Do you believe Spencer is a good man who messed up or a messed-up man trying to do good? Would you date/ marry him?

9. Did Arizona owe Mercedes's marriage respect? If you were the mistress, would you call the police on the Mrs. if she trespassed into your home?

10. Have you ever had a vaginal detox or a ThermiVa treatment? If not, would you? If you have, how was your experience?

11. Bing had lots of money. He could've married almost any woman. Why do you think Bing proposed to and married Blake?

12. Was Devereaux in love with being in love with a man? Was she the type of woman who had to have a man? Was Antonio a good fit for her?

13. Is it okay for a woman to take her secrets to her grave? Do you have secrets you've never shared with anyone?

How Well Do You Know Mary B. Morrison?

1. What's Mary's favorite color?

2. At what age did Mary get married?

3. What's Mary's ex-husband's name?

4. What city did Mary attend community college?

5. If Mary weren't an author, what would she do for a living?

6. How many corsets does Mary own?

7. What's Mary's favorite adult toy?

8. Would Mary choose love over money or money over love, if she were to remarry?

9. How many full lace wigs does Mary own?

10. Why did Mary move from Laurel, Maryland (DC area), back to Oakland, California, in 2001?

11. What's Mary's Yorkshire Terrier's name and age?

12. What dessert would Mary serve at a dinner party?

13. What's Mary's favorite MBM novel and why?

14. What inspired Mary B. Morrison to write *Soulmates Dissipate?*

For answers and more about Mary, visit www.kensingtonbooks.com and www.MaryMorrison.com
   Follow Mary on:
   Facebook at TheRealMaryB
   Instagram and Snapchat at MaryHoneyBMorrison
   Twitter at MaryBMorrison

DON'T MISS Mary B. Morrison's

If I Can't Have You series

If I Can't Have You
What really makes a man plunge headlong into obsession?
And what does he do once he's past the point of no return?
Find out in this seductive, mesmerizing tale of "love"
gone dangerously wrong.

I'd Rather Be with You
With Madison's marriage on the rocks, Loretta couldn't
resist looking after Chicago's interests and reigniting his
passion for life. But now Madison wants to take back
what's no longer hers. . . .

If You Don't Know Me
The scandalous story of two women, a sizzling wager, and the
fallout that's turned lives upside down. Now, with the only
man they've ever wanted at stake, who will go one step too
far to claim him?

Available wherever books and ebooks are sold.